Acclaim for N

ELEMENTARY PARTICLES

"A novel that casts klieg lights onto the pathologies of late-twentieth-century life. Every once in a while an artist comes along who is both enlightened and deeply damaged, whose vision is penetrating exactly to the degree that is dangerously and brutally honed. Blake . . . Van Gogh . . . Emily Dickinson, and, more recently, Céline. This is the frame in which to see Michel Houellebecq." —*Elle*

"Insolent and misunderstood, politically incorrect, Tournieresque in its ambition, this is a novel which hunts big game while others settle for shooting rabbit." —Julian Barnes

"Extraordinary. . . . A novel of evident stature, which immediately invites comparison with writers such as Céline, Beckett, and Camus. . . . Finishing this book, one is genuinely excited by its author's daring and conviction." —*The Guardian*

"France's biggest literary sensation since Françoise Sagan, people are saying, since Albert Camus. . . . The passing to a new generation of the literary flame—albeit, in this instance, a blowtorch." —*The Economist*

"A novel on the grand scale. It is almost Balzacian in its attention to detail, and dauntingly ambitious in its determination to tackle 'big themes.' . . . It is also . . . a very funny book."

—*Times Literary Supplement*

"Full of provocative ideas, powerfully expressed."

—*The Christian Science Monitor*

"Darkly funny and surprisingly touching. . . . Its ferocious comedy pertains to us, whether we want it to or not." —*Slate*

"Extravagantly opinionated and pessimistic and, at times, extremely funny. . . . One must also salute Houellebecq's sure narrative pace—the book is a page-turner—as well as his moving descriptions of loneliness, childhood cruelty, sexual frustration, social anomie and our inability to connect."

—*L.A. Weekly*

"A major achievement in contemporary fiction." —*ArtForum*

"A tragically beautiful book that constitutes a kind of epitaph for the hopes of the twentieth century [with] an almost mystical aspiration towards a more loving society. . . . Intelligent people should soon be divided into those who have and haven't read it yet." —*The Sunday Times* (London)

Michel Houellebecq

THE ELEMENTARY PARTICLES

A poet and novelist, Michel Houellebecq is the author of numerous books, including *Whatever* (*Extension du domaine de la lutte*). His awards include the Grand prix national des lettres and, for *The Elementary Particles*, the Prix novembre. He lives in Ireland.

INTERNATIONAL

ALSO BY MICHEL HOUELLEBECQ

Whatever

Platform

THE ELEMENTARY PARTICLES

THE ELEMENTARY PARTICLES

Michel Houellebecq

TRANSLATED FROM THE FRENCH
BY FRANK WYNNE

VINTAGE INTERNATIONAL
Vintage Books
A Division of Random House, Inc.
New York

FIRST VINTAGE INTERNATIONAL EDITION, NOVEMBER 2001

 Published in the United States by Vintage Books, a division of Random House, Inc., New York, and simultaneously in Canada by Random House of Canada Limited, Toronto. Originally published in hardcover in France as *Les particules élémentaires* by Flammarion, Paris, in 1998. This translation was first published in the United Kingdom under the title *Atomised* by William Heinemann, an imprint of The Random House Group Limited, London, and subsequently in the United States by Alfred A. Knopf, a division of Random House, Inc., New York, in 2000.

The publisher wishes to thank Asya Muchnick for her comprehensive assistance in translating and editing this text.

The Library of Congress has cataloged the Knopf edition as follows:
Houellebecq, Michel.
[Particules élémentaires. English]
The elementary particles / Michel Houellebecq ; translated by Frank Wynne.
p. cm
ISBN 0-375-40770-7 (alk. paper)
I. Wynne, Frank. II. Title.
PQ2668.077 P3713 2000
843'.914—dc21 00-040568

Vintage ISBN: 0-375-72701-9

Book design by Virginia Tan

www.vintagebooks.com

Printed in the United States of America
20 19 18 17 16 15 14 13

Prologue

This book is principally the story of a man who lived out the greater part of his life in Western Europe, in the latter half of the twentieth century. Though alone for much of his life, he was nonetheless occasionally in touch with other men. He lived through an age that was miserable and troubled. The country into which he was born was sliding slowly, ineluctably, into the ranks of the less developed countries; often haunted by misery, the men of his generation lived out their lonely, bitter lives. Feelings such as love, tenderness and human fellowship had, for the most part, disappeared. The relationships between his contemporaries were at best indifferent and more often cruel.

At the time of his disappearance, Michel Djerzinski was unanimously considered to be a first-rate biologist and a serious candidate for the Nobel Prize. His true significance, however, would not become apparent for some time.

In Djerzinski's time, philosophy was generally considered to be of no practical significance, to have been stripped of its purpose. Nevertheless, the values to which a majority subscribe at any given time determine society's economic and political structures and social mores.

Metaphysical mutations—that is to say radical, global transformations in the values to which the majority subscribe—are rare in the history of humanity. The rise of Christianity might be cited as an example.

Once a metaphysical mutation has arisen, it tends to move inexorably toward its logical conclusion. Heedlessly, it sweeps away economic and political systems, aesthetic judgments and social hierarchies. No human agency can halt its progress—nothing except another metaphysical mutation.

It is a fallacy that such metaphysical mutations gain ground only in weakened or declining societies. When Christianity appeared, the Roman Empire was at the height of its powers: supremely organized, it dominated the known world; its technical and military prowess had no rival. Nonetheless, it had no chance. When modern science appeared, medieval Christianity was a complete, comprehensive system which explained both man and the universe; it was the basis for government, the inspiration for knowledge and art, the arbiter of war as of peace and the power behind the production and distribution of wealth—none of which was sufficient to prevent its downfall.

Michel Djerzinski was not the first nor even the principal architect of the third—and in many respects the most radical—paradigm shift, which opened up a new era in world history. But, as a result of certain extraordinary circumstances in his life, he was one of its most clear-sighted and deliberate engineers.

We live today under a new world order,
The web which weaves together all things envelops our bodies,
Bathes our limbs,
In a halo of joy.
A state to which men of old sometimes acceded through music
Greets us each morning as a commonplace.
What men considered a dream, perfect but remote,
We take for granted as the simplest of things.
But we are not contemptuous of these men;
We know how much we owe to their dreaming,
We know that without the web of suffering and joy which was their history, we would be nothing,
We know that they kept within them an image of us, through their fear and in their pain, as they collided in the darkness,
As little by little, they wrote their history.
We know that they would not have survived, that they could not have survived, without that hope somewhere deep within,

They could not have survived without their dream.
Now that we live in the light,
Now that we live in the presence of the light
Which bathes our bodies,
Envelops our bodies,
In a halo of joy,
Now that we have settled by the water's edge,
And here live in perpetual afternoon

Now that the light which surrounds our bodies is palpable,
Now that we have come at last to our destination
Leaving behind a world of division,
The way of thinking which divided us,
To bathe in a serene, fertile joy
Of a new law,
Today,
For the first time,
We can revisit the end of the old order.

PART ONE
The Lost Kingdom

1

The first of July 1998 fell on a Wednesday, so although it was a little unusual, Djerzinski organized his farewell party for Tuesday evening. Bottles of champagne nestled among containers of frozen embryos in the large Brandt refrigerator usually filled with chemicals.

Four bottles for fifteen people was a little miserly, but the whole party was a sham. The motivations that brought them together were superficial; one careless word, one false glance, would break it up and send his colleagues scurrying for their cars. They stood around drinking in the white-tiled basement decorated only with a poster of the Lakes of Germany. Nobody had offered to take photos. A research student who had arrived earlier that year—a young man with a beard and a vapid expression—left after a few minutes, explaining that he had to pick up his car from the garage. A palpable sense of unease spread through the group. Soon the term would be over; some of them were going home to visit family, others on vacation. The sound of their voices snapped like twigs in the air. Shortly afterward, the party broke up.

By seven-thirty it was all over. Djerzinski walked across the parking lot with one of his colleagues. She had long black hair, very white skin and large breasts. Older than he was, she would inevitably take his position as head of the department. Most of her published papers were on the DAF3 gene in the fruit fly. She was unmarried.

When they reached his Toyota he offered his hand, smiling. (He had been preparing himself mentally for this for several seconds, remembering to smile.) Their palms brushed and they shook hands gently. Later, he decided the handshake lacked warmth; under the circumstances, they could have kissed each other on both cheeks like visiting dignitaries or people in show business.

After they said their goodbyes, he sat in his car for what seemed to him an unusually long five minutes. Why had she not driven off? Was she masturbating while listening to Brahms? Perhaps she was thinking about her career, her new responsibilities: if so, was she happy? At last her Golf pulled out of the lot; he was alone again. The weather had been magnificent all day, and it was still warm now. In the early weeks of summer everything seemed fixed, motionless, radiant, though already the days were getting shorter.

He felt privileged to have worked here, he thought as he pulled out into the street. When asked "Do you feel privileged to live in an area like Palaiseau?" sixty-three percent of respondents answered "Yes." This was hardly surprising: the buildings were low, interspersed with lawns. Several supermarkets were conveniently nearby. The phrase "quality of life" hardly seemed excessive for such a place.

The expressway back into Paris was deserted, and Djerzinski felt like a character in a science fiction film he'd seen at the university: the last man on earth after every other living thing had been wiped out. Something in the air evoked a dry apocalypse.

Djerzinski had lived on the rue Frémicourt for ten years, during which he had grown accustomed to the quiet. In 1993 he had felt the need for a companion, something to welcome him home in the evening. He settled on a white canary. A fearful animal, it sang in the mornings though it never seemed happy. Could a canary be happy? Happiness is an intense, all-consuming feeling of joyous fulfillment akin to inebriation, rapture or ecstasy. The first time he took the canary out of its cage, the frightened creature shit on the sofa before flying back to the bars, desperate to find a way back in. He tried again a month later. This time the poor bird fell from an open window. Barely remembering to flutter its wings, it landed on a balcony five floors below on the building opposite. All Michel could do was wait for the woman who lived there to come home, and fervently hope that she didn't have a cat. It turned out that she was an editor at *Vingt Ans* and worked late; she lived alone. She didn't have a cat.

Michel recovered the bird after dark; it was trembling with cold and fear, huddled against the concrete wall. He occasionally saw the woman again when he took out the garbage. She would nod in greeting, and he would nod back. Something good had come of the accident—he had met one of his neighbors.

From his window he could see a dozen buildings—some three hundred apartments. When he came home in the evening, the canary would whistle and chirp for five or ten minutes. Michel would feed the bird and change the gravel in its cage. Tonight, however, silence greeted him. He crossed the room to the cage. The canary was dead, its cold white body lying on the gravel.

He ate a Monoprix TV dinner—monkfish in parsley sauce, from their Gourmet line—washed down with a mediocre Valdepeñas. After some hesitation, he put the bird's body into a plastic bag, which he topped off with a beer bottle and dumped in the trash chute. What was he supposed to do—say mass?

He didn't know what was at the end of the chute. The opening was narrow (though large enough to take the canary). He dreamed that the chute opened onto vast garbage cans filled with old coffee filters, ravioli in tomato sauce and mangled genitalia. Huge worms, as big as the canary and armed with terrible beaks, would attack the body, tear off its feet, rip out its intestines, burst its eyeballs. He woke up trembling; it was only one o'clock. He swallowed three Xanax. So ended his first night of freedom.

2

On 14 December 1900, in a paper to the Berlin Academy entitled "Zur Theorie des Gesetzes der Energieverteilung in Normalspektrum," Max Planck introduced the idea of quantum energy. It was a concept that would play a decisive role in the evolution of physics. Between 1900 and 1920, Einstein, Bohr and their contemporaries developed a number of ingenious models which attempted to reconcile this idea with previous theories. Not until the 1920s did it become apparent that such attempts were futile.

Niels Bohr's claim to be the true founder of quantum mechanics rests less on his own discoveries than on the extraordinary atmosphere of creativity, intellectual effervescence, openness and friendship he fostered around him. The Institute of Physics, which Bohr founded in Copenhagen in 1919, welcomed the cream of young European physicists. Heisenberg, Pauli and Born served their apprenticeships there. Though some years their senior, Bohr would spend hours talking through their hypotheses in detail. He was perceptive and good humored but extremely rigorous. However, if Bohr tolerated no laxity in his students' experiments, he did not think any new idea foolish a priori; no concept was so established that it could not be challenged. He liked to invite his students to his country house in Tisvilde, where he also welcomed politicians, artists and scientists from other fields. Their conversations ranged easily from philosophy to physics, history to art, from religion to everyday life. Nothing comparable had happened since the days of the Greek philosophers. It was in this extraordinary environment, between 1925 and 1927, that the basic premises of the Copenhagen Interpretation—which called into question established concepts of space, time and causality—were developed.

Djerzinski had singularly failed to foster such an environment around him. The atmosphere in his research facility was like an office, no better, no worse. Far from the popular image of molecular biologists as Rimbauds with microscopes, research scientists were not great thinkers but simple technicians who read *Le Nouvel Observateur* and dreamed of going on vacation to Greenland. Molecular biology was routine. It required no creativity, no imagination and only the most basic second-rate intellect. Researchers wrote theses and studied for Ph.D.'s when a baccalauréat and a couple of years in college would have been more than enough for them to handle the equipment. "There's no mystery to decoding the genome," Desplechin, the director of the biology department, liked to say. "Discovering the principle of protein synthesis, now that takes some real work. It's hardly surprising that Gamow, the first person to figure it out, was a physicist. But decoding DNA, pfff . . . You decode one molecule, then another and another, feed the results into a computer and let it work out the subsequences. You send a fax to Colorado—they're working on gene B27, we're working on C33. It's like following a recipe. From time to time someone comes up with an inconsequential improvement in equipment and they give him the Nobel Prize. It's a joke."

The first of July was oppressively hot. In the afternoon a storm was forecast, which would send the sunbathers scattering. Desplechin's office on the quai Anatole-France looked out onto the river. Opposite, on the quai des Tuileries, homosexuals, many of them wearing thongs, walked around in the sunshine. They chatted in pairs and groups, and shared towels. Suntan lotion glistened on their biceps; their buttocks were rounded and sleek. While they talked, some massaged their genitals through nylon briefs, or slipped a finger under their waistbands, revealing pubic hair or the root of the penis. Desplechin had set up a telescope beside the bay window. Rumor had it that he was homosexual; in reality, in recent years, he was simply a garden-variety alcoholic.

On one such afternoon he had twice tried to masturbate, his eye glued to the eyepiece, staring at an adolescent who had taken off his thong and whose cock had begun to rise. Desplechin's penis fell, wrinkled and flaccid; he abandoned the attempt.

Djerzinski arrived punctually at four o'clock, when Desplechin had summoned him. The case was intriguing. Certainly, it was common for a researcher to take a year's sabbatical to work in Norway or Japan, or another of those sinister countries where middle-aged people commit suicide en masse. Others—especially in the Mitterrand years, when greed reached its dizziest heights—went to venture capitalists and set up companies to exploit some molecule or another commercially. Many of them had succeeded in basely profiting from the knowledge they had acquired during their years of pure research to amass considerable fortunes. But for Djerzinski to take a sabbatical with no plan, no goal nor the merest hint of an excuse, was incomprehensible. At forty, he was already head of the department, with fifteen researchers working under him. He reported directly to Desplechin—in theory at least. His team was widely considered to be one of the best in Europe, and their results excellent. What was wrong with the man?

Desplechin forced himself to be upbeat: "So, any idea what you're going to do with yourself?" There was a long silence before Djerzinski answered soberly, "Think." This was hardly a promising start, but Desplechin kept up his cheerful façade. "Any personal projects?" He stared into the thin face, his sad, serious eyes, and suddenly felt intensely embarrassed. What personal life? He had plucked Djerzinski from the University of Orsay fifteen years ago. It had proved to be an excellent choice: Djerzinski was a disciplined, inventive and rigorous researcher who had built up an impressive body of work in the intervening years. The reputation of the faculty as a leader in molecular biology was due in no small part to his work. He had kept his side of the bargain.

"Well," Desplechin concluded, "we'll keep your log-in to the faculty server active indefinitely, of course. You'll have access to the results and the Intranet and so forth. If you need anything, please don't hesitate to get in touch."

After Djerzinski left, Desplechin went back to the bay window. He was sweating slightly. On the far bank, a young, dark-haired Arab boy was taking off his shorts. Fundamental questions remained to be answered in biology. Biologists acted as though molecules were separate and distinct entities linked solely by electromagnetic attraction and repulsion. Not one of them, he was sure, had even heard of the EPR paradox or the Aspect experiments, nor taken the trouble to study developments in physics since the beginning of the century. Their view of the atom had evolved little from that of Democritus. They accumulated reams of repetitive statistics in the hope of finding some immediate industrial application, never realizing that their very methods were now threatened. He and Djerzinski were probably the only members of the National Scientific Research Center who had studied physics and who understood that once biologists were forced to confront the atomic basis of life, the very foundations of modern biology would be blown away.

Desplechin thought about this as night fell over the Seine. He could not begin to imagine where Djerzinski's thinking might lead; he did not even feel able to discuss it with him. He was almost sixty years old and, intellectually, he felt that he was over the hill. The homosexuals had left now, and the bank was deserted. Desplechin couldn't remember when he last had an erection. He waited for the storm.

3

The storm broke at about nine o'clock that evening. Djerzinski listened to the rain and sipped cheap Armagnac. He had just turned forty—perhaps he was having a midlife crisis. Improved living standards meant that a forty-year-old nowadays was in excellent physical shape. The first signs that one had crossed a threshold—whether in physical appearance or in the slowing of the body's responses—and begun the long decline toward death, tended to appear at forty-five, perhaps fifty. In any case, the typical midlife crisis was sexual—a sudden frantic pursuit of young girls. This was hardly the case for Djerzinski. He used his cock to piss, nothing more.

The following morning he got up at seven, took his copy of Werner Heisenberg's autobiography, *Physics and Beyond*, and headed for the Champ-de-Mars. The dawn was limpid and cool. He'd owned the book since he was seventeen. He sat under a plane tree on the Allée Victor-Cousin and reread the chapter in which Heisenberg, recounting his years as a student, tells of his first encounter with atomic theory:

> It must have been in the spring of 1920. The end of the First World War had thrown Germany's youth into a great turmoil.

The reins of power had fallen from the hands of a deeply disillusioned older generation, and the younger one drew together in an attempt to blaze new paths, or at least to discover a new star by which they could guide their steps in the prevailing darkness. And so, one bright spring morning, some ten or twenty of us, most of them younger than myself, set out on a ramble which, if I remember correctly, took us through the hills above the western shore of Lake Starnberg. Through gaps in the dense emerald screen of beech we caught occasional glimpses of the lake beneath, and of the tall mountains in the far distance. It was here that I had my first conversation about the world of atoms which was to play such an important part in my subsequent life.

At around eleven the heat began to become oppressive, and Michel went back to his apartment. He undressed completely and lay down. In the three weeks that followed he barely moved. It is easy to imagine that a fish, bobbing to the surface to gulp the air, sees a beautiful but insubstantial new world. Then it retreats to its world of algae, where fish feed on one another. But for a moment it has a glimpse of a different, a perfect world—ours.

On the evening of 15 July he phoned Bruno. His half brother's voice on his answering machine was coolly ironic over a jazz riff. Bruno had a leather jacket and a goatee. To enhance his streetwise image he smoked cigarillos, worked on his pecs and talked like a character from a second-rate cop show. Bruno was definitely in the throes of a midlife crisis. Was Michel? A man in a midlife crisis is asking only to live, to live a little more, a little longer. Michel, on the other hand, had had enough; he could see no reason to go on.

That evening he stumbled on a photo taken at his primary school in Charny and he cried. The child in the photograph sat at his desk holding a textbook open in front of him. The boy smiled straight at the camera, happily, confidently; it seemed unthinkable to Michel that he was that boy. The child did his homework, worked hard in class with an assured seriousness. He was just beginning to discover the world, and what he saw did not frighten him; he was ready to take his place in society. All of this was written on the boy's face. He was wearing a jacket with a narrow collar.

For several days Michel kept the photograph beside him on his bedside table. The mysteries of time were banal, he told himself, this was the way of the world: youthful optimism fades, and happiness and confidence evaporate. He lay on his Bultex mattress, struggling to come to terms with the transience of life. There was a small round dimple on the boy's forehead—a scar, from chickenpox, that had accompanied him down the years. Where was truth? The heat of midday filled the room.

4

Born to illiterate peasants in central Corsica in 1882, Martin Ceccaldi seemed destined for the undistinguished life of a farmer, which had been the lot of his ancestors for countless generations. It is a way of life long since vanished, and is fondly remembered only by a handful of radical environmentalists. A detailed description of this pastoral "idyll" is of limited interest, but to be comprehensive I will outline it broadly. You are at one with nature, have plenty of fresh air and a couple of fields to plow (the number and size of which are strictly fixed by hereditary principle). Now and then you kill a boar; you fuck right and left, mostly your wife, whose role is to give birth to children; said children grow up to take their place in the same ecosystem. Eventually, you catch something serious and you're history.

Martin Ceccaldi's singular destiny was entirely symptomatic of the role played by secularism, throughout the Third Republic, in integrating citizens into French society and promoting technological progress. His teacher quickly realized that he was an exceptional pupil, a child of considerable intelligence with a gift for abstract thought—qualities which would have little opportunity to develop in peasant society. Martin's teacher was keenly aware that there was more to his job than spoon-feeding elementary facts and figures to every untrained citizen. His task was to seek out the qualities that allowed a child to join the elite of the

Third Republic. He managed to persuade Martin's parents that their son could fulfill his destiny only if he were to leave Corsica.

In 1894, supported by a scholarship, the boy started school at Thiers de Marseille, an institution faithfully described in the autobiography of Marcel Pagnol (the author's well-written, realistic reconstruction of the ideals of an era through the rags-to-riches story of a gifted young man would remain Martin's favorite). In 1902 his teacher's faith was rewarded when he was admitted to the École Polytechnique.

In 1911 he accepted a position which would change the course of his life forever. He was to create an efficient system of waterways throughout French Algeria. For more than twenty-five years he calculated the curve of aqueducts and the diameter of pipes. In 1923 he married Geneviève July, a secretary whose family had come from the Languedoc to settle in Algeria two generations before. In 1928 their daughter, Janine, was born.

The story of a life can be as long or as short as the teller wishes. Whether the life is tragic or enlightened, the classic gravestone inscription marking simply the dates of birth and death has, in its brevity, much to recommend it. However, in the case of Martin Ceccaldi, it seems appropriate to set his life in a socioeconomic context, to say less about the individual than about the society of which he is symptomatic. Carried forward by the sweep of history and their determination to be a part of it, *symptomatic* individuals lead lives which are, in the main, happy and uncomplicated. A couple of pages are sufficient to summarize such a life. Janine Ceccaldi, on the other hand, belongs to a different and dispiriting class of individuals we can call *precursors*. Well adapted to their time and way of life on the one hand, they are anxious, on the other hand, to surpass them by adopting new customs, or proselytizing ideas still regarded as marginal. Precursors, therefore, require a more detailed study—especially as their lives are often tortuous or confused. They are, however, merely catalysts—generally of some form of social breakdown—without the power to impose a new direction on events; which role is the preserve of *revolutionaries* and *prophets*.

From an early age, it was clear to Martin and Geneviève Ceccaldi that their daughter was extraordinarily intelligent—at least as brilliant as her father. She was an independent girl. She lost her virginity at the age of thirteen—a remarkable achievement given the time and place. She spent the war years (uneventful, for the most part, in Algeria) going to dances and balls in Constantine and, later, Algiers while somehow managing to sustain flawless grades term after term. So it was that, with a first-class baccalauréat and considerable sexual experience, Janine left Algiers for Paris in 1945 to study medicine.

Postwar France was a difficult and troubled society: industrial production was at an all-time low and rationing would continue until 1948. Even so, a privileged few on the margins of society already showed symptoms of the mass consumption of sexual pleasure—a trend originating in the United States—that would sweep through the populace in the decades that followed. As a student in Paris, Janine had a ringside seat during the existential years. She danced to bebop at the Tabou with Jean-Paul Sartre. Though unimpressed by the philosopher's work, she was struck by his ugliness, which almost amounted to a handicap; they did not meet again. She herself was a stunning Mediterranean beauty and had many lovers before she met Serge Clément in 1952, while he was completing his surgical internship.

"You want to know what my dad was like?" Bruno liked to say, years later. "Give a gorilla a mobile phone and you've got the general idea." Obviously, Serge Clément could not possibly have had a mobile phone at the time, but he was, it has to be admitted, somewhat hirsute. Though certainly not handsome, he had a simple, uncomplicated virility which seduced Janine. Moreover, he had plans. While traveling in the United States, he had become convinced that plastic surgery offered excellent career prospects for an ambitious young surgeon. The use of sex in marketing and the simultaneous breakdown of the traditional couple, together with the economic boom he sensed was coming to postwar Europe, suggested a vast untapped market which Serge Clément was among the first in Europe—certainly the first in France—to identify. His only problem was money: he needed funds to start out in business. Martin Ceccaldi, impressed by his future son-in-law's entrepreneurial spirit, agreed to lend him the money. Clément's first clinic opened in Neuilly in 1953. Promoted in a series of positive articles in women's magazines—then rapidly expanding—it proved an outstanding success, and Serge opened a second clinic in 1955 in the hills above Cannes.

Janine and Serge were what would later be called a "modern" couple and it was something of an accident that Janine got pregnant by her husband. She decided, however, to have the child, believing that maternity was something every woman should experience. It was an uneventful pregnancy, and Bruno was born in March 1956. The couple quickly realized that the burden of caring for a small child was incompatible with their ideal of personal freedom, so in 1958 they agreed to send Bruno to Algeria to live with his maternal grandparents. By then Janine was pregnant again, this time by Marc Djerzinski.

Lucien Djerzinski had left Katowice in 1919 hoping to find work in France—or, more exactly, fled the misery and famine of the small mining community into which he had been born twenty years earlier. In France he found work on the railways as a laborer before being promoted to track maintenance. He married Marie le Roux, also employed by the railways, who was the daughter of a newspaperman from Burgundy, and fathered four children before dying in an Allied bombing raid in 1944.

Marc, their third child, was fourteen when his father died. He was an intelligent boy, serious, perhaps a little sad. In 1946, with the help of a neighbor, he got a job as a junior electrician at the Pathé studios in Joinville, where it was immediately apparent that he had a talent for film. Given the most rudimentary instructions, he could set up and light a set before the lighting cameraman had even arrived. Henri Alekan was impressed by the boy's work, and when he joined the ORTF, shortly after broadcasting began in 1951, he invited Marc to be his assistant.

When he met Janine, in 1957, Marc was shooting a documentary on the "Tropezians." Focusing principally on Brigitte Bardot (*Et Dieu créa la femme*, released in 1956, marked the beginning of the Bardot legend), it also covered the artistic and literary scene around Saint-Tropez with particular emphasis on what would later be called *la bande à Sagan*. Janine was fascinated by this milieu, which despite her wealth was closed to her. She seemed to be genuinely in love with Marc. She convinced herself that he had the makings of a great director—which probably was true. Marc made cinéma vérité documentaries. Using minimal lighting and the careful placement of objects, he could conjure disturbing scenes reminiscent of Edward Hopper: calm, prosaic but quietly desperate. Though he was surrounded by celebrities, his gaze never seemed more than indifferent. He filmed Sagan and Bardot as he might a lobster or a squid, with the same attention to detail. He spoke to no one, befriended no one; he was genuinely fascinating.

Janine had divorced Serge in 1958, shortly after they had packed Bruno off to her parents. It was an amicable separation, with both parties admitting fault. Serge was generous, giving Janine his share of the Cannes clinic, which guaranteed her a comfortable income. Marc proved no less a loner after he and Janine moved into a villa in Sainte-Maxime. She nagged him constantly, telling him he should work on his career as a director. He agreed but did nothing, simply waiting for the next documentary opportunity to come his way. If she arranged a dinner party, he would eat in the kitchen before the guests arrived and then go walking on the beach. He would return just as the guests were leaving and explain that he was editing a film.

The birth of his son in 1958 clearly disturbed him. He would stand for minutes at a time staring at the child, who bore an uncanny resemblance to him: the same angular face, high cheekbones and piercing green eyes. Shortly afterward, Janine began to be unfaithful. He was probably hurt by her infidelity, but it was impossible to tell as he spoke less and less. He spent his time building and photographing small altars of pebbles, driftwood and seashells under the blazing sky.

His documentary about Saint-Tropez was well received in the industry, but he turned down an interview request from *Les Cahiers du Cinéma*. His reputation reached new heights in 1959 with the broadcast of a short, acerbic documentary about the film *Salut les copains* and the "yeah, yeah" phenomenon. He had no interest in drama and twice refused an invitation to work with Jean-Luc Godard. Janine had by now taken up with a group of Americans staying on the Riviera. Something radical was happening in California. At Esalen, near Big Sur, people were living together in communes based upon sexual liberation and the use of psychedelic drugs said to expand the realm of consciousness. Janine and Francesco di Meola became lovers. An Italian-American, he had met Ginsberg and Aldous Huxley and was one of the founding members of the Esalen commune.

In January 1961 Marc traveled to China to shoot a documentary about the new communist society emerging in the People's Republic. He arrived back in Sainte-Maxime on the afternoon of 23 June. The house seemed deserted. A girl of about fifteen sat naked and cross-legged on the floor of the living room. "Gone to the beach," she finally said, listlessly, before sinking back into torpor. In Janine's bedroom he found a large, bearded man, naked and visibly drunk, lying snoring across the bed. Listening, Marc thought he could hear cries or moans.

Pushing open the door of one of the upstairs bedrooms, he smelled a retch-inducing stench. The sun flared violently through the huge bay window onto the black and white tiles where his son crawled around awkwardly, slipping occasionally in pools of urine or excrement. He blinked against the light and whimpered continuously. Sensing a human presence, the boy tried to escape; when Marc picked him up, the child trembled in his arms.

Marc left the house and bought a child's car seat from a nearby shop. He wrote a short note to Janine, strapped his son into his car, climbed in and headed north. When he reached Valence, he turned into the Massif Central. It was getting dark. From time to time, between the hairpin bends, he glanced back at his sleeping son and felt overcome by a strange emotion.

Subsequently, Michel's grandmother, who had retired to live in the Yonne, brought him up. His mother moved to America shortly afterward to join di Meola's commune. He would not see her again until he was fifteen. He saw little of his father, either. In 1964 Marc went to Tibet to film a documentary about the Chinese occupation. He wrote to his mother to say he was well, and to tell her how much he admired Tibetan Buddhism—which the Chinese were brutally eradicating; after that, silence. The French government registered a protest with the Chinese authorities, but there was no response. Though no body was ever found, he was officially presumed dead a year later.

5

It is the summer of 1968; Michel is ten years old. He has lived with his grandmother since he was three, in the village of Charny in the Yonne, near the border with the Loiret. Every morning he gets up early to make his grandmother's breakfast. He has made a list: how long the tea should brew, how many slices of bread and butter and so on.

He often stays in his room all morning reading Jules Verne, *Pif le chien* or *The Famous Five,* but he spends most of his time poring over a magazine he collects, *The Universe Explained.* There are articles about the structure of the elements, about how clouds form and bees swarm. He reads about the Taj Mahal, a palace built by an ancient king to honor his dead queen; about the death of Socrates; about Euclid's invention of geometry three thousand years ago.

In the afternoon, sitting in the garden with his back to the cherry tree, he can feel the springiness of the grass and the heat of the sun. The lettuces soak up the sun's rays and water from the ground. He has to water them when it gets dark. He sits in the garden reading *The Universe Explained,* or one of the books in a series called *One Hundred Facts About . . .* He absorbs knowledge.

Sometimes he cycles cross-country, pedaling as hard as he can, filling his lungs with a taste of the infinite. He doesn't know it yet, but the infinity of childhood is brief. The countryside streams past.

. . .

There is nothing left in Charny but a small grocer's shop. Every Wednesday, though, the butcher's van comes around; the fishmonger's every Friday. His grandmother often makes creamed cod for lunch on Saturday. Michel does not know that this is his last summer in Charny. His grandmother suffered a heart attack some months ago, and her daughters are already looking for a house in the suburbs of Paris where she can be closer to them. She is not strong enough to cope on her own anymore, nor to tend the garden all year long.

Though Michel rarely plays with boys his own age, he gets along with his peers well enough. They consider him a bit of a loner. His schoolwork is excellent—he seems to understand everything effortlessly—and he is first in all his classes. Naturally, his grandmother is very proud. Yet he is neither bullied nor hated by his classmates; he is happy to let them copy his work in class, always waiting for the boy next to him to finish before turning the page. Despite his excellent academic record, he always sits at the back of the class. His is a fragile kingdom.

6

One summer while he was still living in the Yonne, Michel spent an afternoon running through the fields with his cousin Brigitte. A pretty, gentle girl of sixteen, she some years later would marry a complete bastard. It was the summer of 1967. She grabbed his hands, swinging him round and round until they collapsed in a heap on the freshly mown grass. He pressed himself into her warm breast; she was wearing a short skirt. Next morning they were covered in spots and itched all over.

Thrombidium holosericum, also called the chigger, is plentiful in summer meadows. Two millimeters in diameter, with a fat, fleshy, bright red body, it embeds its beak in the skin of mammals, causing unbearable itching. *Linguatula rhinaria*, or tongue worm, is a parasite which lives in the frontal and maxillary sinuses of dogs and, occasionally, humans. The larva is oval and has a short tail and a sharp spike near the mouth; two pairs of limbs are armed with long claws. The body of the adult is between eighteen and eighty-five millimeters long, flat, ribbed, translucent and covered in barbed spines.

In December 1968 Michel's grandmother moved to Seine-et-Marne to be closer to her daughters. Michel's daily life changed little at first. Fifty kilometers from Paris, Crécy-en-Brie was a still pretty country village; its old and dignified houses had been painted by Corot. Tourist brochures referred to it, hopefully, as "Venice on the Brie," a reference to the network of canals that brought water from the Grand Morin. Few villagers commuted to Paris, most working for local businesses or in nearby Meaux.

Two months after the move, at a time when advertising had barely begun on France's then only channel, his grandmother bought a television. And so, on 21 July 1969, Michel was able to watch the first steps of man on the moon, live. Six hundred million people across the world watched with him. The broadcast, which lasted three or four hours, probably represents the culmination of the first stage of the great Western technological dream.

Though he joined the local school in Crécy in midterm, Michel adapted quickly and had no difficulty passing his end-of-year exams. Every Thursday he bought *Pif*, newly relaunched, with its free "gadget" every week. Unlike most children his age, he did not buy it for the gadget but for the adventure stories. Through a dazzling sweep of history and costume these tales played out some simple moral values. Michel slowly realized that this moral system ran through all the stories: "Ragnar the Viking"; "Teddy Ted and the Apache"; "Rahan, Son of a Savage Age"; and "Nasdine Hodja," who duped viziers and caliphs. It was a realization that would profoundly affect him. Later, reading Nietzsche provoked only a brief irritation, and Kant served only to confirm what he already knew: that perfect morality is unique and universal. Nothing is added to it and nothing changes over the course of time. It is not dependent on history, economics, sociology or culture; it is not dependent on anything. Not determined, it determines; not conditioned, it conditions. It is, in other words, absolute.

Everyday morality is always a blend, variously proportioned, of perfect morality and other more ambiguous ideas, for the most part religious. The greater the proportion of pure morality in a particular system, the happier and more enduring the society. Ultimately, a society governed by the pure principles of universal morality could last until the end of the world.

Michel liked all of the heroes in *Pif*, but his favorite was Black Wolf, the Lone Indian. He was a synthesis of the noblest qualities of the

Apache, the Sioux and the Cheyenne. Black Wolf roamed the prairies ceaselessly with his horse Chinook and his wolf Toopee, instinctively coming to the aid of the weak. Black Wolf continually commented on the transcendent ethic which underpinned his actions. Often, he referred to poetic proverbs from the Lakota and the Cree; sometimes, more prosaically, to the "law of the prairie." Years later, Michel still considered him Kant's ideal hero: always acting "as if he were by his maxims a legitimating member in the universal kingdom of ends." Some episodes—like "The Leather Bracelet," in which the extraordinary character of the old Cheyenne chief searches for the stars—broke free of the straitjacket of the "adventure story" for a world that was more poetic, more moral.

He was less interested in television. Every week, however, his heart in his mouth, he watched *The Animal Kingdom*. Graceful animals like gazelles and antelopes spent their days in abject terror while lions and panthers lived out their lives in listless imbecility punctuated by explosive bursts of cruelty. They slaughtered weaker animals, dismembered and devoured the sick and the old before falling back into a brutish sleep where the only activity was that of the parasites feeding on them from within. Some of these parasites were hosts to smaller parasites, which in turn were a breeding ground for viruses. Snakes moved among the trees, their fangs bared, ready to strike at bird or mammal, only to be ripped apart by hawks. The pompous, half-witted voice of Claude Darget, filled with awe and unjustifiable admiration, narrated these atrocities. Michel trembled with indignation. But as he watched, the unshakable conviction grew that nature, taken as a whole, was a repulsive cesspit. All in all, nature deserved to be wiped out in a holocaust—and man's mission on earth was probably to do just that.

In April 1970 *Pif* gave away a free gift which was to become famous: Sea Monkeys. Each copy came with a sachet of *poudre de vie*—the eggs of a tiny marine crustacean, *Artemia salina*, which had spent thousands of years in suspended animation. The process of bringing them back to life was complicated: water had to be allowed to settle for three days, then warmed. Only then was the powder added and the water stirred gently. In the days that followed, the bowl had to be kept near a source of light; warm water had to be added regularly to compensate for evaporation and the water stirred to keep it oxygenated. Some weeks later, the bowl was swarming with a multitude of translucent crustaceans, indisputably alive if faintly revolting. Not knowing what to do with them, Michel ended up tipping them into the river Morin.

The complete adventure story in the same issue concerned the boyhood of Rahan, and told how he had come to his vocation as a lone hero in Palaeolithic Europe. When still a child, he had seen his tribe wiped out by an erupting volcano. As he knelt by his dying father, Crâo the Wise, the old man gave him a necklace of three hawk's talons. Each talon symbolized one of the qualities of "those who walked upright"—the first loyalty, the second courage and the third, and most important, kindness. Rahan had worn the necklace ever since, always trying to prove himself worthy of it.

In the long narrow garden of the house in Crécy was a cherry tree only slightly smaller than the one in Michel's garden in the Yonne. There he would sit and read *The Universe Explained* and *A Hundred Facts About . . .* For his twelfth birthday, his grandmother gave him "My First Chemistry Set." Chemistry was mysterious and strange; it was much more exciting than mechanics or electricity. Each substance came in a separate tube. Each had its own color and texture, elements forever distinct from each other, but simply juxtaposing them could produce violent reactions, which in a flash could create some new substance.

As he was reading in the garden one afternoon in July, Michel realized that the chemical bases of life could've been completely different. Atoms with identical valency but higher atomic weight could have taken the place of the carbon, oxygen and nitrogen which made up all living things. On another planet, with different temperature and atmospheric pressure, the stuff of life could be silicon, sulfur and phosphorus; or germanium, selenium and arsenic; or even tin, tellurium and antimony. He had no one he could really talk to about these things. At his request, his grandmother bought him several books on biochemistry.

7

Bruno's earliest memory was one of humiliation. He was four years old and attending the Parc Laperlier nursery school in Algiers. It was an autumn afternoon and the teacher had shown the boys how to make necklaces out of leaves. The girls, most of them in white dresses, sat on a small bank watching, their faces already betraying a hint of dumb female resignation. The ground was strewn with golden leaves, mostly chestnut and plane. One after another, his friends finished their necklaces and went to place them around the necks of their little girlfriends, but he could not seem to finish his. The leaves broke and crumbled in his hands. How could he tell them that he, too, needed love? How could he let them know without a necklace? He started to cry with rage, yet the teacher did not come to help. Class had finished, and the children stood up and began to file out of the park. The nursery school closed shortly afterward.

His grandparents lived in a beautiful apartment on the boulevard Edgar-Quinet. Like many in the center of Algiers, it was designed in the bourgeois style of the great Haussmann buildings in Paris. A central hall, twenty meters long, ran the length of the apartment, ending in a drawing room from whose balcony the whole of the "White City" was at one's feet. Many years later, when Bruno was already an embittered middle-aged cynic, he could still remember himself, aged four, pedaling furiously down the dark hallway toward the shimmering portal of the balcony. It was at moments like this that he had come closest to true happiness.

His grandfather died in 1962. In temperate climates, the body of a bird or mammal first attracts specific species of flies (*Musca, Curtoneura*), but once decomposition sets in, these are joined by others, particularly *Calliphora* and *Lucilia*. Under the combined action of bacteria and the digestive juices disgorged by the larvae, the corpse begins to liquefy and becomes a ferment of butyric and ammoniac reactions. In three short months, the flies will have completed their work. They are succeeded by hordes of coleoptera, specifically *Dermestes*, and lepidoptera like *Aglossa pinguinalis*, which feed on fatty tissue. Larvae of the *Piophila petasionis* feed on the fermenting proteins with other coleoptera called *Corynetes*.

The now-decomposed cadaver becomes a host to *Acaridae*, which absorb the last traces of residual moisture. Desiccated and mummified, the corpse still harbors parasites, the larvae of beetles, *Aglossa cuprealis* and *Tineola biselliella* maggots, which complete the cycle.

Bruno could still see the beautiful deep black coffin with a silver cross. It was a soothing, even happy image: he knew his grandfather would be at peace in such a magnificent coffin. He did not learn about *Acaridae* and the host of parasites with names like Italian film stars until later. But even now the image of his grandfather's coffin remained a happy one.

He remembered his grandmother, sitting on a suitcase in the middle of the kitchen on the day they arrived in Marseilles. Cockroaches scuttled between the cracks in the tiles. It was probably then that she began to lose her mind. The litany of troubles in those few short weeks had overwhelmed her: the slow agony of her husband's death, the hurried departure from Algiers and the arduous search for an apartment, finding one at last in a filthy housing project in the northeast of Marseilles. She had never set foot in France before. Her daughter had deserted her, and hadn't even attended her father's funeral. Deep down, Bruno's grandmother felt certain there had been a mistake. Someone, somewhere, had made a dreadful mistake.

She picked herself up and carried on for another five years. She bought new furniture, set up a bed in the dining room for Bruno and enrolled him in a local primary school. Every afternoon she came to collect him. He was ashamed of the small, frail, shriveled woman who took his hand to lead him home. All the other children had parents; divorce was still rare in those days.

At night she would replay her life over and over, trying to discover how it had ended like this. She rarely managed to find sleep before dawn. The apartment had low ceilings and, in the summer, the rooms were stuffy and unbearably hot. During the day she puttered around in old slippers, talking to herself without realizing it. Sometimes she would repeat a sentence fifty times. Her daughter's memory haunted her: "Her own father's funeral and she didn't come." She went from one room to another carrying a washrag or a saucepan whose purpose she had already forgotten. "Her own father's funeral . . . Her own father's funeral." Her slippers scuffled on the tiled floors. Terrified, Bruno curled himself into a ball in his bed. He knew things could only get worse. Sometimes she would get up early, still in dressing gown and curlers, and whisper to herself, "Algeria is French," and then the scuffling would begin. She walked back and forth in the tiny two-room apartment staring at some fixed, faraway point. "France . . . France . . ." she repeated slowly, her voice dying away.

She had always been a good cook; here it became her only pleasure. She would cook lavish meals for Bruno, as though entertaining a party of ten: peppers marinated in olive oil, anchovies, potato salad; sometimes there would be five hors d'oeuvres before a main course of stuffed zucchini or rabbit with olives, from time to time a couscous. The one thing she had never succeeded in mastering was baking, but every week when she collected her pension she would bring home pastries, boxes of nougat, candied chestnuts and almond cakes. As time went by, Bruno became a fat, fearful child. She herself ate little or nothing.

On Sunday mornings she would sleep in, and Bruno would climb into her bed and press himself against her emaciated body. Sometimes he dreamed of getting up in the night, taking a knife and stabbing her through the heart; he could see himself break down in tears beside the body. In his imagination, he always died soon after her.

Late in 1966 she received a letter from her daughter. Bruno's father—with whom she still exchanged cards at Christmas—had given her their address in Marseilles. In the letter, Janine expressed no real regret about the past, which she mentioned in the following sentence: "I heard Daddy died and you moved to France." She explained that she was leaving California and returning to the south of France. She gave no forwarding address.

One morning in March 1967, while making deep-fried zucchini, the old woman knocked over the pan of boiling oil. She managed to drag herself into the hallway, where her screams alerted the neighbors. When Bruno came home from school, Madame Haouzi, who lived upstairs, met him at the door. She took him to the hospital, where for a few minutes he was allowed to see his grandmother. Her burns were hidden beneath the sheets. She had been given a great deal of morphine, but she recognized Bruno and took his hand in hers. Some minutes later the child was led away. Her heart gave out later that night.

For the second time, Bruno found himself face to face with death, and for a second time he almost completely failed to grasp its significance. Years later, when he was praised for a composition or a history essay, his first thought was to tell his grandmother. He would remember, then, that she was dead, but only rarely did he face this fact; it did not interrupt the dialogue between them. When offered a place at the university to study modern literature, he discussed this with her, though by now he was losing faith. He had bought two boxes of candied chestnuts for the occasion, which proved to be their last major conversation. Once he'd completed his studies and taken his first teaching job, he realized something had changed: he could not reach her anymore. The image of his grandmother dissolved and disappeared.

On the morning after her funeral he witnessed something strange. His father and mother—neither of whom he had seen before—were discussing what should be done with him. They were in the main room of the Marseilles apartment; Bruno sat on his bed and listened. To hear other people talk about him was disconcerting, especially as they seemed completely oblivious to his presence. He could almost forget that he was there—not an unpleasant feeling. Though the conversation was to have a profound impact on his life, at the time what they were saying did not seem to concern him directly. Later, when he thought about the conversation, as he often did, he felt nothing. As he sat listening to them that day, he could feel no link, no physical connection between himself and these two impossibly tall and youthful people.

It was decided that he should be enrolled at boarding school in September. He would spend weekends with his father in Paris. His mother would try to take him on vacation from time to time. Bruno did not object: these people did not seem hostile. In any case, his real life was the one he had shared with his grandmother.

8

THE OMEGA MALE

Bruno leans against the sink. He has taken off his pajama top, and the folds of his pale stomach press against the cold porcelain. He is eleven years old. About to brush his teeth, as he does every night, he hopes to get out of the bathroom without anything happening. When Wilmart comes up from behind and pushes him, Bruno backs away, trembling; he knows what will happen next. "Leave me alone," he says feebly.

Now Pelé also comes over. He is short, stocky and very strong. He slaps Bruno hard and the boy starts to cry. They push him to the ground, grab his feet and drag him across the floor to the toilets. They rip off his pajama bottoms. His penis is hairless, still that of a child. The two hold him by the hair and force his mouth open. Pelé takes a toilet brush and scrubs Bruno's face. He can taste shit. He screams.

Brasseur joins the others; at fourteen, he is the oldest boy in the *sixième*. He takes out his prick, which to Bruno seems huge, then stands over the boy and pisses on his face. The night before he'd forced Bruno to suck him off and lick his ass, but he doesn't feel like it tonight. "This'll put hair on your chest," he jokes, "and your balls." He nods and the others spread shaving cream on his genitals. Brasseur opens a straight razor and brings the blade close. Terrified, Bruno shits himself.

. . .

One night in March 1968, a prefect found him curled up on the floor of the toilets in the courtyard, naked and covered in shit. He found a pair of pajamas for the boy and took him to see Cohen, the housemaster. Bruno was terrified of being forced to squeal on Brasseur, but Cohen was calm, though he'd been dragged out of bed in the middle of the night. Unlike the prefects who reported to him, he treated the boys with the same respect he extended to his colleagues. This was his third boarding school and certainly not the toughest. He knew that victims almost always refused to inform on their tormentors. The only thing he could do was penalize the prefect in charge of the *sixième* dormitory. Most of the boys were ignored by their parents, making Cohen the sole authority figure in their lives. He tried to keep a close eye on his pupils and preempt trouble, but with only five prefects for two hundred boys, this was impossible. After Bruno left he made himself a cup of coffee and leafed through his files. Though he could prove nothing, he knew the culprits were Pelé and Brasseur. If he caught them, he would have them expelled. One or two cruel elements were enough to reduce the others to a state of savagery. In early adolescence, boys can be particularly savage; they gang up and are only too eager to torture and humiliate the weak. Cohen had no illusions about the depths to which the human animal could sink when not constrained by law. He had built a fearsome reputation since his arrival at the school in Meaux. He knew he represented the ultimate sanction, without which the treatment meted out to boys like Bruno would know no bounds.

Bruno was happy to repeat a year, since Pelé, Brasseur and Wilmart had graduated to the *cinquième* and would be in a different dormitory. Unfortunately, a ministerial directive taken after the riots of 1968 introduced an autodisciplinary system in boarding schools and a reduction in staffing. The decision was very much of its time, and resulted in considerable savings in salaries. It became easier for pupils to move about at night, and soon the bullies took to staging raids on the younger boys' dormitories at least once a week. They would bring one or two victims back to the *cirquième* dormitory, where the ceremonies would begin. Toward the end of December, Jean-Michel Kempf, a nervous, skinny boy who had arrived earlier that year, threw himself out the window to escape his tormentors. The boy was lucky to escape with multiple fractures; the fall easily could've been fatal. His ankle was badly broken, and though surgeons worked hard to reassemble the bone fragments, he would be crippled for the rest of his life.

Cohen organized an inquiry, which confirmed his suspicions; and despite the boy's protestations of innocence, he suspended Pelé for three days.

For the most part, animal societies are structured according to a hierarchy in which rank relates directly to the physical strength of each member. The most dominant male in the group is known as the *alpha male*, his nearest rival the *beta male*, and so on down to the weakest of the group, the *omega male*. Combat rituals generally determine status within the group; weaker animals try to better their position by challenging those above them. A dominant position confers certain privileges: first to feed and to couple with females in the group. The weakest animal, however, can generally avoid combat by adopting such submissive postures as crouching or presenting the rump.

Bruno, however, found himself in a less auspicious position. While dominance and brutality are commonplace in the animal kingdom, among higher primates, notably the chimpanzee (*Pan troglodytes*), weaker animals suffer acts of gratuitous cruelty. This tendency is at its greatest in primitive human societies and among children and adolescents in developed societies. *Compassion*, the capacity to identify with the suffering of others, develops later; this is quickly systematized into a *moral order*. At the boarding school in Meaux, Jean Cohen personified that moral order and did not intend to deviate from it. He did not believe that the Nazis had perverted Nietzsche's philosophy. In Cohen's opinion, the ideas manifest in Nietzsche's philosophy—the rejection of compassion, the elevation of individuals above the moral order and the triumph of the will—led directly to Nazism. Given his qualifications and his time at the school, Cohen could have been headmaster; he remained a housemaster by choice. He wrote repeatedly to the Ministry of Education to complain about the cutback in boarding school staff, but received no reply.

In captivity, a male kangaroo—*Macropus*—will often interpret the zookeeper's upright posture as a threat. If the keeper hunches his shoulders, adopting the nonaggressive stance of a peaceful kangaroo, the animal's violent impulse is defused. Jean Cohen did not intend to become a peaceful kangaroo. The savagery of Michel Brasseur, a normal stage in the development of the ego even in lesser animals, had crippled one of his classmates; boys like Bruno would probably be psychologically scarred for life. When he summoned Brasseur to his office, he fully intended to make his contempt obvious, to let the boy know he was about to be expelled.

On Sunday evenings, when his father drove him back in the Mercedes, Bruno would start to tremble as they reached the outskirts of Nanteuil-les-Meaux. The school hall was decorated with bas-reliefs of illustrious former pupils: Courteline and Moissan. Georges Courteline was a French writer whose stories parodied the absurdities of the bourgeoisie. Henri Moissan, a chemist who was awarded the Nobel Prize in 1906, had isolated silicon and fluorine, and pioneered the use of the electric oven. Bruno's father always arrived just in time for dinner at seven o'clock. Bruno usually only managed to eat at lunchtime, when they ate with the day pupils. At dinner only the boarders were present; they sat in groups of eight, with a senior at the head of each table. The seniors served themselves and then spat into the bowl so the younger boys wouldn't touch it.

Every Sunday, Bruno tried to talk to his father, and each time he decided it was hopeless. His father believed it was good for a boy to learn to defend himself; and it was true that other boys—some no older than Bruno—fought back. They kicked and punched until, eventually, they earned the respect of their elders.

At forty-two, Serge Clément was a success. While his parents ran a small grocer's shop in Petit-Clamart, Serge already owned three clinics specializing in plastic surgery—one in Neuilly, another in Vésinet and a third near Lausanne in Switzerland. When his ex-wife left to live in California, he had taken over the management of the clinic in Cannes, sending her half of the profits. He had not done any surgical work for some time but was, as they say, "a good manager." He didn't really know how to behave with his son, though. He wanted to do his best for the boy, as long as it did not require too much of his time; and he felt a certain guilt. He usually would arrange not to see his girlfriends when Bruno came for the weekend. He bought prepared meals from the delicatessen and they ate together, then watched television. Serge had no idea how to play games. Sometimes Bruno would get up in the middle of the night and go to the fridge. He would pour cornflakes into a bowl, add milk and cream and a thick layer of sugar. Then he would eat. He would eat bowl after bowl of cornflakes until he felt sick. His stomach felt heavy. He felt almost happy.

9

From a moral standpoint, 1970 was marked by a substantial increase in the consumption of the erotic, despite the intervention of vigilant censors. The musical *Hair,* which was to bring the "sexual liberation" of the 1960s to the general public, was a huge success. Bare breasts spread quickly across the beaches of the Riviera. In a few short months, the number of sex shops in Paris leapt from three to forty-five.

In September, Michel started the *quatrième* and took German as his second language. It was in German class that he met Annabelle.

At the time, Michel had only the most modest idea of what happiness might be. In fact, he had never thought about it. His views were those of his grandmother, who had instilled them in her children. His grandmother was Catholic and voted for de Gaulle; both her daughters had married communists, but this had not changed her view of the world. She was of the generation who as children had suffered the hardships of war and then, at twenty, celebrated the Liberation. These are the ideas they wished to bequeath to their children: a woman stays at home and does the housework (her work made easier by a variety of electrical appliances, allowing her plenty of time to spend with her children). A man goes off to his job but, thanks to automation, works shorter hours, and his work is less arduous. Couples are happy and faithful; they live in a nice house in the suburbs. In their spare time, they may enjoy gardening and crafts and appreciate the arts, or they may prefer to travel and discover other countries, other cultures, other lifestyles.

Jacob Wilkening was born in Leeuwarden, in the Netherlands. He arrived in France at the age of four, and had only a vague recollection of his Dutch childhood. In 1946 he married the sister of one of his best friends. She was seventeen years old, and had never been with a man. He worked for a time in a factory making microscopes before setting up his own business crafting precision lenses, principally subcontracting for Angénieux and Pathé. The business flourished. There was no competition from Japan in those days, and France produced lenses that were the equal of Schneider and Zeiss. The couple had two sons, born in 1948 and 1951, and, much later, in 1958, a daughter, Annabelle.

Born into a happy family—in the twenty-five years they had been married, her parents had never had a serious argument—Annabelle knew that she was destined for the same. She began to think about such things the summer before she met Michel, when she was going on thirteen. Somewhere in the world was a boy she had never met, a boy who knew nothing about her, but with whom she would spend the rest of her life. She would try to make him happy, and he would try to make her happy as well. But she was disturbed that she didn't have the slightest idea what he would look like. A girl her age had expressed the same concern in a letter to the Disney comic *Le Journal de Mickey*. The answer was meant to be reassuring, and ended with these words: "Don't worry, little Coralie; when you see him, you'll know."

They began to spend time together doing their German homework. Michel lived just across the street, barely fifty meters away. More and more often, they spent Thursdays and Sundays together. Michel would arrive at Annabelle's house just after lunch, when her little brother would look out the window and announce, "Annabelle, it's your fiancé . . . ," she would blush; but her parents did not make fun of her. She realized that she really liked Michel.

An odd boy, he knew nothing about soccer or rock music. He was not unpopular at school, but although he talked to a number of people, he kept his distance. Before Annabelle, he had never invited anyone to his house. He was a solitary child, used to his own thoughts and dreams. Little by little, he grew accustomed to her presence. They often set out on their bicycles up the hill at Voulangis, then walked through the woods and fields until they came to the cliff that towered above the valley of the Grand Morin. They walked back through the meadows, slowly getting to know each other.

10

CAROLINE YESSAYAN IS TO BLAME FOR EVERYTHING

That same year, things improved a little for Bruno when he went back to school. Now in the *quatrième*, he was one of the big boys. From the *quatrième* to the final year, the boys slept in a different wing in dormitories divided into four-bed cubicles. To the bullies, he had already been destroyed, humiliated; they moved on to new victims. This was also the year Bruno discovered girls. Sometimes—not often—there was a joint outing for the local boarding schools. On Thursday afternoons, if the weather was good, they would go to a sort of man-made beach on the banks of the Marne outside Meaux. There was a café nearby with pinball machines and table soccer, though its real attraction was a python. The boys liked to torment the animal, tapping their fingers on the sides of the vivarium. The vibrations drove the snake wild and it would throw itself against the glass until it knocked itself unconscious.

One afternoon in October, Bruno found himself talking to Patricia Hohweiller. She was an orphan and had to stay in school year-round, except for the holidays, when she went to stay with her uncle in Alsace. She was blonde and thin and talked very quickly, her animated face occasionally slipping into an odd smile. The following week he was shocked to see her sitting, legs spread, on Brasseur's knee. His arm was around her waist and he was kissing her. Bruno drew no particular conclusions from this. If the thugs who had terrorized him for years were popular with the girls, it was because they were the only ones who dared to hit on them. He had noticed that Pelé, Wilmart and even Brasseur himself never bullied the younger boys if there were girls around.

Pupils in the *quatrième* were allowed to join the film society, which held screenings every Thursday evening in the boys' assembly hall, though girls were allowed to attend. One night in December, just before *Nosferatu: A Symphony of Horror* started, Bruno took the seat next to Caroline Yessayan. Toward the end of the film—having thought about it for more than an hour—he very gently placed his left hand on her thigh. For a few wonderful seconds (five? seven? surely no more than ten) nothing happened. She didn't move. Bruno felt a warm glow flood his body and thought he might faint. Then, without saying a word, she brushed his hand away. Years later—fairly often, actually—when some little whore was sucking him off, Bruno would remember those few seconds of terrifying joy; he also remembered the moment when Caroline Yessayan moved his hand away. What the boy had felt was something pure, something gentle, something that predates sex or sensual fulfillment. It was the simple desire to reach out and touch a loving body, to be held in loving arms. Tenderness is a deeper instinct than seduction, which is why it is so difficult to give up hope.

If Bruno had touched Caroline Yessayan's arm that evening, she almost certainly would have let him, and it probably would have been the beginning of something. While they were waiting in line, she had deliberately struck up a conversation and had kept a seat free to give him an opportunity to sit beside her. During the film, she had put her arm on the armrest between them. She had noticed Bruno before and she fancied him; that evening, she was hoping against hope that he would hold her hand. Why did Bruno touch her thigh? Probably because Caroline Yessayan's thigh was bare, and in his innocence he could not imagine it was bare for no reason. As he grew older and remembered his boyhood with disgust, he came to see this as the defining moment of his life. It all appeared to him in the light of cold and unchangeable fact. On that December evening in 1970, Caroline Yessayan had it in her power to undo all the humiliation and the sadness of his childhood. After this first failure (for after she gently removed his hand, he never spoke to her again), everything became much more difficult. Of course, it was not really Caroline Yessayan's fault. Rather the reverse: Caroline Yessayan—a little Armenian girl with doe eyes and long, curly black hair who had found herself, after endless family wranglings, among the dark and gloomy buildings of the boarding school in Meaux—Caroline Yessayan alone gave Bruno a reason to believe in humanity. If it all had ended in a terrible emptiness, it was because of something so trivial that it was grotesque. Thirty years later, Bruno was convinced that, taken in context, the episode could be summed up in one sentence: Caroline Yessayan's miniskirt was to blame for everything.

In putting his hand on Caroline Yessayan's thigh, Bruno might as well have been asking her to marry him. The beginning of his adolescence coincided with a period of social change. Aside from a handful of *precursors*—of whom his parents, of course, were a depressing example—the previous generation had made a fierce and unwavering connection between marriage, sex and love. The rise of the bourgeoisie and the rapid economic changes of the 1950s had led to a decline in *arranged marriages*—except in the rapidly dwindling aristocracy, where lineage was still of real significance. The Catholic Church, which had always frowned upon sex outside of marriage, welcomed this shift toward the *love match*. It was closer to Catholic doctrine ("Male and female created He them"), and brought its ideal world of peace, fidelity and love a step closer. The Communist party, which was the only spiritual power that could rival the church at the time, was fighting for almost identical objectives. Consequently, young people in the 1950s, without exception, waited impatiently to *fall in love*, as the desertion of the countryside and the concurrent disappearance of village communities allowed the choice of a future spouse to be made from an almost infinite selection, just as the choice itself became of the utmost importance. (At Sarcelles, in September 1955, a new political movement dedicated to the preservation of the "extended family" was launched; proof in itself that society had now been reduced to the nuclear family.) It would be fair to say that the late 1950s and early 1960s were *the golden age of romantic love*—a time we remember today through the songs of Jean Ferrat and early Françoise Hardy.

But it was at precisely this time that the consumption of prurient mass-market entertainment from North America (the songs of Elvis Presley, the films of Marilyn Monroe) was spreading all over Western Europe. Along with the refrigerators and washing machines designed to make for a happy couple came the transistor radio and the record player, which would teach the adolescent how to *flirt*. The distinction between true love and flirtation, latent during the sixties, exploded in the early seventies in magazines like *Mademoiselle Âge Tendre* and *Vingt Ans*, and crystallized around the central question of the era: "How far can you go before you get married?" The libidinal, hedonistic American option received great support from the liberal press (the first issue of *Actuel* appeared in October 1970, and *Charlie-Hebdo* in November). Although their politics were notionally left-wing, these magazines embraced the ideals of the entertainment industry: the destruction of Judeo-Christian values, the supremacy of youth and individual freedom. Torn between these conflicting pressures, teen magazines hastily cobbled together a compromise that can be summed up in the following life history.

In the first stage (say, from twelve to eighteen), a girl would *go out with* several boys (the semantic ambivalence of the term reflected a very real behavioral ambiguity: what did *going out with* a boy actually mean? Did it mean kissing, or did it include the more profound joys of *petting* or of *heavy petting*, or even of full sexual intercourse? Should you allow a boy to touch your breasts? Should you take off your panties? And what should you do with his *thing*?) For Patricia Hohweiller and Caroline Yessayan the problem was far from simple; their favorite magazines gave vague, often contradictory answers. In the second stage (once she left high school), the same girl needed a *serious relationship* (referred to in German magazines as "big love"). Now the defining question was: "Should I move in with Jeremy?" This was the second and final stage. The flaw in the solution offered by girls' magazines—arbitrarily recommending contradictory forms of behavior in consecutive periods of a girl's life—only became apparent some years later with the inexorable rise in the divorce rate. Nevertheless, for many years girls, naïve and already disoriented by the speed of social change, accepted these improbable rules and tried their best to stick to them.

. . .

Things were very different for Annabelle. Last thing at night, before she went to sleep, she thought about Michel and every morning she was overjoyed to see him again. If something funny or interesting happened at school, her first thought was of the moment she could tell Michel about it. On days when they could not see each other for some reason, she was worried and upset. During the summer holidays (her family had a house in the Gironde), she wrote to him every day. The letters were more sisterly than passionate, and her feelings more a glow than a consuming fire, but even if she were reluctant to admit it to herself, the truth slowly dawned on her: on the first try, without looking, without really wanting to, she had found *true love*. Her first love was the real thing; there would not be another, and such a question did not even arise. It was a plausible scenario, according to *Mademoiselle Âge Tendre*, but one did well to be cautious as it almost never happened. There were, however, rare, almost miraculous cases that demonstrated it was possible. And if it happened to you it was the most wonderful thing in the whole world.

11

Michel still had a photograph taken in the garden of Annabelle's house during the Easter holidays of 1971. Her father had hidden Easter eggs in the bushes and flower beds. In the photo, Annabelle was standing in the middle of a bed of forsythias, parting the tall stems, intent on her search with all the gravity of childhood. She had just begun to mature; her face was delicate, and it was obvious even then that she would be exceptionally beautiful. The gentle swell of her sweater hinted at her breasts. This would be the last time there was an egg hunt at Easter; the following year they would be too old to play these games.

At about the age of thirteen, progesterone and estrogen secreted by the ovaries in a girl's body produce pads of fatty tissue around the breasts and buttocks. When perfectly formed, these organs have a round, full, pleasing aspect and produce violent arousal in the male. Like her mother at that age, Annabelle had a beautiful body. Her mother's face was charming but plain, and nothing could have prepared her for the painful shock of Annabelle's beauty; she was quite frightened by it. Annabelle owed her big blue eyes and the dazzling shock of blonde hair to her father's side of the family, yet only the most extraordinary fluke of morphogenetics could account for the devastating purity of her face.

Without beauty a girl is unhappy because she has missed her chance to be loved. People do not jeer at her, they are not cruel to her, but it is as if she were invisible—no eyes follow her as she walks. People feel uncomfortable when they are with her. They find it easier to ignore her. A girl who is exceptionally beautiful, on the other hand, who has something which too far surpasses the customary seductive freshness of adolescence, appears somehow unreal. Great beauty seems invariably to portend some tragic fate.

At fifteen, Annabelle was one of those rare beauties who can turn every man's head—regardless of age or physical fitness. She was one of the few who could send pulses racing in young and middle-aged alike and cause old men to groan with regret simply by walking down the street. She quickly noticed the silence that followed her appearance in a café or a classroom, but it would be years before she completely understood it. At the school in Crécy-en-Brie, it was common knowledge that she and Michel were "together," but even if they hadn't been, no boy would have dared to try. The terrible predicament of a beautiful girl is that only an experienced womanizer, someone cynical and without scruple, feels up to the challenge. More often than not, she will lose her virginity to some filthy lowlife in what proves to be the first step in an irrevocable decline.

In September 1972 Michel entered the *seconde* at the Lycée de Meaux, leaving Annabelle, who was in the *troisième*, in Crécy for another year. Every evening Michel took the train home, changed at Esbly and usually arrived in Crécy on the 6:33 p.m. train, where Annabelle would be waiting at the station. They would walk through the small town and along the banks of the canals. Sometimes—though not often—they would go to the café. Annabelle knew that one day Michel would want to take her in his arms, kiss her and caress her body, which she could feel was changing. She waited patiently for that day, and wasn't unduly worried; she was confident it would happen.

Many fundamental aspects of sexual behavior are innate, though experiences during the formative years of life play an important role in birds and mammals. Early physical contact with members of the same species seems to play a vital role in the development of dogs, cats, rats, guinea pigs and rhesus monkeys (*Macaca mulata*). Male rats deprived of maternal contact during infancy exhibit serious disturbances in sexual behavior, especially in mating rituals. If his life had depended on it (and, in a very real sense, it did), Michel could not have kissed Annabelle. Often, when he arrived at Crécy station Annabelle would be so overjoyed to see him that she threw her arms around him. For a moment they were held in a state of happy paralysis; only afterward would they begin to talk.

Bruno was also in the *seconde* at Meaux, though not in Michel's class. He knew that his mother had a son by a different father, but no more than that. He saw little of his mother. He twice had spent his holidays in the villa in Cassis where she now lived. She regularly entertained hitchhikers and sundry young men passing through. The popular press would have characterized them as *hippies*. It was true that they were unemployed, and that Janine—who by now had changed her name to Jane—provided for them during their stay. They lived off the profits of the plastic surgery clinic her ex-husband had set up—in other words, off the desire of well-to-do women to fight the ravages of time, or correct certain natural imperfections. They would swim naked in the creeks. Bruno always refused to take off his trunks; he felt small, pale, fat and repulsive. Sometimes his mother would take one of the boys to her bed. She was forty-five years old and her vulva was scrawny and sagged slightly, but she was still a very beautiful woman. Bruno jerked off at least three times a day. Here he was surrounded by the vulvas of young women, sometimes less than a meter away, but Bruno understood that they were closed to him: other boys were bigger, stronger, more tanned. Much later, Bruno would come to realize that the petit-bourgeois world of employees and middle managers was more accepting, more tolerant, than the alternative scene—represented at that time by hippies. "If I dress up as a middle manager, they'll accept me as one," Bruno liked to say. "All I need is a suit, a shirt and tie—all for eight hundred francs on sale at C&A. In fact, all I really have to do is learn to tie a necktie. Not having a car is a bit of a problem—the only real problem middle managers face in life. But it can be done: take out a loan, work for a couple of years to pay it off and there you go. But there's no point in trying to pass myself off as a dropout. I'm not young or good-looking enough and I'm certainly not cool enough. My hair's falling out, I'm getting fat. Worse than that, the older I get, the more terrified I am of rejection. I'm just not *natural* enough, not enough of an *animal*. It's a permanent handicap because no matter what I say or do, no matter what I buy, I can never overcome it, because it's a natural handicap."

From the first time he went to stay with his mother, Bruno knew he would never be accepted by the hippies; he was not and never would be a noble savage. At night, he dreamed of gaping vaginas. It was about then that he began reading Kafka. The first time, he felt a cold shudder, a treacherous feeling, as though his body were turning to ice; some hours after reading *The Trial* he still felt numb and unsteady. He knew at once that this slow-motion world—riddled with shame, where people passed one another in an unearthly void in which no human contact seemed possible—precisely mirrored his mental world. The universe was cold and sluggish. There was, however, one source of warmth—between a woman's thighs; but there seemed no way for him to reach it.

It was becoming increasingly clear that something was wrong with Bruno. He had no friends, he was terrified of girls, his entire adolescence was a disaster. His father realized this with a growing sense of guilt. He insisted that his ex-wife join them for Christmas 1972 so they could discuss the problem. As they talked, it became clear that Bruno's half brother was at the same school (in a different class) and that the boys had never met. This single fact hit Bruno's father hard, for it epitomized the utter breakdown of their family, a breakdown for which they were both to blame. Asserting his authority for the first time, he insisted that Janine contact her other son and try to salvage what she could.

Janine had no illusions as to Michel's grandmother's opinion of her, but it was to prove even worse than she expected. Just as she was parking the Porsche outside the house in Crécy-en-Brie, the old woman came out carrying a shopping bag. "I can't stop you from seeing him," she said curtly, "he's your son. Now I'm off to do some shopping. I'll only be a couple of hours, and I don't want to find you here when I get back." Then she turned on her heel.

Michel was in his room. Janine pushed open the door and went in. She had intended to kiss him, but when she moved toward him he jumped back nearly a meter. He had grown to look strikingly like his father: the same fine blond hair, the same sharp features and high cheekbones. She had brought him a present: a record player and some

Rolling Stones albums. He took them without a word. He kept the record player, but smashed the records some days later. His room was austere, without a single poster on the wall. A math book lay open on his desk. "What are you working on?" she asked. "Differential equations," he answered reluctantly. She had wanted to talk to him about his life, invite him on vacation; obviously that was out of the question. She simply told him that his brother would be coming to visit him, and he nodded. She had been there almost an hour, and the silences were becoming more drawn out, when they heard Annabelle's voice from the garden. Michel ran to the window and shouted for her to come in. Janine watched the girl as she opened the gate. "She's pretty, your girlfriend," she said, her mouth twisting slightly. The word lashed Michel like a whip, and his whole expression changed. Annabelle passed as Janine was climbing into the Porsche; the woman stared at her, her eyes filled with loathing.

Michel's grandmother felt no antipathy toward Bruno. In her blunt but essentially accurate opinion, he was another victim of Janine's parenting skills. Every Thursday afternoon Bruno would go to see Michel, taking the train from Crécy-la-Chapelle. If it was possible—and it almost always was—he would find a girl on her own and sit facing her. Most of them wore see-through blouses or something similar and crossed their legs. He would not sit directly opposite but at an angle, sometimes sharing the same seat a couple of feet away. He would get a hard-on the moment he saw the sweep of long blonde or dark hair. By the time he sat down, the throb in his underpants would be unbearable. He would take a handkerchief out of his pocket as he sat down and open a folder across his lap. In one or two tugs it was over. Sometimes, if the girl uncrossed her legs just as he was taking his cock out, he didn't even need to touch himself—he came the moment he saw her panties. The handkerchief was a backup; he didn't really need it. Usually he ejaculated across the folder, over pages of second-order equations, diagrams of insects or a graph of coal production in the USSR. The girl would keep reading her magazine.

Years later, Bruno could never see himself in that boy. He knew these things had happened and that they were directly connected to the fat, timid boy in the photographs of his childhood. The little boy was clearly related to the sexually obsessed adult he had become. His childhood had been difficult and his adolescence ghastly. He was forty-two now; objectively, death was still a long way off. What was left? Oh, there would be other blow-jobs and he would come to accept having to pay for them. A life lived in pursuit of a goal leaves little time for reminiscence. As his erections became shorter and more infrequent, Bruno felt himself succumb to a sad decline. His only goal in life had been sexual, and he realized it was too late to change that now. In this, Bruno was characteristic of his generation. While he was a teenager, the fierce economic competition French society had known for two hundred years abated. The prevailing opinion was that economic conditions tended toward a certain equality. The Swedish model of democratic socialism was referred to by politicians and businessmen alike. In such a society, Bruno was not motivated to distinguish himself through financial success. His sole professional objective was—quite reasonably—to fade into the "vast, amorphous mass of the middle classes," as President Giscard d'Estaing would later refer to it. But human beings are quick to establish hierarchies and keen to feel superior to their peers. Denmark and Sweden, which then provided the socioeconomic models for European democracies, also obliged with a model of sexual liberation. Unexpectedly, this great middle class of laborers and office workers—or, rather, their sons and daughters—were to discover a new sport in which to compete. At a language course which Bruno attended in 1972 in Traunstein, a small Bavarian village near the Austrian border, Patrick Castelli, a young French boy in his class, succeeded in fucking thirty-seven girls in the space of three weeks. Over the same period, Bruno managed to score zero. In the end he flashed his prick at a shop assistant in a supermarket; luckily, the girl broke out laughing and did not press charges. Like Bruno, Patrick Castelli was a good student from a respectable family, and their career prospects were almost identical. Bruno's memories of his adolescence were all of this kind.

Later, the rise of the global economy would create much fiercer competition, which swept away all the dreams of integrating the populace into a vast middle class with ever-rising incomes. Whole social classes fell through the net and joined the ranks of the unemployed. But the savage sexual competition did not abate as a result—quite the reverse.

Bruno had known Michel for twenty-five years now. Over the course of this terrifyingly long period, he felt he had hardly changed at all: he firmly believed in the concept of a kernel of personal identity, some immutable core which defined him. It was true, however, that vast tracts of his intimate history had sunk without trace from his memory. There were months—years, in fact—that seemed as though he had never lived them. This was not true of his adolescence, which was a rich seam of memories and formative experiences. The human memory, his brother explained to him much later, resembles Griffiths's Consistent Histories. It was in May and they were drinking Campari in Michel's apartment. They usually talked about social and political issues, and rarely discussed the past; that evening was an exception. "Each person has a set of memories of different points in their lives," Michel explained. "The memories come in different forms; thoughts, feelings, faces. Sometimes you only remember a name—like that girl Patricia Hohweiller you were talking about earlier, you probably wouldn't be able to recognize her today. Sometimes you remember a face without knowing why. Everything you remember about Caroline Yessayan is compacted into the precise seconds when your hand was resting on her thigh.

"Griffiths's consistent-history approach was introduced in 1984 to create coherent narratives from quantum information. A Griffiths's history is constructed from a succession of more or less random quantum measurements taken at different moments. Each measurement defines a specific physical mass at a precise moment with reference to a specific set of values. As an example, in a time t_1 an electron moves at a certain speed approximately determined depending on the method of measurement. At a time t_2 it is situated at a certain point in space. At a time t_3, it has a certain spin value. From this collection of measurements it is possible to construct a *history* which is logically consistent. It cannot be said to be *true*; simply that it can be sustained without contradiction. Under a given set of experimental conditions, a finite number of possible histories can be recreated using Griffiths's method; these are called

Griffiths's Consistent Histories. In these, the world behaves as though composed of separate objects, each having fixed, intrinsic properties. However, the number of consistent histories that can be created from a single set of data is generally greater than one. As a being you are self-aware, and this consciousness allows you to hypothesize that the story you've created from a given set of memories is a *consistent history*, justified by a single narrative voice. As a unique individual, having existed for a particular period and been subjected to an ontology of objects and properties, you can assert this with absolute certainty, and so automatically assume that it is a Griffiths's history. You make this hypothesis about real life, rather than about the domain of dreams."

"I'd like to believe that the self is an illusion," said Bruno quietly, "but if it is, it's a pretty painful one." Michel, who knew nothing about Buddhism, couldn't answer. It was not an easy conversation; they saw each other twice a year at most. In September 1973 they had both started in the *première* C, and for two years they took the same math and physics classes. Michel was far ahead of the rest of his class. Human reality, he was beginning to realize, was a series of disappointments, bitterness and pain. He found in mathematics a happiness both serene and intense. Moving through the half-light, he would suddenly find a way through—with some formula, some audacious factorization—and be transported to a plane of luminous serenity. The first equation in any proof was the most poignant, because the truth fluttering in the distance was still precarious; the last was the most thrilling, the most joyful.

That same year Annabelle entered the *seconde* at the Lycée de Meaux. The three spent their afternoons together after class, before Bruno headed back to the school, Michel and Annabelle to the train station. Then events took a sad, strange turn. At the beginning of 1974 Michel wandered into Hilbert spaces; launched himself into the theory of measurements, discovered the integrals of Riemann, Lebesgue and Stieltjes. At the same time Bruno was reading Kafka and masturbating on the commuter train. One afternoon in May he had the pleasure of letting his towel fall open and flashing his cock at a couple of twelve-year-old girls at the new swimming pool at La Chapelle-sur-Crécy. The pleasure was heightened as he watched them elbow one another, clearly interested in the show. He caught the eye of one of them—a short brunette with glasses—and held it for a long time. Though he was too miserable and frustrated to be especially interested in the psychology of others, Bruno realized nonetheless that his half brother's situation was worse than his own. They often went to the café together; Michel would wear anoraks and caps that made him look ridiculous, he was hopeless at table soccer, and Bruno did all the talking. Michel barely moved, barely said a word; he simply stared at Annabelle, his gaze attentive but lifeless. Annabelle did not give up; for her, Michel's face was like a commentary from another world. At about that time she read *The Kreutzer Sonata* and, for a moment, thought she understood him. Twenty-five years later it was clear to Bruno that everything about their relationship had been lopsided, out-of-kilter, abnormal—there had never been a future in it. But the past always seems, perhaps wrongly, to be predestined.

12

A BALANCED DIET

In revolutionary times, those who accord themselves, with an extraordinary arrogance, the facile credit for having inflamed anarchy in their contemporaries fail to recognize that what appears to be a sad triumph is in fact due to a spontaneous disposition, determined by the social situation as a whole.

—AUGUSTE COMTE,
Cours de philosophie positive, Leçon 48

France in the 1970s was marked by the controversy surrounding *Phantom of the Paradise, A Clockwork Orange* and *Les Valseuses*—three very different films whose success firmly established the commercial muscle of a "youth culture," based principally on sex and violence, which would redefine the market in the decades that followed. Those who had made their fortunes in the 1960s, now in their thirties, found their lives mirrored in *Emmanuelle*, released in 1974. In the context of a Judeo-Christian culture, Just Jaeckin's film, with its mixture of fantasy and exotic locations, appeared as a manifesto for the leisure class.

A number of other important events in 1974 further advanced the cause of moral relativism. The first Vitatop club opened in Paris on 20 March; it was to play a pioneering role in the cult of the body beautiful. The age of majority was lowered to eighteen on 5 July, and divorce by mutual consent was officially recognized on the eleventh, thus removing adultery from the penal code. Lastly, on 28 November, after a stormy debate described by commentators as "historic," the Veil act legalizing abortion was adopted, largely thanks to lobbying by the left. Christian doctrine, which long had been the dominant moral force in Western civilization, accorded unconditional importance to every human life from conception to death. The significance was linked to the belief in the existence within the body of a *soul*—which was by definition immortal and would ultimately return to God. In the nineteenth and twentieth centuries, advances in biology gave rise to a more materialist anthropology, radically different in its assumptions and significantly more moderate in its ethical counsel. On the one hand, this change meant that the fetus, a small collection of steadily subdividing cells, was no longer acknowledged as a viable individual except by consensus (absence of genetic defects, parental consent). On the other hand, the new concept of *human dignity* meant that the elderly person, a collection of steadily failing organs, had the right to life only as long as it continued to function well enough. The ethical problems posed by the extremes of youth and age (abortion and, some decades later, euthanasia) would become the battleground for different and radically antagonistic worldviews.

The agnosticism at the heart of the French republic would facilitate the progressive, hypocritical and slightly sinister triumph of the materialist worldview. Though never overtly discussed, the question of the *value* of human life would nonetheless continue to preoccupy people's minds. It would be true to say that in the last years of Western civilization it contributed to a general mood of depression bordering on masochism.

For Bruno, who had just recently turned eighteen, the summer of 1974 was a significant, possibly crucial period in his life. Years later it would recur in sessions with his psychiatrist, who seemed to enjoy the story immensely. Sometimes Bruno altered or refined the details, but this is his standard version:

"It was the end of July. I was staying on the coast with my mother for a week. The house was full of people coming and going. My mother was sleeping with some Canadian guy at the time—young, built like a lumberjack. The day I was supposed to leave, I got up early. It was already pretty hot. I went into her room. They were still asleep. I hesitated for a second or two and then I pulled the sheet off them. My mother moved and for a minute I thought she was going to open her eyes; her thighs parted slightly. I knelt down in front of her vagina. I brought my hand up close—a couple of centimeters away—but I didn't dare touch her. Then I went outside and jerked off. There'd always been cats hanging around the house, mostly strays. A black cat lay sunning itself on a rock. The land around the house was stony and white, a merciless white. The cat looked over at me from time to time while I was whacking off, but closed its eyes just before I came.

"I bent down and picked up a rock. The cat's skull shattered and some of its brains spurted out. I covered the body with a pile of stones and went back inside. There was still nobody awake. Later that morning, driving me back to my father's house about fifty kilometers away, my mother talked to me about di Meola for the first time. Apparently, he'd left California four years earlier and had bought a big place on the hills of Ventoux near Avignon. In the summer he took in young people from all over Europe and America. She thought maybe I could go there one summer; she said it would broaden my horizons. According to her, di Meola's commune wasn't a cult, it simply passed on the teachings of the Brahman. Di Meola knew a lot about cybernetics and communication skills and used deprogramming techniques he'd developed at Esalen. It was all about liberating the individual's innate potential—'Because we only use ten percent of our brain, you know.'"

"Anyway," said Jane as they drove through the pine forests, "there'd be kids your own age there. It would be good for you. We all thought you were pretty hung up about sex while you were here this summer."

The Western concept of sexuality was perverse and unnatural, she went on. In many primitive societies, sexual initiation was a natural thing that took place early in adolescence under the supervision of the tribal elders. "I am your mother," she stressed. She did not mention that she had initiated di Meola's son David in 1963. David was thirteen at the time. In the first encounter, she had undressed in front of him and encouraged him to masturbate. The second afternoon, she had masturbated him and sucked him off. On the third and final afternoon, he had been able to penetrate her. Jane had pleasant memories of it; the young boy's rock-hard cock never seemed to go down, even after he had come several times. It was probably this experience which converted her to young men. "Of course," she went on, "the initiation should always take place outside of the immediate family—that's very important. It opens the world up to the adolescent."

Bruno jumped, afraid that his mother had been awake that morning as he was staring at her vagina. In fact, his mother's remark was banal: the incest taboo is well documented in the animal kingdom, especially among mandrills and gray geese. The car sped toward Sainte-Maxime.

"When I got to my father's house I realized that he wasn't well," Bruno would go on. "He had only taken a couple of weeks off that summer. I didn't know it at the time, but for the first time the business was doing badly and he had money problems. He told me later that it was because he had completely missed out on the market for silicone breast implants. He thought it was a passing fad that would never catch on outside the U.S. Which was utterly stupid. Nothing has ever caught on in America that didn't engulf Western Europe a couple of years later—nothing. One of his junior associates had left the clinic and set up on his own. He'd poached a lot of my father's clients simply by offering silicone implants as his specialty."

Bruno's father was seventy when he made this confession. He would die shortly afterward of cirrhosis of the liver. "History repeats itself," he told Bruno, tinkling the ice in his glass. "That idiot Poncet . . . [He was talking about the dynamic young surgeon who twenty years earlier had been his ruination.] That idiot Poncet just refused to diversify into penis enlargement—thinks it's too much like butchery. He doesn't think the men's market will catch on in Europe. Moron. Almost as much of a moron as I was twenty years ago. If I was thirty years old now, I'd set myself up in prick enlargement." Having said this, he usually slipped back into a daydream at the edge of consciousness. Conversation tended to stagnate at his age.

In July 1974 Bruno's father was only at the beginning of a long, slow decline. He would spend the afternoons locked in his room with a pile of cigars and a bottle of bourbon. He would come downstairs at seven and heat up something, his hands shaking. It was not that he didn't want to speak to his son, but that he couldn't; he really couldn't. After two days, the atmosphere had become oppressive. Bruno started to go out; he would spend whole afternoons at the beach.

The psychiatrist was less interested in the part of the story that followed, but Bruno thought it was important and had no intention of passing over it. After all, he was paying the bastard to listen to him, wasn't he?

"She was alone," Bruno went on. "She went to the beach every afternoon on her own. She was seventeen, a poor little rich girl—a bit like me. A chubby little thing, she was shy and very pale and had pimples. The fourth afternoon—it was the day before I left, in fact—I put down my towel and sat beside her. She was lying on her stomach and she'd unfastened her bikini top. I remember the only thing I could think to say was 'You on vacation?' She looked up. I'm sure she wasn't expecting brilliant conversation, but maybe not something quite so moronic. Anyway, we introduced ourselves: her name was Annick. I knew she would have to sit up sooner or later and I wondered would she try to fasten her bikini top behind her? Would she sit up and show me her breasts? She did something midway between the two; she turned over, holding the ends of her top together. When she'd finished, the bra was a bit lopsided and only half covered her breasts. She had big tits, which were already sagging a bit and must have got a lot worse later. I thought she was very brave. I reached over and slipped my hand under her bra, feeling her breast as I did. She didn't move, but she stiffened a little and closed her eyes. I went on stroking her tits; her nipples were hard. It was one of the most beautiful moments of my life.

"Things got complicated after that. I took her back to my house and we went up to my room. I was scared my father would see her. He had been with a lot of beautiful women in his life, but he was asleep—actually, he was completely drunk, he didn't wake up until ten o'clock that night. Strangely, she wouldn't let me take off her panties. She told me she'd never done it before, in fact she'd never really done anything with a boy before. But she was quite happy to jerk me off, she was pretty enthusiastic; I remember she was smiling. Then I moved my cock up to her mouth; she sucked it a little bit but she didn't really like it. I didn't push it. I straddled her, and when I slipped my cock between her tits she moaned a bit and seemed happy. I was really turned on. I pushed down her underpants—she didn't stop me this time, she even lifted herself up to help me. She wasn't particularly pretty, but her pussy was as beautiful as any pussy in the world. Her eyes were closed. When I slipped my hands under her ass, she parted her thighs completely. I was so excited that I came right there before I could even put it in her. There was jism in her pubic hair. I was really upset, but she said that it didn't matter, that she was happy.

"We didn't really have much time to talk. It was nearly eight o'clock and she had to get back to her parents. I remember she told me she was an only child, I don't know why. She seemed so happy, so proud to have a good reason to be late for dinner that I nearly cried. We kissed for a long time in the garden in front of the house. The next day I went back to Paris."

When he finished his story, Bruno paused for a moment. The psychiatrist discreetly shifted in his chair and said, about nothing in particular, "Good." Depending on how much of the hour had elapsed, he would prompt Bruno again, or simply say, "We'll leave it there for today?" stressing the last word a little to make this a question. As he said this, his smile was polished and effortless.

13

In that same summer of 1974, at a disco in Saint-Palais, Annabelle let a boy kiss her. She had just read an article about boy-girl relationships in *Stéphanie*. The article had propounded a miserable rationalization on the subject of childhood friendships. It was extremely rare that a childhood friend became a boyfriend, according to the magazine. His natural role was to become a friend—a *loyal friend;* he might perhaps be a confidant and offer emotional support through the trials of first *boyfriends*.

In the seconds that followed that first kiss, despite the assertions of the article, Annabelle was horribly sad. She felt flooded by some new, painful sensation. She left the Kathmandu and refused to let the boy come with her. She was trembling slightly as she unlocked her moped. She had worn her prettiest dress that evening. Her brother's house was only a kilometer away. It was barely eleven o'clock when she arrived, and there was a light on in the living room. When she saw the light, she started to cry. It was here, on a July night in 1974, that Annabelle accepted the painful but unequivocal truth that she was an *individual.* An animal's sense of self emerges through physical pain, but individuality in human society only attains true self-consciousness by the intermediary of *mendacity,* with which it is sometimes confused. At the age of sixteen, Annabelle had kept no secrets from her parents, nor—and she now realized that this was a rare and precious thing—from Michel. In a few short hours that evening, Annabelle had come to understand that life was an unrelenting succession of lies. It was then, too, that she became aware of her beauty.

Individuality, and the sense of freedom that flows from it, is the natural basis of *democracy*. In a democratic regime, relations between individuals are commonly regulated by a social contract. A pact which exceeds the natural rights of one of the co-contractors, or which does not provide a clear retraction clause, is considered de facto null and void.

If he was willing to talk in some detail about the summer of 1974, Bruno talked little about his final year at school. In truth, all he remembered of that year was a growing sense of unease. His memories of that time were vague and a little gray. He continued to see Michel and Annabelle regularly, and to all intents and purposes they remained close, but their baccalauréat was fast approaching and they would inevitably go their separate ways at the end of the year. Michel had changed: he was very intense, listened to Jimi Hendrix and rolled around on the carpet. Long after his peers, he was finally beginning to show visible signs of adolescence. He and Annabelle seemed more awkward with each other and held hands less and less frequently. In short, as Bruno summed up the situation for his psychiatrist, "everything was going to hell in a handbasket."

Since his episode with Annick, which in hindsight he had a tendency to embroider (he had sensibly avoided telephoning her), Bruno felt a little more confident despite the fact that he had had no encounters since. In fact, he had been brutally rejected when he had tried to kiss Sylvie, a pretty little brunette in Annabelle's class. Still, a girl had found him attractive, and if one girl could, there might be others. He began to feel protective toward Michel. After all, he was the older brother. "You have to do something. Everyone knows Annabelle is in love with you—she's just waiting for you to make the first move. And she's the prettiest girl in school." Michel would fidget in his chair and say "Yes." Weeks passed. He was visibly faltering on the threshold of adulthood. Kissing Annabelle was the only way for both of them to avoid crossing that threshold, though he did not realize it, lulled as he was by a sense that there would always be time. In April he vexed his teachers when he failed to fill out his matriculation papers. It was clear to everyone that, more than anyone, he stood an excellent chance of being accepted into one of the Grandes Écoles. With his baccalauréat barely a month away, Michel seemed to be coasting. He would sit and stare through the narrow bars of the classroom window at the clouds, the trees, the other pupils; it was as though human affairs could not really touch him.

Bruno, on the other hand, had decided to apply to study the humanities: he was bored with the developments of Taylor–Maclaurin; moreover, in liberal arts there would be girls—lots of girls. His father did not object. Like all old libertines, he had become maudlin with age and bitterly regretted that his selfishness had ruined his son's life—which was not entirely untrue. In May he separated from his last mistress, Julie, though she was a remarkably beautiful woman. Her name was Julie Lamour, but she had taken the stage name Julie Love. She starred in the first French porn films, long-forgotten films by Burd Tranbaree and Francis Leroi. She looked a little like Janine but was considerably more stupid. "I'm cursed . . . cursed . . ." Bruno's father murmured over and over when, happening on a photograph of his ex-wife as a young woman, he saw the resemblance. Julie had become intolerable. Since meeting Deleuze at one of Bénazéraf's dinner parties, she had taken to giving lengthy intellectual justifications of porn. In any case, she was costing him a fortune: on the set, she demanded a chauffeured Rolls-Royce, a fur coat, all of the erotic trappings, which as he grew older became more and more of a drain. Late in 1974 he had to sell the house in Sainte-Maxime. Some months later he bought an apartment for his son—a bright, peaceful studio—near the gardens at the Observatoire. Taking Bruno to view it, he did not think of it as a gift, but rather as a way of making amends; besides, it was obviously a bargain. But as he looked around the apartment he became excited. "You could have girls over," he said inadvertently, and, seeing his son's face, regretted it at once.

Michel eventually enrolled in the university at Orsay to study math and physics. He had been attracted by the dormitories on campus; that was how he thought. Unsurprisingly, both boys passed their baccalauréat. When they went to get their results, Annabelle went with them, her face solemn. She had matured a lot over the year. A little thinner, and with an inward smile, she was, unfortunately, more beautiful than ever. Bruno decided to take an initiative: the house in Sainte-Maxime was gone, but he could go and stay at di Meola's commune, as his mother had suggested, and he asked if they might come with him. A month later, toward the end of July, they set off.

14

SUMMER OF '75

They will not frame their doings to turn unto their God: for the spirit of whoredoms is in the midst of them, and they have not known the LORD.

—*Hosea* 5:4

The man who met them at the bus station at Carpentras seemed weak and ill. The son of an Italian anarchist who immigrated to America in the 1920s, Francesco di Meola's life was a success story—at least in the financial sense. Like Serge Clément, the young Italian realized that the society emerging at the end of the Second World War would be radically different, and that many pursuits once considered marginal or elitist would become economically important. While Bruno's father was investing in plastic surgery, di Meola was becoming involved in the music business. He did not make as much money as many in the industry, but he made his fair share. At forty, like many people in California, he sensed a new movement, something deeper than simply a passing fad, calling for the sweeping away of Western civilization in its entirety. It was this insight which brought luminaries like Alan Watts, Paul Tillich, Carlos Castañeda, Abraham Maslow and Carl Rogers to his villa at Big Sur. A little later, he had the privilege of meeting Aldous Huxley, the spiritual father of the movement. By then old and almost blind, Huxley paid him scant attention, but the meeting was to leave a profound impression on di Meola.

He himself was unclear as to the reason he left California in 1970 and bought a property in Haute-Provence. Later, close to the end, he came to think that he had wanted, for some obscure reason, to *die in Europe*, though at the time, he was aware only of the most superficial reasons. The events of May '68 had impressed him, and as the hippie movement began to ebb in California, he turned his attention to the youth of Europe. Jane encouraged him in this. Young people in France were particularly repressed, a time bomb of resentment under the legacy of Gaullist patriarchy, which, according to Jane, a single spark would be enough to detonate. For some years now, Francesco's sole pleasure had been to smoke marijuana cigarettes with very young girls attracted by the spiritual aura of the movement and then fuck them among the mandalas and the smell of incense. The girls who arrived at Big Sur were, for the most part, stupid little WASP bitches, at least half of whom were virgins. Toward the end of the sixties the flow began to dwindle and he thought that perhaps it was time to go back to Europe. He found it strange that he thought of it as "going back," since he had left Italy when he was no more than five years old. If his father had been a militant revolutionary, he was also a cultivated man, an aesthete who loved his mother tongue. This had undoubtedly left its mark on Francesco. In truth, he had always thought of Americans as idiots.

He was still a handsome man, with a tanned, chiseled face and long, thick, wavy white hair, but his cells had begun to reproduce in a haphazard fashion, destroying the DNA of neighboring cells and secreting toxins into the body. The specialists he consulted differed on most points, but on one they were agreed: he was dying. The cancer was inoperable and would continue inexorably to metastasize. Overall his consultants were of the opinion that he would die peacefully and, with medication, probably would not suffer any physical pain; and to date he had experienced only a general tiredness. However, he refused to accept the diagnosis; he could not even imagine accepting it. In contemporary

Western society, death is like *white noise* to a man in good health; it fills his mind when his dreams and plans fade. With age, the noise becomes increasingly insistent, like a dull roar with the occasional screech. In another age the sound meant waiting for the kingdom of God; it is now an anticipation of death. Such is life.

Huxley, he would always remember, had seemed detached about the prospect of his own death, though perhaps he was simply numbed or drugged. Di Meola had read Plato, the Bhagavad-Gita and the Tao Te Ching, but none of them had brought him the slightest comfort. He was barely sixty, but he was dying; the signs were there, there could be no doubt about it. He had even begun to be less interested in sex, and it was with a certain detachment that he noticed how beautiful Annabelle was. He did not notice the boys at all. He had lived around young people for a long time, and it was probably habit which made him curious to meet Jane's sons, though in fact he couldn't have cared less. He dropped them off in the middle of the estate and told them they could pitch their tent anywhere. He wanted to go to bed, preferably without meeting anyone. Physically, he was still the epitome of a sensual man, a man of the world; his eyes twinkled with irony and perception, a look certain exceptionally stupid girls thought of as radiant and benevolent. He did not feel in the least benevolent, and moreover thought of himself as a mediocre actor. How could they all be so easily taken in? Decidedly, he thought sometimes, a little sadly, these young people searching for spiritual values were really idiots.

Moments after they climbed down from the Jeep, Bruno realized he had made a mistake. The estate sloped gently toward the south, scattered with shrubs and flowers. A waterfall tumbled into a clear green pool; nearby, a woman lay naked, sunning herself on a flat rock while another soaped herself before diving in. Closer to them, on a rug, a bearded man was meditating or sleeping; against his tanned skin, his long blond hair was striking—he looked a little like Kris Kristofferson. Bruno felt depressed. But then, what had he expected? Perhaps they could still leave, as long as they did so immediately. He glanced across at his friends. Annabelle was calmly unfolding her tent; sitting on a tree stump, toying with the straps on his backpack, Michel seemed miles away.

Water follows the path of least resistance. Human behavior is predetermined in principle in almost all of its actions and offers few choices, of which fewer still are taken. In 1950 Francesco di Meola had a son by an Italian starlet, a second-rate actress who would never rise above playing Egyptian slaves; eventually, in the crowning achievement of her career, she had two lines in *Quo Vadis*. They called the boy David. At fifteen, David dreamed of being a rock star. He was not the only one. Though richer than bankers and company presidents, rock stars still managed to retain their rebel image. Young, good-looking, famous, desired by women and envied by men, rock stars had risen to the summit of the social order. Nothing since the deification of the pharaohs could compare to the devotion European and American youth bestowed upon their heroes. Physically, David had everything he needed to achieve his ends: he had an animal, almost diabolical beauty; his eyes were a deep blue; his face masculine but refined; his long hair thick and black.

With the help of his father's contacts, David recorded his first single at seventeen; it was a complete flop. It was released, it must be said, in the same year as *Sgt. Pepper* and *Days of Future Passed*, to name only two. Jimi Hendrix, the Rolling Stones and the Doors were at the height of their powers; Neil Young had just begun recording and great things were still expected of Brian Wilson. There was little room then for a bassist who was good but not gifted. David persisted. He played in four different groups, changed musical styles, and three years after his father, he too decided to try his luck in Europe. He got a regular gig in a club on the Riviera; that was no problem. Every night girls waited for him in his dressing room; that was no problem either. However, no one from any of the record companies so much as listened to his demos.

When David met Annabelle he had already slept with more than five hundred women; nevertheless, he could not remember ever seeing such supple perfection. For her part, Annabelle found herself attracted to him like all the rest. For days she resisted, finally giving in to him a week after they arrived. There were about thirty of them dancing outside at the rear of the house; the night was warm and starry. Annabelle was wearing a white skirt and a T-shirt with a sun drawn on it. David danced beside her, sometimes twirling her in rock-and-roll fashion. They danced tirelessly for more than an hour to the beat of a tambourine—sometimes fast, sometimes slow. Bruno leaned against a tree, alert, vigilant, his heart in his mouth. At times Michel appeared at the edge of the bright circle, at others he disappeared into the darkness. Suddenly there he was, barely five yards away. Bruno watched Annabelle break away from the dancers and go over to him, and distinctly heard her ask, "Aren't you dancing?" Her face as she said it was terribly sad. Michel declined, his gesture immeasurably slow, like some prehistoric animal recently roused. Annabelle stood looking at him for five or ten seconds longer, then turned and went back to the dancers. David put his hand on her waist and pulled her to him. She placed her hands on his shoulders. Bruno looked at Michel again and thought he saw a smile play on his lips; he looked down, and when he looked up again, Michel had disappeared. Annabelle was in David's arms, their lips close together.

Lying in his tent, Michel waited for daybreak. In the early hours a fierce storm broke and he was surprised to discover that he was a little afraid. When at last the storm subsided, a steady rain began to fall. Raindrops splashed dully on the canvas; though only inches from his face, they could not touch him here. He had a sudden premonition that all his life would be like this moment. Emotion would pass him by, sometimes very close. Others would experience happiness and despair, but such things would be unknown to him, they would not touch him. Several times that evening Annabelle had looked over at him while she danced. Though he had wanted to, he simply could not move; he felt as though his body were slipping into icy water. Still, everything seemed strangely calm. He felt separated from the world by a vacuum molded to his body like a shell, a protective armor.

15

The following morning Michel's tent was empty. His things were gone, but he had left a note which read, simply, *Don't worry*. Bruno himself left a week later. As he boarded the train, he realized that since arriving he hadn't tried to flirt with anyone, or even talk to anyone.

Late in August, Annabelle noticed that her period was late. She thought it was probably best this way. There was no problem; David's father knew a doctor in Marseilles, a fervent champion of family planning. The guy's name was Laurent, he was about thirty, expansive, with a little red mustache. He insisted that she call him Laurent. He showed her the instruments and explained to her the procedure of dilation and curettage. He liked to establish a rapport with his clients, thinking of them almost as friends. He had been an advocate of women's rights from the beginning, and believed there was still a long way to go. The operation was scheduled for the following day; the costs would be covered by the family planning clinic.

By the time she returned to her hotel, Annabelle was distraught. She would have the abortion the following day and stay overnight at the hotel before going home; that was what she had decided. Every night for three weeks she had slept in David's tent. The first time it had been painful, but afterward she enjoyed it. She had never thought that sexual pleasure could be so overpowering. But she felt no particular affection for the guy; she knew he would quickly find someone else, was probably with someone now.

At a dinner party that same evening, Laurent talked enthusiastically about Annabelle's case. This was precisely what they had been fighting for, he remarked, to ensure that a seventeen-year-old girl—"and a pretty girl, too," he almost added—did not have her life destroyed by a holiday romance.

Annabelle was apprehensive about returning to Crécy-en-Brie, but her fears were unfounded. When she got back on 4 September her parents complimented her on her tan. Michel had already left, they told her, moving into the university dormitory in Bures-sur-Yvette; they obviously did not suspect a thing. She went to visit Michel's grandmother. Though the old woman seemed tired, she greeted Annabelle warmly and managed to find her grandson's address for her. Yes, it was a little strange that Michel had come back from vacation before the others; and she thought it odd that he should go to the university weeks before he was due to start, but then Michel had always been a strange boy.

In the midst of nature's barbarity, human beings sometimes (rarely) succeed in creating small oases warmed by love. Small, exclusive, enclosed spaces governed only by love and shared subjectivity.

Annabelle spent the fortnight that followed writing to Michel. It was hard work; several times she crossed out what she had written and started again. When finished, it ran to forty pages; it was her first *love letter*. She posted it on 17 September, the day she went back to school; then she waited.

The University of Paris IX—Orsay—is the only one in the Paris area modeled on the American campus system. Both undergraduates and graduate students stay in dormitories set in quads. Orsay University also has an exceptional physics research facility dedicated to the study of elementary particles.

Michel lived at the top of building 233, in a corner room on the fourth floor where he felt immediately at home. There was a small bed, a desk and some shelves for his books. His window looked out onto a lawn which ran down to the river. If he leaned out and craned his neck, he could see the gray concrete expanse of the particle accelerator on the right. With a month to go before lectures began, the dorms were almost empty. There were some African students, whose problem was where to stay in August, when the dormitories closed completely. Michel sometimes talked to the concierge and during the day he walked by the river. He didn't suspect that he would be here for more than eight years.

One morning, at about eleven o'clock, he lay down on the grass beneath some indeterminate trees. He was surprised at how miserable he felt. Far removed from Christian notions of grace and redemption, unfamiliar with the concepts of freedom and compassion, Michel's worldview had grown pitiless and mechanical. Once the parameters for interaction were defined, he thought, and given the initial conditions, events took place in an empty, spiritless space, each inexorably predetermined. What happened was meant to happen; it could not be otherwise; no one was to blame. At night Michel dreamed of abstract snow-covered spaces—his body, bandaged from head to foot, drifting beneath lowering skies between steel mills. During the day he would sometimes run into one of the African students, a short Malian boy with sallow skin, and they would nod to each other. The university cafeteria was not yet open, so Michel bought tins of tuna at the supermarket in Courcelles-sur-Yvette and went back to his room. Night fell. He walked the empty corridors.

In mid-October Annabelle wrote to him again—a shorter letter this time. She had phoned Bruno only to discover that he had no news either; all he could tell her was that Michel telephoned his grandmother regularly but probably would not be home before Christmas.

One evening in November, coming out of a lecture on analysis, Michel found a note in his pigeonhole at the dorm. It read: *Phone your aunt, Marie-Thérèse. URGENT.* He had not seen his aunt or his cousin Brigitte for two years. He phoned back immediately. His grandmother had had another stroke and she was in a hospital in Meaux. It was serious, very serious. Her aorta was weak; her heart might fail at any time.

. . .

It was around 10 p.m. when he walked through Meaux, past the lycée. At the same time, Annabelle was inside reading a passage by the Greek thinker Epicurus: brilliant, liberal and, to be honest, a pain in the ass. The sky was dark and the river Marne filthy and turbulent. He found the Hôpital Saint-Antoine easily, a complex of modern glass-and-steel buildings which had opened the previous year. His aunt Marie-Thérèse was waiting for him, with his cousin Brigitte, in the hall on the seventh floor; they had clearly been crying. "I don't know if you should see her," Marie-Thérèse said. He ignored the suggestion. What had to be endured, he would endure.

She was in intensive care, in a room of her own. The sheet was a bright white against her exposed shoulders and arms; he could scarcely tear his eyes away from the bare flesh, wrinkled, pale and terribly old. Her arms, perforated with tubes, were bound to the bedrails with straps. Her throat had been intubated, and wires ran from under the sheets to monitoring devices. They had taken away her nightdress and had not allowed her to redo her chignon, as she had every morning for years. With her long gray hair undone, she no longer seemed like his grandmother but simply a creature of flesh and blood who seemed both very young and very old, given up into the hands of the medical profession. Michel took her hand; it was the one thing he still recognized. He often held her hand, even now at seventeen. She did not open her eyes, but perhaps she sensed it was his touch, despite everything. He did not squeeze her hand, but simply took it in his as he had always done; he dearly hoped that she knew it was him.

Her childhood had been grim. From the age of seven she had labored on the farm surrounded by semialcoholic brutes. Her adolescence was too short for her to have any precise memories of it. After the death of her husband, she worked in a factory and brought up her four children; in midwinter she drew water from the pump in the courtyard so they could wash. At sixty, having just retired from the factory, she agreed to look after her son's only child. He had wanted for nothing—clean clothes, good Sunday lunches and love. All these things she had done for him. Any analysis of human behavior, however rudimentary, should take account of such phenomena. Historically, such human beings have existed. Human beings who have worked—worked hard—all their lives with no motive other than love and devotion, who have literally given their lives for others, out of love and devotion; human beings who have no sense of having made any sacrifice, who cannot imagine any way of life other than giving their lives for others, out of love and devotion. In general, such human beings are generally women.

Michel had been in the room for about fifteen minutes, holding his grandmother's hand in his, when an intern came in and told him that he would be in the way if he were to stay any longer. There might be something they could do; not an operation, it was past that, but something, maybe. He shouldn't give up hope.

They headed back in silence; Marie-Thérèse drove the Renault 16 mechanically. They ate without saying much, occasionally evoking a memory. Marie-Thérèse cooked and served, needing to keep busy; now and again she would stop and cry a little and then go back to cooking.

Annabelle had been there when the ambulance came and when the Renault came back. At about one a.m., she rose and dressed—her parents were asleep—and walked to the gate of Michel's house. The lights were still on, and everyone was probably in the living room, but it was impossible to make out anything through the heavy curtains. A light rain fell. Ten minutes passed. Annabelle knew she could ring the doorbell and see Michel, but she could also do nothing. She did not know that these ten minutes were a concrete example of *free will*; she knew only that they were terrible and that when they had elapsed, she would never be quite the same again. Many years later Michel proposed a theory of human freedom using the flow of superfluid helium as an analogy. In principle, the transfer of electrons between neurons and synapses in the brain—as discrete atomic phenomena—is governed by quantum uncertainty. The sheer number of neurons, however, statistically cancels out elementary differences, ensuring that human behavior is as rigorously determined—in broad terms and in the smallest detail—as any other natural system. However, in rare cases—Christians refer to them as *acts of grace*—a different harmonic wave form causes changes in the brain which modify behavior, temporarily or permanently. It is this new harmonic resonance which gives rise to what is commonly called *free will*.

Nothing of the sort happened on this occasion, and Annabelle went home. She felt much older. It would be almost twenty-five years before she saw Michel again.

At three a.m. the telephone rang; the nurse seemed truly sorry. Everything possible had been done, but very little was possible. Her heart was too weak. At least they could be sure that she had not suffered. But, she had to tell them, it was over now.

Michel went back to his room, taking short steps, barely twenty centimeters at a time. Brigitte moved to get up but Marie-Thérèse prevented her. For a minute or two there was silence, and then a sort of mewing or howling from his room. Brigitte hurried to him. Michel was rolled into a ball at the foot of his bed. His eyes were wide open, but his expression was not one of grief, nor of any recognizable human emotion. His face was filled with abject, animal fear.

PART TWO
Strange Moments

1

Bruno lost control of the car just outside Poitiers. The Peugeot 305 skidded across the expressway and hit the guardrail, spun 180 degrees, righted itself, then stopped. "Christ!" he muttered numbly, "Jesus fucking Christ!" A Jaguar hurtled toward him, doing 220 km; the driver braked sharply and swerved, narrowly missing the other guardrail, then drove off leaning on his horn. "Bastard!" screamed Bruno, climbing out and shaking his fist. "Fucking bastard!" Then he got back into his car, made a U-turn and continued on his way.

The Lieu du Changement was founded in 1975 by a group of '68 veterans (in fact, they were more "spirit of '68," since none of them had actually been involved in the riots). It was just south of Cholet on a vast estate scattered with pine forests that belonged to one of the members' parents. Their plan, inspired by the liberal values of the early seventies, was to create an authentic utopia—a place where the principles of self-government, respect for individual freedom and true democracy could be practiced in the "here and now." The Lieu was not a commune, but had the more modest aim of providing a place where like-minded people could spend the summer months living according to the principles they espoused. It was intended that this haven of humanist and democratic feeling would create synergies, facilitate the meeting of minds and, in particular, as one of the founding members put it, provide an opportunity to "get your rocks off."

Just before Cholet Sud, Bruno took the exit off the expressway and drove for ten kilometers along country roads. The map was not very clear, and he felt hot. It was pure chance, he thought, that he finally saw the sign. In large, multicolored letters it read LIEU DU CHANGEMENT and, underneath: *I am properly free when all the men and women about me are equally free* (Mikhail Bakunin). On the right, two teenage girls were walking up a path that led to the sea and dragging a plastic duck. The sluts were wearing nothing under their T-shirts. Bruno watched them as they passed; his cock ached. Wet T-shirts, he thought solemnly, were a wonderful thing. The girls turned off the road; they were clearly heading to the nearby campsite.

He parked the 305 and walked over to a small wooden hut with a WELCOME sign. Inside, a woman of about sixty sat in the lotus position. Her thin, wrinkled breasts hung over her thin cotton tunic; Bruno felt sorry for her. She gave him a big, somewhat stilted smile. "Welcome to the Lieu du Changement," she said at last. She smiled broadly again; was she demented? "Have you got your reservation form?" Bruno took his papers out of his wallet. "Perfect!" muttered the hag, still smiling like a half-wit.

It was forbidden to drive cars within the grounds of the campsite so he decided to work in stages: first he would find a place to pitch his tent, then he would get his things from the car. He had bought a tent from La Samaritaine before setting off ("Made in the People's Republic of China, 2/3 persons, 449FF").

The first thing Bruno noticed when he arrived in the clearing was the pyramid. It was twenty meters high and twenty meters along the base: exactly equilateral. The sides were constructed of glass panes in heavy wood frames. The dying sun glinted on some of them, while through others it was possible to see the internal framework of levels and partitions, also constructed of dark wood. It was intended to symbolize a tree.

In the center, a large cylinder housed the central staircase. A stream of people—some alone, others in small groups; some dressed, others naked—was leaving the building. With the sunset flaring through the long grass, the whole scene looked like a science fiction movie. Bruno observed the scene for two or three minutes, then took his tent under his arm and started up the first hill.

The land was hilly and wooded with clearings here and there; the ground was carpeted with pine needles, and there were communal sanitary facilities at regular intervals. No plots were marked out. Bruno started to sweat, and he had gas; he'd eaten too much at the rest stop. He was finding it difficult to think clearly, but he knew that the choice of where to pitch his tent could make all the difference in the success of his stay.

He was concluding as much when he noticed a clothesline strung between two trees. An evening breeze moved gently through the panties that had been hung out to dry. It might be a good idea to camp here, he thought, since it's easy to get to know your neighbors when camping. Not necessarily to fuck them, just to get acquainted. It was a start. He put down the tent and began to study the instructions. The French translation was abominable, the English not much better; he assumed that the other European languages were just as bad. Fucking Chinks. What the hell did *upturn the demipoles to stable the dome* mean?

He was standing staring hopelessly at the diagrams when a sort of squaw appeared, dressed in a miniskirt of animal pelt, her large breasts dangling in the twilight. "Just got here?" the apparition asked. "Need a hand setting up your tent?"

"I'll be okay," he said in a strangled voice. "I'll be okay, thanks . . . It's very good of you," he whispered. He had the impression this was a trap. Moments later, a wailing erupted from the neighboring wigwam (where the hell had they bought this thing—or had they made it themselves?). The squaw ran off, returned with two little brats, one on each hip, and rocked them gently. They screamed louder. The squaw's brave trotted up, his cock dangling in the breeze. He was about fifty, a stocky guy with long gray hair and a beard. He took one of the little monkeys in his arms and started tickling it. Disgusting. Bruno moved a little way off—that was a close call. With little monsters like that, he wouldn't get a wink of sleep. She was obviously breast-feeding, the cow; nice tits, though.

He walked a couple of meters away from the wigwam, but didn't want to stray too far from the panties. They were delicate, lacy and transparent, and he couldn't imagine they belonged to the squaw. He finally found a spot between two Canadian girls (cousins? sisters? school friends?) and set to work.

It was almost dark by the time he had finished. In the half-light, he went back to get his suitcases. He met a number of people on the way: both couples and singles, and quite a few single women in their forties. At regular intervals there were signs nailed to the trees reading MUTUAL RESPECT. He walked up to one of them; underneath was a small dish full of condoms conforming to French specifications. Below, there was a white plastic trash can. He stepped on the pedal and turned on his flashlight; the trash can was mostly full of empty beer cans, but there were also used condoms. That's reassuring, thought Bruno; it looks like this place is humming.

The trip back was difficult; he was out of breath and the suitcase handles cut into his hands. He had to stop halfway up. Some people were still circulating, the beams from their flashlights crossing in the darkness. There was still a lot of traffic on the coast road. The Dynasty on the way to Saint-Clément had a topless night, but he didn't feel up to it. He stood motionless for half an hour. This is my life, thought Bruno, I'm watching the cars' headlights through the trees.

When he got back to his tent he poured himself a whiskey and jerked off slowly, flicking through a copy of *Swing*—"pleasure is a right"—having bought a copy at a service station near Angers. He had no intention of really replying to any of the small ads; he couldn't hack a *gang bang* or a *sperm fest*. The women seeking single men were generally looking for black guys, and in any case he did not come close to the minimum size they required. Issue after issue, he came to the conclusion that his cock was too small for the porn circuit.

In general, however, he was not unhappy with his body. The hair transplant had taken well—luckily he'd found a good surgeon. He worked out regularly and, frankly, thought he looked good for forty-two. He poured another whiskey, ejaculated on the magazine and fell asleep, almost content.

2

A THIRTEEN-HOUR FLIGHT

The Lieu du Changement rapidly ran into the problem of aging. In the eighties young people found its ideals dated. There were theater workshops and massage therapy, but it basically was a campsite; the accommodations and facilities were not up to resort standards. Apart from that, the anarchic spirit of the place made it difficult to control access and collect payments; its finances, which had always been precarious, became even more problematic.

Their first response—a decision passed unanimously by the founding members—was to establish preferential rates for the young, but this did not prove sufficient. At the annual board meeting in the beginning of the 1984 fiscal year, Frédéric Le Dantec made a proposal that turned out to be the Lieu's salvation. He suggested that business was the leisure industry of the 1980s. Each of them had acquired valuable experience in humanist therapy (Gestalt, rebirth, walking on hot coals, transactional analysis, Zen meditation, communication skills . . .). Why not invest that experience in developing a series of residential courses aimed at businesses? After fierce debate, the proposal was adopted. Once it was accepted, work began on building the pyramid, together with fifty bungalows—basic but comfortable—where visitors could stay. At the same time, the founders organized an extensive mailing, targeting human resources directors in multinational companies. Some of the more left-wing of the founders found this transition difficult to accept. After a brief internal power struggle, the Lieu ceased to be an association under the act of 1901 and became a publicly traded corporation in which Frédéric Le Dantec was principal shareholder. After all, it was his parents' land, and Crédit Mutuel in Charente-Maritime seemed willing to back the project.

Five years later, the Lieu du Changement had an excellent client list (the National Bank of Paris, IBM, the Ministry of Finance, the Paris transit authority, Bouygues telecommunications). Inter- and intracompany courses were offered year-round and the campsite—maintained principally for reasons of nostalgia—accounted for less than five percent of the company's annual turnover.

Bruno woke with a crippling headache and no illusions. He had heard about the place from a secretary who had been on a "Personal Development—Positive Thinking" course at five thousand francs a day. He had asked her for the brochure. Friendly, open-minded, liberal; he got the picture. But one statistic at the bottom of the page attracted his attention: in July–August of the previous year, sixty-three percent of visitors to the Lieu du Changement were female. That was almost two women to every man: an excellent ratio. He decided to check it out, and booked a week there in July; especially as camping would be cheaper than going to a Club Med. Of course, he could guess what sort of women went there: deranged old lefties who were probably all HIV-positive. But still, with two women to every man, he stood a chance; if he worked it properly, he might even bag two.

The year had started well from a sexual point of view. The influx of girls from Eastern Europe had meant prices had dropped. For two hundred francs you could get a little personal relaxation, down from four hundred francs some months earlier. Unfortunately, he crashed his car in April and the repairs were expensive; worse still, it had been his fault. The bank started to squeeze him and he had to economize.

He lifted himself on his elbow and poured himself his first whiskey. The copy of *Swing* was still open at the same page. A guy who kept his socks on—his name was Hervé—was thrusting his cock toward the camera with visible effort.

Not my thing, thought Bruno, not at all. He put on a pair of boxer shorts and walked toward the shower block. After all, he thought hopefully, the squaw from last night was more or less fuckable. In fact her big, sagging breasts were perfect for a tit-job; it had been three years since his last time. Bruno had always liked jerking off between a girl's tits, but whores didn't really go for it. Was it the fact that you came in their faces that turned them off? Did it require more time and personal investment than a blow-job? Whatever, a tit-job wasn't generally on the menu, so it was difficult to get girls to do it. They seemed to think of it as personal. Often, when he requested one, Bruno had to make do with a hand-job or maybe a blow-job. He sometimes managed to coax a tit-job out of a girl, but as far as Bruno was concerned there were not nearly enough to go around.

might accidentally brush against his prick. At this thought he felt increasingly dizzy and had to hold on to the porcelain sink. At the same instant two boys arrived, laughing a little too loudly; they were wearing black shorts with fluorescent stripes. Suddenly Bruno's hard-on was gone; he put his penis back into his shorts and returned to picking at his teeth.

Later, still in a state of shock, he went down to the breakfast tables. He sat apart from the others and spoke to no one. As he chewed his vitamin-enriched cereal, he thought about the Faustian nature of sexual pursuit, its vampirism. For example, Bruno thought, people are wrong to talk about homosexuals. He had never—or very rarely—met a homosexual; on the other hand, he knew a great many *pederasts*. Some pederasts—thankfully, very few—prefer little boys; they wind up in prison for a long stretch and no one ever talks about them again. Most pederasts, however, are attracted to youths between fifteen and twenty-five. Anyone older than that is, to them, simply an old, dried-up asshole. Watch two old queens together, Bruno liked to say, watch them closely: they may be fond of each other, they may even be affectionate, but do they really want each other? No. As soon as some tight fifteen-to-twenty-five-year-old ass walks past, they will tear each other apart like panthers; each will rip the other to pieces just for that tight little ass—so Bruno thought.

In this, as in many things, so-called homosexuals had led the way for society as a whole, Bruno figured. Take him, for example—he was forty-two years old. Did he want women his own age? Absolutely not. On the other hand, for young pussy wrapped in a miniskirt he was prepared to go to the ends of the earth. Well, to Bangkok at least. Which was, after all, a thirteen-hour flight.

3

Sexual desire is preoccupied with youth, and the progressive influx of ever-younger girls onto the field of seduction was simply a return to the norm; a restoration of the true nature of desire, comparable to the return of stock prices to their true value after a run on the exchange. Nonetheless, women who turned twenty in the late sixties found themselves in a difficult position when they hit forty. Most of them were divorced and could no longer count on the conjugal bond—whether warm or abject—whose decline they had served to hasten. As members of a generation who—more than any before—had proclaimed the superiority of youth over age, they could hardly claim to be surprised when they, in turn, were despised by succeeding generations. As their flesh began to age, the cult of the body, which they had done so much to promote, simply filled them with an intensifying disgust for their own bodies—a disgust they could see mirrored in the gaze of others.

The men of their generation found themselves in much the same position, yet this common destiny fostered no solidarity. At forty, they continued to pursue young women—with a measure of success, at least for those who, having skillfully slipped into the social game, had attained a certain position, whether intellectual, financial or social. For women, their mature years brought only failure, masturbation and shame.

Dedicated exclusively to sexual liberation and the expression of desire, the Lieu du Changement naturally became a place of depression and bitterness. Farewell to limbs entwined in a clearing under the full moon! Farewell to the quasi-Dionysian spectacle of oiled bodies glistening under the midday sun. That, at least, is what the forty-somethings muttered as they regarded their flaccid pricks and rolls of fat.

In 1987 the first quasi-religious workshops appeared at the Lieu. Christianity was excluded, of course, but a sufficiently nebulous, exotic mysticism—for these rather weak-minded beings—dovetailed neatly with the cult of the body beautiful which, against all sense, they continued to promote. There were still workshops on sensual massage and the liberation of the orgone, but interest in the esoteric—astrology, Egyptian tarot, chakras—boomed. There were Encounters with the Angel and courses on crystal healing. Siberian shamanism made a conspicuous debut when, in 1991, during the long initiation in a sweat lodge fired by sacred coals, an initiate died of heart failure. Tantric Zen, which combined profound vanity, diffuse mysticism and sexual frottage, flourished. In a matter of years, the Lieu—like many centers throughout France and Western Europe—became a relatively popular New Age institution while maintaining its reputation as a "1970s-style" hedonist's paradise, which became its unique selling point.

After breakfast Bruno retired to his tent. He considered masturbating (the image of the teenagers was still vivid), but finally decided against it. The enticing girls must be the offspring of the regiments of flower children he had passed around the Lieu, so clearly some of the old hags had succeeded in reproducing after all. This realization plunged Bruno into vague, unpleasant reflections. He tore open the flap of his tent; the sky was blue, small clouds floated like spatters of sperm between the pines, the day promised to be dazzling. He glanced at the program for the week: he had chosen option one—"Creativity and Relaxation." There was a choice of three workshops that morning: mime and psychodrama, painting in watercolors and creative writing. Psychodrama, he decided, was best avoided. He had been there and done that, on a weekend course in Chantilly where he had watched fifty-year-old social workers rolling around on the floor whining for daddy to bring them their teddy bears. Painting sounded more interesting, but would probably be outdoors: did he really want to squat among pine needles, insects and God knows what else, only to turn out some crap?

The woman who led the creative writing workshop had long black hair and a full, sensual mouth outlined in carmine red (what he usually referred to as "blow-job lips"); she wore a black tunic and stretch pants. A good-looking woman, she had class. Probably just a slut, though, thought Bruno, crouching down in the ill-defined circle of disciples. To his right a fat, sallow, gray-haired woman with thick glasses breathed noisily. She reeked of wine and it was only ten-thirty.

"To salute our collective presence," began the leader, "to salute the Earth and the five ways, we will begin the workshop with the hatha-yoga movement called 'the sun salutation.'" She followed this with a description of an unlikely posture; the wino on Bruno's right belched. "You look tired, Jacqueline," said the yogi. "You shouldn't do any exercise if you don't feel up to it. Lie down; the group will join you in a while."

They all had to lie down while the teacher delivered a long, vacuous speech in the style of Contrexéville: "You are plunging into beautiful, crystal water. You can feel it enveloping your limbs, flowing over your stomach. You give thanks to your mother, the Earth. Confidently, you press yourself to your mother, the Earth. Feel your desire. You give thanks to yourself for giving you this desire," etc. Lying on the filthy Japanese mat, Bruno ground his teeth together angrily. The dipso beside him belched regularly. Between burps, she exhaled with a great "Haaaaaa," which presumably was intended to express her relaxation. The karma queen went on with her routine, conjuring tellurian energies to revitalize the stomach and groin. After meandering through the four elements, and satisfied with her performance, she concluded: "Now that you have broken the barrier of the rational and made contact with your deepest desires, open yourself to the limitless power of the creative urge." "Urge, schmurge," fumed Bruno as, with difficulty, he got to his feet. The writing session was followed by a presentation in which each of them had to read what they had written. The only halfway decent babe in the whole workshop was called Emma—a fit little redhead wearing jeans and a T-shirt, who had written a completely inane poem about moon-sheep. Most of the group were positively oozing with rapture at having made contact with Mother Earth, Father Sun and family. At last it was Bruno's turn to read. Mournfully he intoned:

Taxi drivers are fucking cunts
They never stop, the little runts

"You feel like that . . ." said the yogi, "you feel like that because you haven't mastered your negative energy. I can feel deep, powerful desires within you. We can help you—here and now. Let's all stand and focus the energies of the group."

Everyone stood, joined hands and formed a circle. Reluctantly, Bruno took the hands of the old bag on his right and a revolting little bearded man who looked like Cavanna. Her whole being focused but calm, the yogi uttered a long "Om" and they were off, everyone droning "Om" as if they'd been doing it all their lives. Bruno was gamely trying to join in the resounding harmony when he suddenly felt himself pitch to the right. Hypnotized, the fat hag was toppling like a stone. He let go of her hand but was unable to break his fall and found himself on his knees in front of the old bitch, now flat on her back and writhing on the mat. The yogi interrupted her meditation and said calmly: "That's it, Jacqueline, just lie down if you feel like it." The two of them seemed to know each other.

The second writing exercise was a little better; inspired by his fugitive vision that morning, Bruno penned the following poem:

I'm tanning my dick
(Hair on my prick)
Down by the pool
(Hair on my tool)

I swear I found God
In Body Space 8
He has a great bod
But his hair is a state

What is our job?
(Hair on my knob)
To praise him in song
(Hair on my dong)

"It's . . . humorous," said the yogi, her tone somewhat disapproving. "And mystical," theorized the drunk, "mystical but empty . . ." What was he going to do, Bruno wondered. How long could he put up with this? Was it really worth the effort? When the workshop ended he rushed back to his tent, not even stopping to try and talk to the little redhead; he needed a whiskey before lunch. Near his tent, he happened across one of the girls he had been eyeing at the showers. With a graceful movement which showed off her breasts, she reached up and took down the lacy panties she had hung out the night before. He felt as though he might explode, showering the campsite in a rain of fatty tissues. What had changed since his adolescence? He still had the same desires, with the knowledge that he probably could never satisfy them. A world that respects only the young eventually devours everyone. For lunch, he chose a Catholic. She was easy to spot: she wore a big iron cross around her neck; besides, her heavy lower lids gave her eyes the fervor common to Catholics or mystics (though, admittedly, also to alcoholics). Long dark hair, pale complexion, a bit skinny but not bad-looking. Facing her sat a girl with reddish blonde hair, the Swiss-Californian type: six feet tall, perfect body, obscenely healthy. She was the leader of the Tantric Zen workshop. In fact, her name was Brigitte Martin and she came from Créteil. She had been initiated into the mysteries of the Orient in California, where she had her breasts done and changed her name. Back in Créteil, she ran a class on Tantric Zen under the name of Shanti Martin; the Catholic was clearly impressed. At first, Bruno found it easy to join in their discussion, which seemed to be about macrobiotics—he had read up on wheat germ—but the conversation quickly turned to more religious themes and soon he was lost. Could Jesus be subsumed into Krishna, or perhaps into some other deity? Was Rin Tin Tin more lovable than Lucky Luke's Rusty? Though Catholic, this woman had no time for the Pope; his medieval outlook, in her opinion, was hindering the spiritual evolution of the Western world. "You're right," said Bruno, "he's a retard." The judgment earned him a new respect from the others.

"And the Dalai Lama can wiggle his ears," he said dolefully as he finished his tofu burger.

Indefatigable, the Catholic got up before coffee was served—she didn't want to be late for her personal development workshop, "The Principles of Yes-Yes." "Ah yes, Yes-yes is cool," said the Swiss-Californian as she got up. "Thanks for the chat," said the Catholic, turning back with a smile. Anyway, he hadn't done too badly, Bruno thought as he headed back to his tent. "Talking to morons like that is like pissing in a urinal full of cigarette butts, like shitting in a toilet full of Tampax: nothing gets flushed, and everything starts to stink." Space separates one skin from another. Words cross the space, the space between one skin and another. Unheard, unanswered, the words hang in the air and begin to decay, to stink; that's the way it is. Seen like this, words could separate, too.

At the pool, he found a pool-chair. The teenage girls danced around like idiots, shivering, hoping a boy might push them in. The sun was at its height; slick, naked bodies moved across the expanse of blue. Without thinking, Bruno launched into a children's book, *The Six Companions and the Gloved Man*, Paul Jacques Bonzon's masterpiece, recently republished by the Bibliothèque Verte. In the unbearable glare of the sun, it was good to find himself back in the mists of Lyons with his stalwart companion, Kapi the dog.

The afternoon program offered a choice between "Sensitive Gestalt-Massage," "Liberating the Voice" and "Rebirthing in Warm Water." In theory, massage sounded the sexiest. He had a brief glimpse of liberating the voice as he walked up to the massage workshop: there were about ten of them, very excited, jumping around to the directions of the Tantric woman and screeching like startled turkeys.

At the top of the hill, arranged in a circle, were trestle tables, each covered with a large towel. The students were naked. In the center of the circle, the instructor, a small, dark-haired man with a slight squint, gave a brief history of sensitive Gestalt-massage. Born out of Fritz Perls's Gestalt—or "Californian"—massage, the method had evolved to integrate aspects of the sensual to become—in his opinion—the most complete form of massage. There were those at the Lieu, he admitted, who did not share his point of view, but he did not wish to become polemical. Whatever the truth of it—and he would like to end on this note—there was massage and then there was massage; in fact one might say that no two massages were alike. Having finished his preamble, he began the demonstration by asking one of the women to lie on the table. "Feel the tension in your partner," he commented as he stroked her shoulders, his cock only centimeters from the girl's long blonde hair. "Harmony, it's all about harmony . . ." he went on, pouring oil on her breasts. "You must respect the wholeness of the body . . ." His hands slipped down her stomach; the girl closed her eyes and parted her thighs, clearly enjoying his work.

"There you go," he concluded. "Now I want you to work in pairs. Take your time, move around the space, get to know each other." Still hypnotized by what he had just seen, Bruno was slow to react, though this was the crucial moment. You simply approached your partner of choice, smiled, and calmly asked her, "Would you like to work with me?" Everyone else seemed to know the drill, and in thirty seconds it was all over. Bruno looked around, panic-stricken, and found himself face to face with a hairy little man with dark hair and a thick penis. He had not realized there were only five girls for seven guys.

Thankfully the other guy didn't look like a queer. Visibly furious, he lay down on his stomach without a word, rested his head on his arms and waited. "Feel the tension . . . respect the wholeness of the body . . ." Bruno poured more oil on but couldn't get past the knees; the guy's body was stiff as a board. Even his buttocks were hairy. The oil was beginning to drip onto the towel, the guy's calves had to be saturated. Bruno looked up. Next to him, two men were lying on their backs. On his left, the man was having his pectorals massaged; the woman's breasts swayed gently, his nose level with her pussy. The instructor's ghetto blaster pumped out synthesizer music; the sky was a perfect blue. All around him oil-slick cocks were beginning to rise toward the light. Everything seemed intensely *real*. He could not bear it any longer. On the far side of the circle, the instructor was advising a couple on technique. Bruno grabbed his backpack and hurried off toward the pool, where it was clearly rush hour. On the nearby lawn, naked women lay chatting, reading or simply taking the sun. Where should he sit? Towel in hand, he wandered erratically across the lawn, tottering as it were between the vaginas. He decided it was time to get off the fence when he spotted the Catholic talking to a dark-skinned rugged little guy with bright eyes and dark curly hair. He made a vague sign of recognition—she did not notice—and flopped down nearby. "Hey, Karim!" someone called to the dark-skinned man as he walked past. Karim waved and went on talking to the Catholic, who lay quietly on her back listening. She had a pretty muff of curly black hair between her thighs. As they chatted, Karim gently kneaded his balls. Bruno rested his head on the grass and concentrated on the gentle world barely a meter away within the Catholic's pubic hair. He quickly fell asleep.

On 14 December 1967 the government passed the Neuwirth Act on contraception at its first reading. Although not yet paid for by social security, the pill would now be freely available in pharmacies. It was this which offered a whole section of society access to the sexual revolution, which until then had been reserved for professionals, artists and senior management—and some small businessmen. It is interesting to note that the "sexual revolution" was sometimes portrayed as a communal utopia, whereas in fact it was simply another stage in the historical rise of individualism. As the lovely word "household" suggests, the couple and the family would be the last bastion of primitive communism in liberal society. The sexual revolution was to destroy these intermediary communities, the last to separate the individual from the market. The destruction continues to this day.

The steering committee of the Lieu du Changement regularly held dinner dances. For a place open to new spiritual ideas, this might seem surprising, but it only confirmed the dinner dance as the inevitable means of sexual selection in noncommunist societies. As Frédéric Le Dantec pointed out, primitive societies also centered their feasts on dancing and the pursuit of collective trance.

A bar and a sound system were installed on the lawn, and people gyrated in the moonlight into the small hours. For Bruno, this was a second chance. Actually, the teenagers at the camp rarely attended these occasions, preferring to go to local clubs (Bilboquet, Dynasty, 2001 and, maybe, Pirates) which hosted theme nights with foam parties, male strip shows and porn stars. A handful of needle-dick dreamers stayed behind, spending their evenings in a tent gently strumming an out-of-tune guitar while their peers despised them. Bruno felt a keen sympathy for these young men. But in the absence of girls he could never hope to attract, he would happily—to quote a reader of *Newlook* he'd met in a café in Angers—"stick his knob in any available hole." It was in this hope that he left his tent at eleven, wearing white trousers and a blue polo shirt, and headed down to the source of the commotion.

Glancing around the mass of dancers, he spotted Karim, who had abandoned the Catholic in favor of a ravishing Rosicrucian. She and her husband, both tall, staid and slim, had arrived that afternoon; they seemed to be from Alsace. The husband had taken four hours to work out the arrangement of the numerous flaps and guylines of their convoluted tent. Earlier, he had taken Bruno aside and initiated him into the hidden mysteries of the Rosy Cross. Eyes glittering behind his small, round glasses, he looked every inch a zealot; Bruno listened without hearing. According to him, the fellowship of the Rosy Cross had been founded in Germany, inspired by the work of the alchemists, but was intrinsically linked to Rhenish mysticism. It was obviously a cabal of queers and Nazis. You can stick your cross up your ass, Bruno thought, distractedly watching that of the man's beautiful wife out of the corner of his eye as she kneeled by the gas stove—not to mention the rose, he added as she stood up, flashing her breasts, and called to her husband to come change the baby.

In any case, now she was dancing with Karim. They made a strange couple: the stocky, cunning little man a good fifteen centimeters shorter than this big Germanic beanpole. He chatted and smiled as they danced, as though he had forgotten why he had picked her up in the first place. Nevertheless, things seemed to be progressing. She smiled back and stared at him, clearly fascinated; once she even laughed out loud. On the far side of the lawn, her husband was explaining the origins of the Rosicrucian fellowship in Lower Saxony in 1530 to another potential convert. At regular intervals his three-year-old son, a blonde-haired, snot-nosed brat, screamed that he wanted to be put to bed. Once again Bruno was faced with a slice of *real life*. He overheard two skinny, priestly individuals commenting on the rake's progress. "He's very expressive, very emotional, you see . . ." said one. "On paper, he's out of his league: he's not good-looking, he's got a beer belly and he's a lot shorter than she is. But he's a charming bastard, and that makes all the difference." The other nodded, seeming to toy mournfully with an imaginary rosary. As he finished his vodka and orange juice, Bruno noticed that Karim had managed to inveigle the Rosicrucian onto a grass bank. One arm around her shoulders, talking all the while, he slipped his other hand up her dress. She's opened her legs for him, the Nazi slut, Bruno thought as he walked away from the dancers. Just as he stepped out of the circle of light, he had a vision of the Catholic girl having her ass felt up by someone who looked like a ski instructor. He still had some cans of ravioli in his tent.

Before heading back, in an act of pure desperation he phoned to check his answering machine. There was one message: "You're probably on vacation," said Michel's voice calmly. "Call me when you get back. I'm on vacation, too—indefinitely."

4

Walking, he reaches the border. A flock of vultures circle over something—probably a corpse. The muscles in his thighs respond to the irregularities of the path. The hills are shrouded in dry grass, stretching out east to the horizon. He has not eaten since the night before; he is no longer afraid.

He wakes, fully dressed, lying across his bed. A truck is unloading a shipment outside the delivery entrance of Monoprix. It is a little after seven o'clock.

For years, Michel had lived a purely intellectual existence. The world of human emotions was not his field; he knows little about it. Nowadays life can be organized with minute precision; supermarket cashiers respond to an imperceptible nod. There has been much coming and going in the ten years he has lived here; from time to time, a couple formed and he watched as the new lover moved in. Friends carrying boxes and lamps up the stairs. They were young and sometimes he heard them laugh. Often (but not always), when they split up the ex-lovers moved out at the same time, leaving an empty apartment. What conclusions could he draw from such things? How should he interpret these comings and goings? It was puzzling.

He himself wanted nothing more than to love. He asked for nothing; nothing in particular, anyway. Life should be simple, Michel thought, something that could be lived as a collection of small, endlessly repeated rituals. Perhaps somewhat empty rituals, but they gave you something to believe in. A life without risk, without drama. But life was not like that. Sometimes he went out and watched the teenagers and the buildings. One thing seemed clear to him: no one knew how to live anymore. Perhaps that was an exaggeration: some people seemed motivated, passionate about some cause, and their lives seemed to have more weight. Hence ACT UP activists thought it was important to run ads which others thought pornographic, depicting homosexual practices in close-up. Their lives seemed busier and more fulfilled, full of exciting incident. They had multiple partners, fucked each other in back rooms; sometimes the condom split or slipped off and they died of AIDS. Even then their deaths seemed radical, dignified. Television gave lessons in dignity, especially TF1. As a teenager, Michel believed that suffering conferred dignity on a person. Now he had to admit he had been wrong. What conferred dignity on people was television.

Despite the constant and pure pleasures of television, he thought it best to go out. In any case, he had to do his shopping. The only conclusion he could draw was that without points of reference, a man melts away.

On the morning of 9 July (the Feast of Saint Amandine) he noticed that ring binders, exercise books and pencil cases were already on display in Monoprix. He found the advertising slogan—"Back to school—no headaches!"—less than persuasive. What was education, what was knowledge, after all, if not one long headache?

The following morning he found the autumn/winter catalogue from 3 Suisses in his mailbox. The massive hardcover was not addressed—had it been hand delivered? As a long-standing subscriber to mail-order catalogues, he was used to the little extras that came with being a loyal customer. Time rolled on. Despite the glorious summer weather, marketing campaigns were already looking to the autumn, though July had barely begun.

As a young man, Michel had read some absurdist literature, focusing on existentialist despair and the motionless emptiness of days; he found such extremes of opinion only half-convincing. At the time he was seeing a lot of Bruno, who dreamed about becoming a writer, covering pages and pages with ink and masturbating continually; he introduced Michel to Samuel Beckett. Presumably he was what they called a *great writer*, though Michel had never managed to finish a single one of his books. That was in the late 1970s; he and Bruno were in their twenties and already felt old. As time went on they would feel older still, and be ashamed by the fact. Their generation was about to make a dramatic shift—substituting the tragedy of death with the more general humiliation of old age. Twenty years later, Bruno had never seriously thought about death and was beginning to wonder if he ever would. He wanted to live to the end, to be a part of life, to fight against physical infirmity and petty everyday misfortunes. With his last breath he would still plead for a postponement, to live a little longer. In particular, he would continue his quest for the ultimate pleasure to the end; one last indulgence. However transitory, a good blow-job was a real pleasure and that—Michel thought as he flicked through the lingerie section ("Sensual Garters!") of his catalogue—was something no one could deny.

He himself masturbated rarely; his fantasies as a young research student, whether inspired by the Minitel or by actual women (usually reps from large pharmaceutical companies), had gradually faded. Now he calmly managed the slow decline of his virility by occasionally jerking off, for which his 3 Suisses catalogue, supplemented now and then by a risqué CD-ROM (79FF), proved more than sufficient. Michel knew that Bruno, by contrast, was frittering away his prime chasing neurotic Lolitas with big breasts, round buttocks and eager mouths; thank God he was a civil servant. It was not absurd, Bruno's world; it was a melodrama where the characters were babes and dogs, cool guys and losers. Michel, on the other hand, lived in a world where everything was precisely regulated, a world without history where all the seasons were commercial ones: the French Open, Christmas, New Year's Eve, the semiannual arrival of the 3 Suisses catalogue. If he were homosexual, he would be able to take part in the AIDS walk or Gay Pride. If he were a libertine, he could look forward to the Salon de l'Érotisme. If he were a sportsman, he would be in the Pyrenees right now, watching a leg in the Tour de France. Though an undiscriminating shopper, he was delighted when his local Monoprix had an "Italian Fortnight." This life was so well organized, on such a human scale; happiness could be found in this; had he wanted for more, he wouldn't have known where to find it.

On the morning of 15 July he took a Christian tract out of the trash can in the hall. It included several life stories, each converging toward an identical happy ending: an encounter with the risen Christ. For some time he had followed the story of a young woman ("Isabelle was in a state of shock—her university career was on the line"), though he had to admit that Pavel's experience was closer to his own ("As an officer in the Czech army, commanding an antiaircraft station was the pinnacle of Pavel's military career"). He had no difficulty identifying with Pavel in the next paragraph: "As a technical expert, who had studied at a distinguished academy, Pavel should have been in love with life. Instead, he was depressed, constantly searching for a reason to live."

The 3 Suisses catalogue, on the other hand, offered a more thoughtful, historically informed insight into Europe's current malaise. The impression of a coming mutation in society in its opening pages is finally given precise formulation on page 17. Michel considered for hours the lines that summed up the theme of the collection: "Optimism, generosity, complicity and harmony make the world go round. THE FUTURE IS FEMALE."

On the eight o'clock news, Bruno Masure announced that an American study had detected signs of fossil life on Mars. The fossils were of bacterial organisms, probably methane-based archaea. It seemed that biological macromolecules had succeeded in forming on earth's closest neighbor, giving rise to nebulous self-replicating life-forms consisting of a nucleus and an ill-defined membrane. It had all ended there, however, presumably the result of climatic changes that made reproduction increasingly difficult to sustain, until eventually it ceased entirely. The story of life on Mars was a modest one. However (and Bruno Masure did not seem to understand this), this brief, feeble misfire brutally refuted all the mythological and religious constructs in which the human race delights. There had been no unique, wondrous act of creation; no chosen people; no chosen species or planet; simply a series of tentative attempts, flawed for the most part, scattered across the universe. It was all so distressingly banal. The DNA of the Martian bacteria seemed identical to that of terrestrial bacteria. More than anything this saddened him, in itself a sign of depression. In normal circumstances a scientist, any scientist in good form, would be excited by the similarities, and see in them the promise of a unifying synthesis. If DNA was everywhere the same, there must be reasons—profound reasons—linked to the molecular structure of peptides, or perhaps to the topological conditions of asexual reproduction. And it must be possible to discover these reasons. Had he been younger, such a prospect would have filled him with enthusiasm.

When he first met Desplechin in 1982, Djerzinski was finishing his doctoral thesis at the University of Orsay. As part of his studies he took part in Alain Aspect's groundbreaking experiments, which showed that the behavior of photons emitted in succession from a single calcium atom was inseparable from the others. Michel was the youngest researcher on the team.

Aspect's experiments—precise, rigorous and perfectly documented—were to have profound repercussions in the scientific community. The results, it was acknowledged, were the first clear-cut refutation of Einstein, Podolsky and Rosen's objections when they claimed in 1935 that "quantum theory is incomplete." Here was a clear violation of Bell's inequalities—derived from Einstein's hypotheses—since the results tallied perfectly with quantum predictions. This meant that only two hypotheses were possible. Either the hidden properties which governed the behavior of subatomic particles were nonlocal—meaning they could instantaneously influence one another at an arbitrary distance—or else the very notion of particles having intrinsic properties in the absence of observation had to be abandoned. The latter opened up a deep ontological void—unless one adopted a radical positivism and contented oneself with developing a mathematical formalism which predicted the observable and gave up on any idea of an underlying reality. Naturally, it was this last option which won over the majority of researchers.

The first paper on Aspect's experiments—"Experimental Realization of Einstein–Podolsky–Rosen *Gedankexperiment*: A New Violation of Bell's Inequalities"—was published in issue 48 of the *Physical Review*. Djerzinski was credited as cowriter of the article. A few days later he had a visit from Desplechin. At forty-three, he was director of the Institute of Molecular Biology at Gif-sur-Yvette. He was increasingly aware that something fundamental was missing in their analysis of gene mutations; and that this was probably related to phenomena at the atomic level.

Their first interview took place in Michel's dorm room. Desplechin was unsurprised by the dreary austerity of the surroundings: they were more or less what he expected. Their conversation continued late into the night. Desplechin pointed out that it was the existence of a finite list of chemical elements which had prompted Niels Bohr's first thoughts on the subject in the 1910s. A planetary theory of the atom based on gravitational and electromagnetic fields should, in principle, led to an infinite number of solutions, and an infinite number of possible chemical elements. The universe, however, was made up of about a hundred elements; a list which was fixed and stable. It was this situation, profoundly anomalous according to Maxwell's equations and the classical laws of electromagnetics, that led to the development of quantum mechanics. In Desplechin's opinion, contemporary biology was now in a similar position. The existence of identical macromolecules and immutable cellular ultrastructures, which had remained consistent throughout evolutionary history, could not be explained by the laws of classical chemistry. In some way as yet impossible to determine, quantum theory must directly impact on biological events. This would create an entirely new field of research.

That first evening, Desplechin was struck by his young interlocutor's calm open-mindedness. He invited Djerzinski to dinner at his home on the rue de l'École-Polytechnique the following Saturday, where one of his colleagues—a biochemist who had published extensively on RNA transcriptases—would join them.

When he arrived at Desplechin's apartment, Michel felt as though he had walked onto a film set. Before this he had scarcely imagined such a milieu: leisure, cultivated with a refined and confident sense of taste. Walnut furniture, Spanish tile, kilims, Afghan rugs, reproductions of Matisse . . . Now he could imagine the rest—the house in Brittany, maybe a small farm in the Luberon. And a boxed set of Bartók quintets, I bet, he thought fleetingly as he began to eat. They had champagne with dinner; dessert was a charlotte of red fruits accompanied by an exceptional semi-dry rosé. It was at this point that Desplechin outlined his project. He could arrange for a post to be created in his department at Gif on a contractual basis. Michel would need to acquire the basic concepts of biochemistry to complement his studies, but that was easily done. Meanwhile, Desplechin would supervise his dissertation personally. Once that was completed, Michel could apply for a permanent post.

Michel glanced at the small Khmer statue on the mantelpiece; the clean lines of the figure of the Buddha touching the ground, asking Nature to witness his resolve to reach enlightenment. Michel cleared his throat and accepted.

In the decade that followed, remarkable technical advances and the use of radioactive markers made it possible to amass a substantial number of results. Though as far as the theoretical questions Desplechin had raised at their first meeting were concerned, thought Djerzinski, there had been zero progress.

In the early hours of the morning, he found himself preoccupied with the Martian bacteria. He found a dozen messages on the Internet, mostly from American universities. Proportions of adenine, guanine, thymine and cytosine had been found to be typical. Randomly, he clicked on the Ann Arbor site where he found a message about aging. Alicia Marcia-Coelho had found evidence to suggest that DNA coding sequences were lost during the repeated subdivision of fibroblasts from nonstriated muscles; this was hardly a surprise. Michel knew Alicia—in fact it was she who had relieved him of his virginity ten years before, after a particularly drunken dinner at a genetics seminar in Baltimore. She had been so drunk that she couldn't help him take off her bra. It had been a difficult moment, painful even. She had just split up with her husband, she confided as Michel struggled with the clasps. After that, everything went normally; he was surprised to discover that he could get a hard-on and even ejaculate inside the researcher's vagina without feeling the slightest pleasure.

5

Many of the people who went to the Lieu du Changement were, like Bruno, over forty, and many, also like him, worked in the public sector or in education and were safeguarded from poverty by their status as civil servants. Most of them would have put themselves on the political left; most of them lived alone, usually as the result of divorce. He was, therefore, a pretty typical visitor. After a few days he noticed that he felt somewhat less bad than usual. The women were intolerable at breakfast, but by cocktail hour the mystical tarts were hopelessly vying with younger women once again. Death is the great leveler. On Wednesday afternoon he met Catherine, a fifty-year-old who had been a feminist of the old school. She was tanned, with dark, curly hair; she must have been very attractive when she was twenty. Her breasts were still in good shape, he thought when he saw her by the pool, but she had a fat ass. She had reinvented herself through Egyptian symbolism, tarot and the like. She was talking about the god Anubis as Bruno lowered his boxer shorts; he decided she probably wouldn't be offended by his erection and that they might become friends. Unfortunately, the erection didn't appear. She had rolls of fat between her thighs, which remained closed. They parted on less than friendly terms.

That evening, just before dinner, a guy called Pierre-Louis introduced himself. He was a math teacher, and looked the part. Bruno had noticed him a couple of days earlier at the theatrical evening; he had done a stand-up routine about a mathematical proof that went around in circles—some kind of comedy of the absurd, not the slightest bit funny. He scribbled furiously on a white board. From time to time he would stop abruptly, marker raised, motionless, bald head furrowed in thought, eyebrows raised in an expression that was supposed to be funny, before scribbling furiously and stammering more than ever. When the sketch ended, five or six people applauded, mostly out of pity. He blushed wildly; it was over.

In the days that followed, Bruno had managed to avoid him on several occasions. He usually wore a sun hat. He was at least six foot four and skinny, but he had a bit of a paunch and made a curious sight walking along the diving board with his fat little belly. He was probably about forty-five.

That evening Bruno again made a quick getaway while the beanpole joined the others in an improvised African dance. He walked up the hill toward the communal restaurant. There was a seat free beside the ex-feminist, who was sitting opposite a sister symbolist. He had barely started his tofu ragout when Pierre-Louis appeared at the far end of the row of tables; he beamed when he noticed a vacant chair opposite Bruno. He had been talking for some time before Bruno noticed, partly because he had a rather bad stammer, and partly because of the shrill nattering of the imbeciles next to them. What about the reincarnation of Osiris? What do you think of Egyptian marionettes? They were paying not the slightest attention to the men. At some point Bruno realized that the poor fool was asking him about his job. "Oh, nothing much . . ." he replied vaguely; he was happy to talk about anything except the national curriculum. The meal was beginning to get on his nerves; he got up to go out for a cigarette. Unfortunately, at precisely that moment the symbolists left, hips swinging, without so much as a glance in their direction. This probably is what triggered the incident.

Bruno was about ten meters from the table when he heard a loud whistle, or rather a strangled cry, high-pitched, almost inhuman. He turned around: Pierre-Louis was red-faced, his fists balled; from a standing start, he leapt onto the table with both feet. He took a deep breath and the wheezing from his chest stopped. He started to pace up and down the table, thumping himself on thc head with his fist as the glasses and plates danced around him. He kicked out at everything within reach, screaming, "You can't do this! You can't treat me like this!" For once he didn't stutter. It took five people to calm him down. He was admitted to the psychiatric ward of the hospital in Angoulême that evening.

At three a.m. Bruno woke with a start and scrabbled his way out of the tent, soaked in sweat. The Lieu was quiet, the moon was full and the monotonous croak of tree frogs filled the air. He sat by the pond and waited for daybreak. Just before dawn, he felt a little cold. The morning sessions would start at ten o'clock. At a quarter past ten he walked down to the pyramid. He hesitated outside the creative writing workshop, then went down to the next floor, where he studied the program for the watercolor class for about twenty seconds before walking up a couple of steps. The stairway was made up of straight flights, each with a curved section in the middle. The steps grew wider toward the middle and narrowed again as one approached the landing. In the curve was a step wider than all the others. It was here that Bruno sat, leaning against the wall. He began to feel well.

As a schoolboy, he would often sit on a step between floors just after class began; these were his rare moments of happiness. Midway between landings, he would lean back against the wall, eyes half-closed, sometimes wide open, and wait. Of course someone might come, in which case he would have to get up, pick up his schoolbag and walk quickly to his classroom, where class already had started. But often no one came, and here on the gray-tiled steps (he wasn't in history class anymore, he wasn't in physics class yet) everything was so peaceful; then gently, almost furtively, his heart soared in short bursts toward joy.

The circumstances were very different now: he had chosen to come to the Lieu; chosen to take part in its activities. Upstairs was a creative writing class; just below the workshop on watercolor; farther down there would be classes on massage or holotropic breathing; farther still, the African dance classes had clearly started up again. All around him human beings were living, breathing, striving for pleasure or trying to develop their personal potential. On every floor, human beings were improving, or trying to improve, their social, sexual or professional skills or find their place within the cosmos. They were "bettering themselves," in the expression commonly used in the Lieu. Bruno was beginning to feel a little sleepy. He had stopped wishing, he had stopped wanting, he was nowhere. Slowly, by degrees, his spirit filled to a state of nothingness, the sheer joy that comes of not being part of the world. For the first time since he was thirteen, Bruno was almost happy.

Would you mind telling me where I might find the nearest candy shop?

He went back to his tent and slept for three hours. When he awoke he was in top form, and he had a hard-on. Sexual frustration in the human male manifests itself as a violent contraction in the lower abdomen as the sperm seems to back up, and pangs shoot toward the chest. The penis itself is painful, constantly hot and slightly sweaty; Bruno had not masturbated since Sunday, which probably had been a mistake. The last remaining myth of Western civilization was that sex was something to do; something expedient, a diversion. He put on a pair of swimming trunks and slipped some condoms into his bag—snorting with laughter as he did so. He had been carrying condoms around for years and had never used one of them—after all, whores always had their own.

The beach at Meschers was crawling with jerk-offs in shorts and bimbos in thongs; this was reassuring. He bought an order of French fries and circulated among the vacationers before settling on a girl of about twenty with beautiful breasts—round, firm and pert, with caramel-colored nipples. "Hello," he said. He waited a beat; the girl frowned nervously. "Hello," he said again. "Would you mind telling me where I might find the nearest candy shop?"

"Hmm?" she said, raising herself up on one elbow. It was then that he noticed she was wearing a Walkman; he backed off, pumping his arm by his side like Peter Falk in *Columbo*. There was no point in pushing it; it was all just too complicated, too second-rate.

As he walked through the crowd toward the surf he tried to keep an image of the girl's breasts in his mind. Suddenly, directly in front of him, three teenage girls stepped out of the waves. They couldn't be more than fourteen, he decided. He noticed their towels and spread his own on the sand a couple of meters away. They hadn't even noticed him. He quickly took off his T-shirt and draped it across his lap, rolled onto his side and took out his penis. With the precision of synchronized swimmers, the girls rolled down the tops of their swimsuits to get the sun on their breasts. Before he had time to touch himself, Bruno came violently onto his T-shirt. He let out a moan and rolled over on the sand. It was done.

The primitive rituals of happy hour

The high point of social life at the Lieu du Changement was over aperitifs, which usually featured live music. That evening there were three guys playing tom-toms to fifty or so guests who danced rooted to the spot and waved their arms in all directions. These were harvest dances, apparently, which some of them had been practicing in the African dance workshop; customarily, after a number of hours, some of them would go into a trance—or pretend to. The archaic or literal sense of the word *trance* is extreme anxiety, fear at the idea of imminent danger. *I would rather leave my home than go on living through such a trance* (Émile Zola). Bruno offered the Catholic girl a glass of Pineau des Charentes. "What's your name?" he asked.

"Sophie," she replied.

"Not dancing?"

"No, I don't really like African dance, it's too . . ."

Too what? He understood her dilemma. Too primitive? Certainly not. Too rhythmic? Even that bordered on racism. There was nothing you could say about African fucking dance. Poor Sophie was trying her best. Her face was pretty: pale-skinned with blue eyes framed by her dark hair. She had small breasts, but they were probably very sensitive. She had to be Breton.

"Are you from Brittany?" he asked.

"Yes—from Saint-Brieuc!" she replied happily. "But I really like Brazilian dance," she added, obviously trying to absolve herself for her disinterest in African dance. Much more of this and Bruno would really get irritated. He was starting to get pissed off about the world's stupid obsession with Brazil. What was so great about Brazil? As far as he knew, Brazil was a shithole full of morons obsessed with soccer and Formula

One. It was the *ne plus ultra* of violence, corruption and misery. If ever a country were loathsome, that country, specifically, was Brazil.

"Sophie," announced Bruno, "I could go on vacation to Brazil tomorrow. I'd look around a favela. The minibus would be armor-plated; so in the morning, safe, unafraid, I'd go sightseeing, check out eight-year-old murderers who dream of growing up to be gangsters; thirteen-year-old prostitutes dying of AIDS. I'd spend the afternoon at the beach surrounded by filthy-rich drug barons and pimps. I'm sure that in such a passionate, not to mention liberal, society I could shake off the malaise of Western civilization. You're right, Sophie: I'll go straight to a travel agent as soon as I get home."

Sophie considered him for a moment, her expression thoughtful, her brow lined with concern. Eventually she said sadly, "You must have really suffered . . ."

"You know what Nietzsche said about Shakespeare, Sophie?" said Bruno. "'The man must have suffered greatly to have such passion for playing the fool!' Personally, I've always thought that Shakespeare was overrated, but now that I think about it, he is a big fool." He stopped and realized to his surprise that he really was beginning to suffer. Sometimes women were so compassionate; they met aggression with empathy, cynicism with tenderness. No man would do any such thing. "Sophie," he said with heartfelt emotion, "I'd like to lick your pussy," but she didn't hear him. She had turned away and struck up a conversation with the ski instructor who had groped her ass three days earlier.

Bruno stood speechless for a moment or two before crossing the lawn to the parking lot. The Leclerc supermarket at Royan was open until ten o'clock. As he wandered through the aisles he thought about Aristotle's claim that small women were of a different species. A *small man still seems to me to be a man*, he wrote, *whereas a small woman appears to me to belong to a new type of animal.* How could you square such a strange assertion with the habitual good sense of the Stagirite? Bruno bought a bottle of whiskey, a box of ravioli and a pack of ginger snaps. By the time he got back, the Lieu was dark. Passing the Jacuzzi, he heard whispering and a muffled laugh. He stopped and peeked through the branches, plastic bag in hand. There were two or three couples; they were quiet now, the only sound the rippling of the water. The moon came out from behind the clouds. At that moment another couple arrived and began to undress. The whispering began again. Bruno put the bag down, took out his penis and started to masturbate. He ejaculated quickly, just as the woman slipped into the warm water.

It was already Friday night. He was going to have to extend his stay by a week. He had to get ahold of himself, find a woman, talk to people.

6

On Friday night Bruno slept badly and had a terrible dream. He was a piglet, his little body fat and sleek. With the other little piglets he was sucked by a vortex into a vast, dark tunnel, its walls rusted, and carried by the slow drift of the current. At times his feet touched the bottom, but then a powerful swell would carry him on. Sometimes he could make out the whitish flesh of one of his companions as it was brutally sucked down. They struggled through the darkness and a silence broken only by the scraping of their hooves on the metal walls. As they plunged deeper, he could hear the dull sound of machines coming from the end of the tunnel. He began to realize that the vortex was pulling them toward turbines with huge, razor-sharp blades.

Later, his severed head was lying in a meadow below the mouth of the drainpipe. His skull had been split from top to bottom, though what remained, lying on the grass, was still conscious. He knew that ants would slowly work their way into the exposed brain tissue to eat away at the neurons and finally he would slip into unconsciousness. As he waited, he looked at the horizon through his one remaining eye. The grass seemed to stretch out forever. Huge cogwheels turned counterclockwise under a metallic sky. Perhaps this was the end of time; at least the world he'd known had ceased to exist.

Over breakfast he met the leader of the watercolor workshop—a veteran of '68 from Brittany. His name was Paul Le Dantec, one of the founding members of the Lieu; his brother was the current director. He was the archetypal old hippie: long gray beard, Indian vest and an ankh on a chain around his neck. At fifty-five this old wreck lived a peaceful life. He would get up at dawn to go bird-watching in the hills, then sit down to a bowl of coffee and Calvados, and roll a cigarette amid the human bustle. The watercolor class didn't start until ten o'clock; he had all the time in the world to chat.

"As a veteran of the Lieu," said Bruno, laughing to establish a sense of complicity, however false, "you must have a lot of stories about this place when it first opened—the seventies, sexual liberation . . ."

"Liberation my ass," groaned the geezer. "There were always women who were wallflowers at orgies, and guys who just stood there waving their dicks. Take it from me, nothing much has changed."

"But I thought AIDS changed everything," said Bruno.

"I suppose it's true that it used to be easier for men," the watercolorist admitted, clearing his throat. "You'd find a mouth or a pussy wide open and you could dive right in—no standing on ceremony. But for that it had to be a proper orgy, invitation only, usually only couples. I tell you, I saw women with their legs wide open, wet and up for it, spending the whole evening masturbating because no one would fuck them. They couldn't even find someone to get them off—you had to be able to get it up first."

"So what you're saying," Bruno said thoughtfully, "is that there never was real sexual liberation—just another form of seduction."

"Oh yeah," the old fart agreed, "there's always been a lot of seduction."

This didn't exactly sound promising. Still, it was Saturday, so there would probably be a crop of newcomers. Bruno decided to chill out, take things as they came, go with the flow. As a result, his day passed without incident; in fact, without the slightest event. At about eleven o'clock that evening he went down to the Jacuzzi. A delicate haze rose above the gentle rumble of the water, lit by the full moon. He approached soundlessly. A couple were entwined on the far side of the pool; it looked as if she had mounted him like a horse. I have as much right as they have, thought Bruno furiously. He undressed quickly and slipped into the Jacuzzi. The night air was cool, the water, by contrast, deliciously warm. Between the twisted branches of the pine trees he could see the stars, and felt himself relax a little. The couple paid no attention to him; the girl continued to pump up and down on the guy, now starting to whimper. It was impossible to see her face. The man began to breathe heavily too. The woman's rhythm began to pick up tempo; she threw her head back and, for a moment, the moon lit up her breasts, her face still hidden behind a dark mass of hair. Then she crushed herself against her partner and wrapped herself around him; his breathing was heavier now, then he let out a long moan and was silent.

They stayed there for a couple of minutes, wrapped around each other, then the man stood up and got out of the pool. He unrolled the condom on his penis before dressing. Bruno was surprised to see that the woman was not leaving with him. The man's footsteps died away and there was silence once more. She stretched out her legs in the water. Bruno did likewise. He felt her foot on his thigh, brushing against his penis. With a soft splash she pushed herself from the edge and came to him. Clouds shadowed the moon; the woman was barely a half meter away but still he could not make out her face. He felt an arm against his thigh and another wrap around his shoulder. Bruno pressed his body to hers, his face against her small, firm breasts. He let go of the edge and gave himself up to her embrace. He could feel her drawing him toward the center of the pool, then slowly she began to turn. He felt the muscles in his neck give, his head suddenly heavy. Below the surface, the gentle murmur of the water became a thunderous roar. He saw the stars as they wheeled slowly overhead. He relaxed into her arms, and his erect penis broke the surface of the water. She moved her hands gently, barely a caress. He was completely weightless. Her long hair brushed his stomach and then her tongue touched the tip of his glans. His whole body shuddered with happiness. She closed her lips and slowly, so slowly, took him in her mouth. He closed his eyes, his body shuddering in ecstasy. The underwater roar was infinitely reassuring. When he felt her lips at the base of his penis, he could feel the movement of her throat. He felt himself flooded with intense waves of pleasure and buoyed up by the whirlpool. All at once he felt very hot. She gently allowed her throat to contract around him; all the energy in his being rushed suddenly to his penis. He howled as he came. He had never felt such fulfillment in his life.

7

CONVERSATION IN A TRAILER

Christiane's trailer was about fifty meters from his tent. She turned the lights on, took out a bottle of Bushmills and poured two glasses. Slim, shorter than Bruno, she probably had been quite pretty once, but her delicate features had faded a little and her skin was blotchy. Only her silky, black hair remained perfect. Her eyes were blue and a little sad. She was probably about forty.

"I just get that way sometimes, I just get it on with everyone," she said. "The only rule is that if they want to fuck, they wear a condom."

She moistened her lips and sipped the whiskey. Bruno watched her. She had thrown on a gray sweatshirt but nothing else. The curve of her mons was beautiful even if her labia sagged a little.

"I'd like to make you come, too," he said.

"There's no rush," she said. "Finish your drink. You can sleep here if you like, there's plenty of room." She nodded at the double bed.

They talked about trailer rentals. Christiane couldn't sleep in a tent, she had back problems. "It's pretty bad," she said. "Most guys prefer a blow-job," she said. "They're not really into fucking, they find it difficult to keep it up. But take some guy's cock in your mouth and he's like a little kid again. I think feminism has hit them harder than they like to admit."

"There are worse things than feminism," Bruno said soberly. He knocked back half of the whiskey before deciding to continue. "Have you known the Lieu long?"

"Pretty much since the beginning. I stopped coming while I was married. Now I come two or three weeks a year. When it started up, it was very alternative, very New Left; now it's more New Age. It hasn't really changed much. They were into oriental mysticism here in the seventies; now it's more about Jacuzzis and massage. It's a nice place—but it's a bit sad. There's a lot less violence here than in the outside world. The whole spiritual thing makes the pickup lines seem less brutal. A lot of women suffer here, though. Men who grow old alone have it easier than older women. They drink cheap booze and fall asleep, their breath stinks, then they wake up and start all over again; they tend to die young. Women take tranquilizers, go to yoga classes, see a shrink; they live a lot longer and suffer a lot more. They try to trade on their looks, even when they know their bodies are sad and ugly. They get hurt but they do it anyway, because they can't give up the need to be loved. That's one delusion they'll keep to the bitter end. Once she's past a certain age, a woman might get to rub up against some cocks, but she has no chance of being loved. That's men for you."

"Christiane," Bruno said gently, "I think you're being a bit harsh . . . I mean, I'm here now and I want to give you pleasure."

"I believe you. I have a feeling you're a nice man. Selfish, but nice."

She took off her sweatshirt and lay across the bed. She placed a pillow under her buttocks and spread her legs. Bruno started by licking around her cunt for a while before tonguing her clitoris in short, quick strokes. Christiane exhaled with a deep moan. "Put your finger in," she said. Bruno did as she asked, turning himself so he could caress her breasts as his tongue continued to flicker over her pussy. He could feel her nipples harden; he looked up. "Don't stop, please," she said. He laid his head on her thigh and stroked her clitoris with his index finger. Her labia minor began to swell. A sudden burst of joy overwhelmed him and he began to lick her eagerly. Christiane let out a little whimper. For an instant he saw his mother's thin, crumpled vagina again and then the image dissolved. He fingered her clitoris faster as his tongue lapped her labia affectionately. Her belly began to redden and her breath came in short gasps. She was wet now and deliciously salty. Bruno paused for a moment and then slipped a finger into her anus and another into her vagina as the tip of his tongue fluttered quickly over her clitoris. Her body shuddered and jolted as she came. He stayed there, face pressed against her moist vulva, then reached his hand toward her and felt her fingers intertwine with his. "Thanks," she said. Then she got up, put on her sweatshirt and filled their glasses again.

"It was really good—in the Jacuzzi just now," Bruno said. "We didn't say a word, and when I felt your lips on my cock I still hadn't really seen your face. There was something pure about it—no seduction."

"It all depends on Krause's corpuscles," Christiane said, smiling. "Sorry—I'm a biology professor." She took a gulp of Bushmills. "The shaft of the clitoris and the glans and ridge of the penis are covered in Krause's corpuscles, rich in nerve endings. When touched, they cause a powerful flow of endorphins in the brain. The penis and the clitoris have about the same number of Krause's corpuscles—sexual equality goes that far, but there's more to it than that, as you know. I was very much in love with my husband. When I stroked his penis or licked it, I worshiped it; I loved to feel him inside me. I was proud that I could make him hard. I kept a photograph of his erect cock in my wallet, it was like a sacred image to me. My greatest joy was to give him pleasure. Then he left me for someone younger. Just now, I could tell you didn't really like my pussy—it already looks a bit like an old woman's cunt. Increased collagen bonding and the breakdown of elastin during mitosis in older people means that human tissue gradually loses its suppleness and firmness. When I was twenty I had a beautiful pussy, now I know the lips are sagging a little."

Bruno drained his glass; he couldn't think of anything to say to her. Shortly afterward, they lay down. He put his arm around Christiane's waist and they fell asleep.

8

Bruno was the first to wake. High up in the trees a bird sang. The covers had slipped off Christiane during the night. Her buttocks were still beautiful, round and very inviting. He remembered a line from *The Little Mermaid*. He had it at home, on a scratched 45 with the Frères Jacques singing "La Chanson des Matelots." She had endured many trials, given up her voice, her home, her beautiful mermaid's tail; all in the hope that she might become a woman and win the love of a prince. In the dead of night, a storm cast her onto a beach and here she drank the magic elixir. A pain ripped through her, so terrible that she felt as though she had been cut in two. She slipped into unconsciousness. At this point, a sequence of chord changes seemed to open up a different world. A woman's voice, the storyteller, said the words which had so marked Bruno as a child: *When she awoke, the sun was shining and the prince stood before her.*

Then he thought about the conversation he'd had with Christiane the night before; he thought he might grow to love her sagging but soft labia. He had a hard-on, as he did every morning, as did almost every man. In the half-light of dawn, Christiane's face seemed very pale surrounded by the thick, disheveled mass of her black hair. Her eyes opened slightly as he entered her. She seemed a little surprised, but she parted her legs. He began to move inside her, though he could feel himself soften as he did. He felt a terrible sadness, mixed with worry and shame. "Do you want me to use a condom?" he asked. "Yeah, please," she said, "they're in that bag of toiletries over there." He tore open the packet—they were Durex Technica. Of course by the time he got the rubber on he had completely lost his hard-on. "I'm sorry, I'm really sorry," he said.

"Don't worry about it," she said gently, "come back to bed." Clearly AIDS had been a blessing for men of his generation. Sometimes by the time the condom was out of the packet, they were completely flaccid. "I never really got used to them . . ." This little ritual over, and their manhood safe, in principle, they could go back to bed, snuggle up against their woman and fall asleep in peace.

After breakfast they walked down past the pyramid. The pond was deserted. They lay down in the sunny meadow. Christiane slipped off his shorts and began to masturbate him. She fondled him gently, delicately. Later, when at her instigation they joined the wife-swapping set, Bruno came to realize that this was a rare quality. Most of the women in the group jerked men off crudely; they had no technique. They gripped the cock too tightly and shook it frantically, probably trying to imitate something they'd seen in a porn film. It might have been spectacular on screen, but on the receiving end it was mediocre and sometimes painful. Christiane, on the other hand, was subtle, wet her fingers regularly, flickered over the most sensitive areas. A woman wearing an Indian tunic passed them and sat at the edge of the water. Bruno inhaled deeply and held back, not wanting to come yet. Christiane smiled at him; the sun was beginning to get warm. He realized that his second week at the Lieu would be very gentle. Perhaps they would even see each other afterward; they might grow old together. From time to time she would offer him a little physical pleasure, and together they could live out their declining libidos. They would go on like that for some years and then it would be over; they would be old, and the comedy of sexual manners finished for good.

While Christiane was taking a shower, Bruno studied the beauty care product ("daily protection for young-looking skin, now in microcapsules") he had bought at Leclerc the day before. The packaging made much of the "new" concept of "microcapsules," but the directions, which were more comprehensive, outlined three principal effects: protection against the sun's harmful rays, all-day moisturizing action and the elimination of free radicals. His reading was interrupted by the arrival of Catherine, the reinvented feminist turned Egyptian tarot reader. She had just come from a workshop on personal development and was itching to talk about it. "Success Through Dance" was about finding your vocation through a succession of symbolic games intended to liberate the "hero within" each student. By the end of the first day, it was apparent that Catherine's personality had aspects of the witch, but also of the lioness, which usually pointed to a career in sales management.

"Hmm . . ." said Bruno.

Just then Christiane came out, a towel around her waist. Catherine trailed off, visibly irritated. She beat a rapid retreat on the pretext that she had a workshop on "Zen and Argentine Tango."

"I thought you were doing 'Tantric Accounting,'" Christiane shouted as she disappeared around the corner.

"Do you know her?"

"Oh, yeah—I've known the bitch for twenty years, pretty much since this place opened."

She shook her hair and wrapped the towel into a turban. They walked back up together. Bruno had the sudden desire to take her hand. He did.

"Never could stand feminists . . ." Christiane continued when they were halfway up the hill. "Stupid bitches always going on about washing dishes and the division of labor; they could never shut up about the dishes. Oh, sometimes they'd talk about cooking or vacuuming, but their favorite topic was washing dishes. In a few short years, they managed to turn every man they knew into an impotent, whining neurotic. Once they'd done that, it was always the same story—they started going on about how there were no real men anymore. They usually ended up ditching their boyfriends for a quick fuck with some macho Latin idiot. I've always been struck by the way intelligent women go for delinquents, brutes and assholes. Anyway, they fuck their way through two or three, maybe more if they're really pretty, and wind up with a kid. Then they start making jam from *Marie Claire* recipe cards. It's always the same story, I've seen it happen dozens of times."

"That's all in the past now," said Bruno in a conciliatory tone.

They spent the afternoon by the pool. On the opposite side, the teenage girls were jumping up and down fighting over to a Walkman. "Cute, aren't they?" said Christiane. "The blonde one, the one with the small breasts, is really pretty . . ." Then she lay down on the bath towel. "Pass me the suntan lotion."

Christiane didn't attend any of the workshops. In fact, she was rather condescending about what she referred to as "that crazy shit." "Maybe I'm being a bit hard," she added, "but I know what the veterans of '68 are like when they hit forty. I'm practically one myself. They have cobwebs in their cunts and they grow old alone. Talk to them for five minutes and you'll see they don't believe any of this bullshit about chakras and crystal healing and light vibrations. They force themselves to believe it, and sometimes they do for an hour or two. They feel the presence of the Angel or the flower blossoming within but then the workshop's over and they're still ugly, aging and alone. So they have crying fits—they do a lot of crying here, have you noticed? Especially after the Zen workshops. They don't have much choice, really—most of them have money problems too. A lot of them have been in therapy and they're completely broke. Mantras and tarot may be stupid, but they're a lot cheaper than therapy."

"Or the dentist," Bruno said obscurely. He laid his head between her open thighs and knew he would fall asleep there.

When it got dark they went back to the Jacuzzi; he asked her not to let him come. Back in the trailer, they made love. "Don't bother," Christiane said when he reached for the condoms. When he entered her, he could tell she was happy. One of the most surprising things about physical love is the sense of intimacy it creates the instant there's any trace of mutual affection. Suddenly—even if you met the night before—you can confide things to your lover that you would never tell another living soul. And so, that night, Bruno told Christiane things he'd told no one—not even Michel, much less his therapist. He talked to her about his childhood, his grandmother's death, how he was bullied at boarding school. He told her about his adolescence, about masturbating on the train with a girl only a few meters away; he told her about the summers he spent at his father's house. Christiane stroked his hair and listened.

They spent the week together, and the evening before Bruno left they had dinner at a seafood restaurant in Saint-Georges-de-Didonne. The air was warm and still; the candles lighting their table barely flickered. The restaurant overlooked the estuary of the Gironde. In the distance they could just make out the headland at Grave. "When I look at moonlight on the water," said Bruno, "it's clear to me we have nothing—absolutely nothing—to do with this world."

"Do you really have to leave?"

"Yeah. I have to spend a couple of weeks with my son. I should've left last week, but now I really have to go. His mother's already booked her vacation—she's flying out the day after tomorrow."

"How old is your son?"

"Thirteen."

Christiane sipped her Muscadet and thought. She was wearing a long dress and had put on makeup. She looked like a girl. Her breasts were just discernible through the lace blouse of the dress; the reflected candles blazed small flames in her eyes. "I think I might be a little bit in love . . ." she said. Bruno waited, hardly daring to breathe, perfectly motionless. "I live with my son in Noyon," she went on. "Things were okay until he was thirteen. I suppose he missed his father, I don't know . . . Do kids really need a father? One thing I do know, his father didn't need him. Oh, he took him to the cinema or to McDonald's a couple of times in the beginning, though he always brought him back early. After a while he came around less and less often. Then he moved down south to be with his new girlfriend, and he stopped visiting altogether. After that, I brought him up on my own. Maybe I let him get away with too much. About two years ago he started going out a lot, hanging around with a bad crowd. Noyon can be pretty violent—you'd be surprised. There're a lot of blacks and Arabs, the National Front got forty percent of the vote in the last election. I live in a condominium in the suburbs. I've had my mailbox broken into, I can't leave anything in the basement. I often get scared. Sometimes I hear gunshots. When I get back from school I basically barricade myself in the apartment and I never go out at night. Sometimes I go on the Minitel and check out the sex sites, that's about it. My son gets in late—sometimes he doesn't come home at all. I don't dare say anything. I'm terrified he'll hit me."

"Are you far from Paris?"

She smiled. "No. Noyon is out in the Oise—it's not even eighty kilometers." She stopped and smiled again, her face for a moment filled with gentleness and hope. "I used to love life," she went on. "I loved life. I was sensitive, affectionate, and I always loved making love. Then something went wrong. I'm not really sure what, but something went wrong with my life."

Bruno had already folded up his tent and packed his things into the car; he spent the last night in her trailer. In the morning, he tried to make love to Christiane but he couldn't; he was too nervous, too agitated. "Come all over me," she said. She smeared his come over her face and breasts. "Stop by and see me," she said as he was going out the door. He promised he would. It was Saturday, the first of August.

9

Unusually, Bruno drove back along country roads. He stopped just before Parthenay. He knew he needed to think, but what exactly did he need to think about? He was parked on a peaceful, boring stretch of countryside by a canal where the water was so still it looked motionless. Water plants sprouted or rotted, it was difficult to say which. The silence was broken by a faint trilling sound—insects, probably. As he stretched out on the grassy bank, he noticed a gentle current; the canal was flowing slowly to the south. He could not see a single frog.

Just before he started university in October 1975, Bruno moved into the studio his father had bought for him. He felt a whole new life was beginning for him. He was quickly disappointed. There were girls, of course, in fact rather a lot of girls enrolled in liberal arts at Censier, but they all seemed to be taken; or if they weren't, they weren't prepared to be taken by him. In an attempt to make friends he went to every lecture, every tutorial, and quickly became a good student. He watched the girls in the cafeteria, listened to them chatting about going out, meeting friends, inviting each other to parties. He started to eat. His diet quickly settled into a nutritious trip down the boulevard Saint-Michel. He would start with a hot dog from the stand on the corner of the rue Gay-Lussac; farther down, he would have a slice of pizza or a kebab. At McDonald's on the boulevard Saint-Germain, he'd devour several cheeseburgers washed down with coke and a banana milk shake before staggering down the rue de la Harpe to finish off with some Tunisian pastries. On his way home he would stop in front of the Cinéma Latin, which showed porn double features. Sometimes he would stand for half an hour pretending to look at the bus timetable in the always vain hope of seeing a woman or a couple go inside. More often than not, he would end up buying a ticket. He always felt better once he was inside; the usherette was the soul of discretion. The men sat far apart, always leaving several seats between them. He would quietly jerk off watching *Naughty Nurses, The Hitchhiker Always Comes Twice, Teacher Spreads Her Legs, The Wild Bunch,* whatever was on. He had to be careful as he left: the cinema was right on the boulevard Saint-Michel, and he could easily bump into a girl from college. Usually he waited for someone else to leave and walked just behind him; it seemed less humiliating that he might have gone to a porn movie with a friend. He usually got back around midnight and read for a while: Chateaubriand or Rousseau. He decided to change his life once or twice a week, to take some radical new direction. This is how it went: first he would take off his clothes and look at himself in the mirror. He had to go to the limit of self-abasement, to face up to the humiliating sight of his fat belly, his flabby cheeks and his sagging buttocks. Then he would turn out the lights and, feet together, arms folded across his chest, he would drop his head forward, the better to go into himself. Then he would breathe slowly, deeply, expanding his revolting belly as far as he could before exhaling slowly, mentally saying a number as he did so. It was essential not to let his concentration waver; every number was important, but the most significant were four, eight and, of course, sixteen, the last one. He would exhale with all his might as he reached the final number; when he raised his head he would be a radically new man, finally ready to live, to swim with the tide of existence. He would no longer feel guilty or ashamed; he would eat normally and behave normally around girls. "Today is the first day of the rest of your life."

This little ritual had no effect whatever on his self-esteem, but could occasionally control his overeating; sometimes he would manage to get through two days before backsliding. He put the failure down to lack of concentration, though soon afterward he would begin to believe again. He was still young.

One evening he ran into Annick as he came out of the Tunisian bakery. He hadn't seen her since their brief meeting in the summer of '74. She was uglier now, practically obese. She wore thick, square glasses with heavy black frames that made her brown eyes seem smaller and accentuated the sickly pallor of her skin. They had coffee together, both of them distinctly uneasy. She was also studying literature, at the Sorbonne; she had a studio apartment nearby, with a view of the boulevard Saint-Michel. She gave him her telephone number when they parted.

In the weeks that followed he went to see her several times. She was too ashamed of her body to get undressed, though she did offer to give him a blow-job the first night. She didn't say it had anything to do with her body, rather that it was because she wasn't on the pill. "Really, I prefer it . . ." She stayed in every night, never went out. She drank herbal tea, tried dieting, yet nothing seemed to work. Several times Bruno tried to take off her trousers, but she just curled up and pushed him away fiercely, without a word. He gave up and took out his penis. She would suck him off quickly, a little brutally, and he would come in her mouth. Sometimes they talked about their studies, but not often; he usually left quickly. True, she wasn't very pretty and he would have been embarrassed to be seen with her on the street, in a restaurant or a movie line. He'd stuff himself with Tunisian pastries until he felt sick and then go to see her, get a blow-job and leave. It was probably best that way.

It was a mild night, the night Annick died. Though the end of March, already it felt like a spring evening. In the patisserie Bruno bought an almond turnover, then walked down along the banks of the Seine. The commentary from the loudspeakers of a *bateau-mouche* filled the air, echoing off the walls of Notre-Dame. He chewed his way through the sticky, honey-covered pastry, only to feel more disgusted with himself than ever. He thought perhaps he should try it right here, in the center of Paris, in the middle of everyone and everything. He closed his eyes, brought his feet together and folded his arms across his chest. Slowly, carefully, with complete concentration, he began to count. When he reached the magic sixteen he opened his eyes, lifted his head. The *bateau-mouche* had disappeared, the riverbank was deserted, the air as mild as before.

Two policemen were trying to disperse a small crowd gathered outside Annick's building. Bruno went a little closer. The girl's body lay smashed and strangely twisted on the sidewalk. Her shattered arms seemed to form two strange limbs around her head. Her face, or what was left of it, lay in a pool of blood. She obviously had brought her hands up to her face in a last, desperate reflex to protect herself from the impact. "Jumped from the seventh floor," said a nearby woman, with odd satisfaction, "killed stone dead." At that moment an ambulance arrived and two men got out carrying a stretcher. As they lifted her body he saw her shattered skull and turned away. The ambulance drove off in a howl of sirens. So ended Bruno's first love.

The summer of '76 was probably the worst time of his life. He had just turned twenty. The heat was stifling, with not a breath of cool air even at night; the summer of '76 would be remembered for this. Girls wore short, flimsy dresses which stuck to their bodies with sweat. He walked around all day, his eyes popping out with lust. At night he would get up and go walking through Paris, stopping at café terraces, hanging around outside nightclubs. He didn't know how to dance. He had a permanent hard-on. He felt as though what was between his legs was a piece of oozing, putrefying meat devoured by worms. Several times he tried to talk to girls in the street, only to be humiliated. At night he would stare at himself in the mirror. He noticed that his hair, plastered to his head with sweat, was already beginning to recede. The folds of his stomach were obvious even through his shirt. He started visiting sex shops and peep shows, which served only to aggravate his suffering. For the first time he turned to prostitutes.

A subtle but definitive change had occurred in Western society during 1974 and 1975, Bruno thought to himself. He was still lying on the grassy bank by the canal; he had rolled up his linen jacket to use it as a pillow. He tore out a clump of coarse, damp grass. During those years when he was desperately trying to fit in, Western society had tipped toward something dark and dangerous. In the summer of 1976 it was already apparent that all of it would end badly. Physical violence, the most perfect manifestation of individuation, was about to reappear.

10

JULIAN AND ALDOUS

When it is necessary to modify or renew fundamental doctrine, the generations sacrificed to the era during which the transformation takes place remain essentially alienated from that transformation, and often become directly hostile to it.

AUGUSTE COMTE,
—*Un Appel aux conservateurs*

Toward noon, Bruno got back into his car and drove into Parthenay. He decided to take the expressway after all. He stopped at a phone booth and called his brother, who answered immediately. He was on his way back to Paris and wondered if he could see him that evening. He wouldn't be free the following evening—he was seeing his son—but he was tonight. It was important.

Michel was impassive. "If you want . . ." he said after a long pause. Like most people, he found he loathed what the sociologists and commentators liked to call the "atomization of society." Also like most, he thought it was important to stay in touch with one's family, even if it meant a certain amount of hassle. For years he had made himself spend every Christmas with his aunt Marie-Thérèse at her house in Raincy, where she was living out her declining years with her husband. His uncle was practically deaf; a kindhearted man, he had voted Communist all his life and refused to go to midnight mass, which always started an argument. Michel listened as the old man talked about emancipating the workingman and sipped gentian tea; from time to time, he would yell something banal in response. Then the others arrived. Michel was fond of his cousin Brigitte; he wanted her to be happy, but the fact that her husband was a bastard made that rather unlikely. He was a sales rep with Bayer and cheated on his wife whenever he had the opportunity; as he was a handsome man and traveled a lot, he had quite a lot of opportunities. Every year, Brigitte's face grew a little more guant.

Michel stopped making his annual visit in 1990, though there was still Bruno. Family relationships last for years, sometimes decades—much longer, in fact, than any other kind of relationship; then, finally, they too gutter out.

When Bruno arrived at about nine o'clock, he had already had a couple of drinks and was eager to talk philosophy. "I've always been struck by how accurate Huxley was in *Brave New World*," he began before he'd even sat down. "It's phenomenal when you think he wrote it in 1932. Everything that's happened since simply brings Western society closer to the social model he described. Control of reproduction is more precise and eventually will be completely disassociated from sex altogether, and procreation will take place in tightly guarded laboratories where perfect genetic conditions are ensured. Once that happens, any sense of family, of father-son bonds, will disappear. Pharmaceutical companies will break down the distinction between youth and age. In Huxley's world, a sixty-year-old man is as healthy as a man of twenty, looks as young and has the same desires. When we get to the point that life can't be prolonged any further, we'll be killed off by voluntary euthanasia; quick, discreet, emotionless. The society Huxley describes in *Brave New World* is happy; tragedy and extremes of human emotion have disappeared. Sexual liberation is total—nothing stands in the way of instant gratification. Oh, there are little moments of depression, of sadness or doubt, but they're easily dealt with using advances in antidepressants and tranquilizers. 'One cubic centimeter cures ten gloomy sentiments.' This is exactly the sort of world we're trying to create, the world we want to live in.

"Oh, I know, I know," Bruno went on, waving his hand as if to dismiss an objection Michel had not voiced. "Everyone says *Brave New World* is supposed to be a totalitarian nightmare, a vicious indictment of society, but that's hypocritical bullshit. *Brave New World* is our idea of heaven: genetic manipulation, sexual liberation, the war against aging, the leisure society. This is precisely the world that we have tried—and so far failed—to create. The only thing in the book that rankles a little with our idea of equal opportunities—or meritocracy—is the idea of dividing society into castes where each performs tasks according to their genetic makeup. But that's also the only point on which Huxley proved a false prophet. Advances in automation and robotics have made the whole idea pointless.

"Oh, Huxley was a terrible writer, I admit. His writing is pretentious and clumsy, his characters are bland ciphers, but he had one vital premonition: he understood that for centuries the evolution of human society had been linked to scientific and technological progress and would continue to be more and more so. He may have lacked style or finesse or psychological insight, but that's insignificant compared with the accuracy of the original concept. Huxley was the first writer to realize that biology would take over from physics as the driving force of society—long before other sci-fi writers."

Bruno stopped and noticed that his brother seemed worried and gaunt. He was clearly tired and had been paying little attention. In fact, he hadn't bothered to go shopping for days. Poverty was usually less oppressive in the summer months, though there were more beggars than ever outside Monoprix this year. What would it be like when war came, Michel wondered as he watched the slow tread of the beggars from his bay window. When would war break out, and what would that mean to the back-to-school rush? Bruno poured himself another glass of wine; he was getting hungry, and was surprised when his brother spoke in a weary voice:

"Huxley came from a large family of English biologists. His grandfather was a friend of Darwin's. He wrote a lot in defense of Darwin's theory of natural selection. His father and his brother Julian were also famous biologists. They were pragmatic, skeptical intellectuals in the English liberal mold—a tradition based more on observation and on experimental methods than was the French Enlightenment. As a boy, Huxley had the opportunity to meet many economists, judges and, particularly, scientists who were regular visitors to his father's house. He was certainly the only writer of his generation who understood the impact biology would have. It would all have happened much faster if it hadn't been for the war. Nazi ideology completely discredited eugenics and the idea of improving the race; it was decades before anyone thought about it again."

Michel went over to the bookshelf and took down *What Dare I Think?* and handed it to Bruno. "It was written by Julian Huxley, Aldous's older brother, and published in 1931, a year before *Brave New World*. All of the ideas his brother used in the novel—genetic manipulation and improving the species, including the human species—are suggested here. All of them are presented as unequivocally desirable goals that society should strive for."

Michel sat down again and wiped his forehead. "In 1946, just after the war, Julian Huxley was appointed director-general of UNESCO, which had just been founded. Aldous Huxley had just published *Brave New World Revisited*, in which he tried to portray the first novel as a social satire. Years later, Aldous would become a pillar of the hippie experiment. He had always been in favor of complete sexual liberation, and he was a pioneer in the use of psychedelic drugs. The founding members of Esalen met him and were taken with his ideas. Then the New Age came along and recycled all the ideas of Esalen. Aldous Huxley is probably one of the most influential thinkers of the century."

They went to a Chinese restaurant on the corner, which offered a set meal for two at 270 francs. Michel had not been out of his apartment in three days. "I haven't eaten today," he said, slightly surprised; he was still carrying the book.

"In 1962," he went on as he stirred his sticky rice, "Huxley published his last book, *Island*. It's set on a utopian tropical island—probably based on Sri Lanka, given the scenery and the vegetation. On the island a civilization has developed which has completely bypassed the great commercial currents of the twentieth century. The civilization is technologically advanced, but still respectful of nature. The natives are pacifists, and completely immune to family neuroses and Judeo-Christian inhibitions. Nudism is accepted as normal, sensuality and sexuality are freely practiced. The book was second-rate, but it was easy to read and it had a enormous effect on hippies and, through them, on New Agers. If you look at it closely, the harmonious society in *Island* has a lot in common with *Brave New World*. Huxley was probably senile by that time. He didn't seem to notice the similarities himself. The society in *Island* is as close to *Brave New World* as hippie liberalism is to bourgeois liberalism—or rather to its Swedish social-democratic variant."

He paused, dipped a shrimp into the chili sauce and then put down his chopsticks. "Like his brother, Aldous was an optimist . . ." he said with something like disgust. "The metaphysical mutation that gave rise to materialism and modern science in turn spawned two great trends: rationalism and individualism. Huxley's mistake was in having poorly evaluated the balance of power between these two. Specifically, he underestimated the growth of individualism brought about by an increased consciousness of death. Individualism gives rise to freedom, the sense of self, the need to distinguish oneself and to be superior to others. A rational society like the one he describes in *Brave New World* can defuse the struggle. Economic rivalry—a metaphor for mastery over space—has no more reason to exist in a society of plenty, where the economy is strictly regulated. Sexual rivalry—a metaphor for mastery over time through reproduction—has no more reason to exist in a society where the connection between sex and procreation has been broken. But Huxley forgets about individualism. He doesn't understand that sex, even stripped of its link with reproduction, still exists—not as a pleasure principle, but as a form of narcissistic differentiation. The same is true of the desire for wealth. Why has the Swedish model of social democracy never triumphed over liberalism? Why has it never been applied to sexual satisfaction? Because the metaphysical mutation brought about by modern science leads to individuation, vanity, malice and desire. Any philosopher, not just Buddhist or Christian, but any philosopher worthy of the name, knows that, in itself, desire—unlike pleasure—is a source of suffering, pain and hatred. The utopian solution—from Plato to Huxley by way of Fourier—is to do away with desire and the suffering it causes by satisfying it immediately. The opposite is true of the sex-and-advertising society we live in, where desire is marshaled and blown up out of all proportion, while satisfaction is maintained in the private sphere. For society to function, for competition to continue, people have to want more and more, until desire fills their lives and finally devours them." He wiped his forehead, exhausted. He hadn't touched his food.

"There are some correctives," Bruno said softly, "some humanist touches which help people forget about death. In *Brave New World*, it's tranquilizers and antidepressants; in *Island* it's hallucinogens, meditation and some vague Hindu mysticism. In our own society, people try to use a mixture of both."

"Julian Huxley gives over the second part of *What Dare I Think?* to discussing religion," retorted Michel, clearly contemptuous. "He's well aware that science and materialism have completely undermined traditional spirituality, but he also realizes that society cannot survive without religion. He spends about a hundred pages trying to set out the principles of a religion which could dovetail with science. The results aren't terribly convincing, and certainly society hasn't followed the route he suggested. In fact, any attempt at fusing science and religion is doomed by the knowledge of physical mortality, so cruelty and egotism cannot fail to spread. In compensation," he concluded bizarrely, "the same is true of love."

11

After Bruno's visit, Michel took to his bed for two weeks. How could society function without religion, he wondered. It seemed difficult enough for an individual human being. For several days he studied the radiator beside his bed. It was a useful and ingenious device—when it was cold, the pipes filled with hot water—but how long could Western civilization continue without some kind of religion? As a child, he liked to water the plants in the kitchen garden. He still had a small black-and-white photograph of himself at the age of six, holding the watering can, watched over by his grandmother. Later, he liked to go on errands; with the change from the bread money, he was allowed to buy a Carambar. Then he would fetch the milk from the farm, swinging the aluminum pail of still-warm milk at arm's length, and he was a little bit afraid as he walked back at nightfall along the deserted path hedged with brambles. Now every trip to the supermarket was torture, though the stock changed regularly and they were always introducing new TV dinners for one. He'd recently—for the first time—seen ostrich steak in the meat section of Monoprix.

To facilitate reproduction, the two helices which make up the DNA molecule separate before each attracts complementary nucleotides. The moment of separation is dangerous, as it is then that random mutations—mostly harmful—occur. The impression of intellectual stimulation created by fasting is real, and by the end of the first week Michel had the intuition that perfect reproduction was impossible while DNA was in the form of a double helix. To obtain an exact replication across an indefinite succession of cellular generations, it would probably be necessary for genetic information to be on a compact structure—for example, a Möbius strip or a torus.

As a child, he could not bear the deterioration of objects, the breakage, the wear and tear. For years he continually taped two broken ends of a plastic ruler together again. With all the layers of tape, the ruler was now lopsided. To draw a straight line was impossible, so it didn't even fulfill the basic function of a ruler. Nevertheless, he kept it. Then it would break again and he would repair it, adding another layer of tape, and put it back in his pencil case.

"One of the marks of Djerzinski's genius," Frédéric Hubczejak would write many years later, "was his ability to go beyond his first intuition that sexual reproduction was, in itself, a source of deleterious mutations. For millions of years, human societies had instinctively made the incontrovertible link between sex and death; a scientist who had irrefutably established such a link in molecular biological terms would normally consider his work done, and leave it at that. Djerzinski, however, understood it was necessary to look past the framework of sexual reproduction to study the general topological conditions of cell division."

From his first week at primary school in Charny, Michel had been struck by the cruelty of boys. It's true that the little beasts were farmers' sons, and therefore closer to animals than most. Nevertheless, it was startling to witness the instinctive, unaffected, joyful way they stabbed frogs with a compass point or a fountain pen; violet ink blossoming beneath the skin of the unfortunate animal as it slowly suffocated to death. They would gather in a circle, their eyes bright, to watch its final agony. Another of their favorite games was to cut the antennae off snails with their round-ended children's scissors. All of the snail's sensory awareness comes from its antennae, crowned by the eyes. Without them the snail is reduced to a pulpous mass, suffering and helpless. Michel quickly realized that he should keep his distance from these young savages; there was little to fear from girls, however, more gentle creatures. This instinctive notion of the world was confirmed every Wednesday night when he watched *The Animal Kingdom*. Amid the vile filth, the ceaseless carnage which was the lot of animals, the only glimmer of devotion and altruism was the protective maternal instinct, which had gradually evolved into mother love. The female squid, a pathetic little thing barely twenty centimeters long, unhesitatingly attacks the diver who comes near her eggs.

Thirty years later he could not come to any other conclusion: women were indisputably better than men. They were gentler, more affectionate, loving and compassionate; they were less prone to violence, selfishness, cruelty or self-centeredness. Moreover, they were more rational, intelligent and hardworking.

What on earth were men for, Michel wondered as he watched sunlight play across the curtains. In earlier times, when bears were more common, perhaps masculinity served a particular and irreplaceable function, but for centuries now men clearly served no useful purpose. For the most part they assuaged their boredom playing tennis, which was a lesser evil; but from time to time they felt the need to *change history*—which basically meant inciting revolutions or wars. Aside from the senseless suffering they caused, revolutions and wars destroyed the best of the past, forcing societies to rebuild from scratch. Without regular and continuous progress, human evolution took random, irregular and violent turns for which men—with their predilection for risk and danger, their repulsive egotism, their irresponsibility and their violent tendencies—were directly to blame. A world of women would be immeasurably superior, tracing a slower but unwavering progression, with no U-turns and no chaotic insecurity, toward a general happiness.

On the morning of 15 August he went out, hoping that the streets would be deserted, which they were. He took some notes which he would stumble across ten years later while writing his most important paper, "Toward a Science of Perfect Reproduction."

At precisely that moment Bruno, exhausted and despairing, was taking his son back to his ex-wife. Anne had just come back from a package tour with Nouvelles Frontières to Easter Island or Benin—he couldn't remember which. She had probably made friends with some of the women on the trip. They would have exchanged addresses, and she would see them once or twice before growing bored with them. She certainly would not have met any men. Bruno had the impression that she had completely given up on everything having to do with men. She would take him aside for a minute or two and ask how things had been. He would say "Fine" in the calm, self-assured tone that women like, before adding, a little facetiously, "though Victor did watch a lot of television." He would quickly feel uncomfortable, as since she had given up smoking, Anne wouldn't tolerate it in her tastefully furnished apartment. As he got up to leave, he would be choked with regret and again wonder what he could do to make things different. He would kiss Victor quickly and then go. His vacation with his son would be over.

In truth, the two weeks they spent together had been a nightmare. Lying on his bed with a bottle of bourbon in his hand, he listened to the sounds of his son in the next room—the toilet flushing after he pissed, the buzz of the remote control. Just like his half brother—though he did not know it—he stared dumbly at the radiator for hours at a time. Victor slept on the sofa bed in the living room and spent fifteen hours a day watching television. The set was already on by the time Bruno woke up every morning—Victor would be watching cartoons on M6 with the sound down and his headphones on. He was not a violent boy and did not mean to be rude, but he and his father had absolutely nothing to say to each other. Twice a day, Bruno would heat something in the microwave and they would eat at the table with hardly a word.

How had it come to this? Victor had just turned fourteen. Some years before, he spent his time drawing pictures he would bring over for his father to see. He copied characters from Marvel Comics—Fatalis, Fantastik, the Pharaoh of the Future—and made up stories for them. Sometimes they would play a game of Mille Bornes, and on Sunday mornings they would go to the Louvre. When he was six, Victor had made a card for his father's birthday. On heavy drawing paper, he had written in big, multicolored letters: I LOVE YOU DAD. Now all that was past, over and done with. Bruno knew that things would only get worse, that they would move from mutual indifference to loathing. In a couple of years his son would try to go out with girls his own age; the same fifteen-year-old girls that Bruno lusted after. They would come to be rivals—which was the natural relationship between men. They would be like animals fighting in a cage; and the cage was time.

On the way home Bruno stopped at a local Arab grocery and bought two bottles of *pastis*. Then, before he drank himself into a stupor, he phoned his brother to arrange to see him the following day. When he arrived at Michel's apartment he found his brother, suddenly famished after weeks of fasting, stuffing himself with Italian salami between great gulps of wine. "Help yourself," he said vaguely, "help yourself." It seemed to Bruno as though he was barely listening. It was like talking to a wall, or a psychiatrist, but he talked nonetheless.

"For years my son turned to me for love and I rejected him. I was depressed, I hated my life, I thought there'd be a time when I felt better. I didn't realize how quickly the years would go by. Between seven and twelve, a child is an astonishing being—kind, rational and open, full of joy and convinced that the world is a logical place. He's full of love, and happy to accept what love we're prepared to give. After that it all goes wrong—it all goes horribly wrong."

Michel gobbled down the last two slices of salami and poured himself another glass of wine. His hands were trembling violently. Bruno continued: "There's nothing more stupid, aggressive, hateful or obnoxious than a teenage boy, especially when he's with boys his own age. He is a monster crossed with an imbecile. He's unbelievably conformist—at puberty a boy is the sudden, malicious and unpredictable (considering the child he was) crystallization of the very worst in mankind. When you think about it, sexuality has to be an absolutely evil force. I don't know how people can live under the same roof as kids like that. I think the only reason they can stomach it is because their lives are completely empty, though I suppose my life is completely empty and I didn't manage it. In any case, the world is full of liars; people spend their lives telling appalling lies. 'We're divorced now, but we're still good friends. I get to see my son every other weekend . . .' That's bullshit. Complete bullshit. In reality, men don't give a damn about their kids, they never really love them. In fact, I'd say men aren't capable of love; the emotion is completely alien to them. The only emotions they know are desire—

in the form of pure animal lust—and male rivalry. There used to be a time when, late in life, a man would come to feel a certain affection for his spouse—though not before she'd borne his children, made a home for them, cooked, cleaned and proved herself in the bedroom. That sort of regard meant they enjoyed sleeping in the same bed. It was probably not what the women were looking for, and it might even have been a delusion—but it could be a powerful feeling. Strong enough that even if men still became excited—though to a decreasing degree—at getting a little piece of ass on the side from time to time, they literally could not live without their wives. When, out of unhappiness, their wives left them, they hit the bottle and died soon afterward—often in a matter of months. Children existed solely to inherit a man's trade, his moral code and his property. This was taken for granted among the aristocracy, but merchants, craftsmen and peasants also bought into the idea, so it became the norm at every level of society. That's all gone now: I work for someone else, I rent my apartment from someone else, there's nothing for my son to inherit. I have no craft to teach him, I haven't a clue what he might do when he's older. By the time he grows up, the rules I lived by will have no value—he will live in another universe. If a man accepts the fact that everything must change, then he accepts that life is reduced to nothing more than the sum of his own experience; past and future generations mean nothing to him. That's how we live now. For a man to bring a child into the world now is meaningless. Women are different, because they continue needing to have someone to love—which is not and has never been true of men. It's bullshit to pretend that men need to fuss over their children, play with them or cuddle them. I know people have been saying it for years, but it's bullshit. After divorce—once the family unit has broken down—a man's relationship with his children is nonsensical. Kids are a trap that has closed, they are the enemy—you have to pay for them all your life—and they outlive you."

Michel got up and went into the kitchen to get a glass of water. He could see colored wheels spinning in midair, and felt like throwing up. First he had to stop his hands from shaking. Bruno was right—paternal love was a lie, a fiction. A lie is useful if it transforms reality, he thought, but if it fails, then all that's left is the lie, the bitterness and the knowledge that it was a lie.

When he came back Bruno was curled up in the armchair, as still as if he were dead. Night was falling over the towers and, after another stifling day, the temperature was bearable again. Suddenly Michel noticed the empty cage where for years his canary had lived; he would have to throw it out, as he had no intention of getting another pet. For a moment, he thought of his neighbor opposite—the girl who worked on *Vingt Ans*—whom he hadn't seen for months. She probably had moved out. He forced himself to concentrate on his hands and saw they were shaking a little less. Bruno still had not moved; the silence between them continued for some minutes.

12

"I met Anne in 1981," Bruno went on with a sigh. "She wasn't really beautiful, but I was tired of jacking off. The good thing, though, was she had big tits. I've always liked big tits . . ." He sighed again. "A WASP with big tits . . ." To Michel's surprise, his eyes were wet with tears. "Later, her tits started to go south and our marriage went with them. I fucked up her whole life. That's one thing I can't forget—I fucked up this woman's life. Is there any wine left?"

Michel went into the kitchen to get another bottle. This was all very strange; he knew Bruno had been seeing an analyst and that he'd stopped. Human beings always do what is least painful. For as long as it is less painful to confess, we talk; then we go silent, we give up, we're alone. If Bruno felt the need to talk about how his life was a failure, it was probably because he was hoping for something, some new beginning; it was probably a good sign.

"I'm not saying she was ugly," Bruno went on, "but her face was plain, charmless. She never had that delicacy, that luminous beauty that can light up a young girl's face. Her legs were too fat for her to wear miniskirts, but I convinced her to wear short tops with no bra; looking at big tits from below is a real turn-on. She was a bit embarrassed at first, but she got used to it. She was very inexperienced sexually; she didn't understand the erotic and didn't know the first thing about lingerie. Here I am going on about her, but you did meet her, didn't you?"

"I came to your wedding . . ."

"That's true," said Bruno, almost stupefied with amazement. "I remember being surprised you turned up. I was sure you didn't want to see me again."

"I *didn't* want to see you again."

Michel thought about the wedding and wondered what on earth had persuaded him to attend that dismal ceremony. He remembered the depressingly austere room in the temple at Neuilly, a little more than half filled with a congregation of the discreetly rich—her father was in finance.

"They were left-wing," said Bruno, "but everyone was left-wing back then. They had no problem with me living in sin with their daughter. We only got married because she was pregnant. The usual story." Michel could still hear the pastor's voice ringing out in the cold, bare room: something about Christ being true God and true man and about the new covenant between the Almighty and his people. In fact, he hadn't really understood what it was about. After three quarters of an hour of this, he was nodding off; he woke with a start at the words: "May the God of Israel bless you, he who had pity on two little children." He had trouble working out what was going on. Were they Jews? He had to think for a moment before registering that it was the same God. The pastor went on smoothly, his voice booming with conviction: "He that loveth his wife loveth himself: for no man ever yet hated his own flesh but nourisheth and cherisheth it, even as the Lord the church: for we are members of his body, of his flesh and of his bones. For this cause shall a man leave his father and his mother and shall be joined unto his wife; and they two shall be one flesh. This is a great mystery: but I speak concerning Christ and the church." It really was a phrase that hit home: *they two shall be one flesh.* Michel considered this for a time and glanced over at Anne: she was calm, focused, and it seemed as though she was holding her breath; she was almost beautiful. Undoubtedly fired up by Saint Paul, the pastor continued with increasing passion: "Lord, send thy blessing upon this thy servant who craves thy protection at the hour of her marriage. Grant that she may be in Christ a pure and faithful wife and that she, like Rachel, will be a comfort to her husband; that, like Rebecca, she will be wise; and that, like Sarah, she will be faithful unto him. Grant that she will remain in the faith and observe thy commandments, cleave to her spouse and renounce all evil. May she be honored for her modesty and respected for her humility and may she be instructed in the ways of the Lord. Grant, Lord, that she shall be fruitful in childbirth and that these two shall see their children's children to the third and fourth generation. May they grow together to a happy old age, and may they know the rest of the chosen in the Kingdom of Heaven. In the name of Jesus Christ, our Lord, Amen." Michel pushed his way through the crowd toward the altar, attracting angry glances as he went. At the third row, he stopped and watched the exchange of rings. Head bowed, the priest took the couple's hands in his own, the intensity of his concentration impressive; the silence in the chapel was total. Then he lifted his head and, in a loud voice sounding both vital and despairing, exclaimed violently: "That which God hath joined together, let no man put asunder."

Later, Michel went up to the priest as he was packing away the tools of his trade. "I was very interested in what you were saying earlier . . ." The man of God smiled urbanely, then Michel began to talk about the Aspect experiments and the EPR paradox: how two particles, once united, are forever an inseparable whole, "which seems pretty much in keeping with what you were saying about one flesh." The priest's smile froze slightly. "What I'm trying to say," Michel went on enthusiastically, "is that from an ontological point of view, the pair can be assigned a single vector state in Hilbert space. Do you see what I mean?"

"Of course, of course . . ." murmured the servant of Christ, looking around. "Excuse me," he said abruptly, and turned to the father of the bride. They shook hands warmly and slapped each other on the back. "Beautiful ceremony . . . magnificent," said the banker, his voice choked with emotion.

"You didn't stay for the reception," said Bruno. "It was a bit embarrassing for me—I was at my own wedding and didn't know anyone there. My father arrived very late, but at least he came: he hadn't shaved and his tie was crooked, he looked the very picture of a decrepit old playboy.

I'm sure Anne's parents would have preferred that she married someone else, but being liberal middle-class Protestants, they had a healthy respect for the teaching profession. Anyway, I was certified and she only had a diploma. The only problem was that her little sister was really pretty. She looked a bit like Anne—she had big tits too—but she wasn't plain at all, she had a beautiful face. It's amazing how the smallest detail in someone's features can make all the difference. Life's a bitch . . ." He sighed again and poured himself another glass.

"I got my first job as a teacher in September '84, at the Lycée Carnot in Dijon. Anne was six months pregnant. There we were—we were teachers, a teaching couple, and now all we had to do was live a normal life.

"We rented an apartment on the rue Vannerie not far from the school. 'You won't be paying Paris prices here,' the realtor told us. 'It's not like life in Paris, either, but it's pretty lively in the summer—we get a lot of tourists here. There's a lot of young people in town now for the Baroque Music Festival.' Baroque music?

"I knew from the start that I was doomed. It wasn't that I missed 'life in Paris.' I couldn't have cared less about that—I'd always been completely miserable in Paris. It was just that I was attracted to every woman except my wife. Like in most provincial towns, there are lots of pretty girls in Dijon; it was much worse than Paris. Those first couple of years the fashions were a real turn-on. It was unbearable, all those cute little girls in their little skirts with their little laughs. At school I saw them in class, at lunchtime I'd see them chatting up boys in the Penalty—the bar next to the school—but I always went home to my wife for lunch. On Saturday afternoons I'd see them in town buying records and clothes. I was always with Anne, who only wanted to look at baby clothes. She had an easy pregnancy and she was really happy. She slept a lot and ate whatever she wanted. We stopped having sex, but I don't think she even noticed. At the prenatal classes she'd made friends with some of the other women. Anne was always very sociable, affable and friendly, she was very easy to live with. I was really shocked when I found out she was expecting a boy. That was the worst—I was going to have to endure the worst. I should've been happy. I was only twenty-eight, but I felt dead inside.

"Victor was born in December. I remember taking him to be baptized at the Église Saint-Michel—I found it incredibly disturbing. 'Those that are baptized shall become the living stones of a spiritual edifice to the glory of the holy mother church,' said the priest. Victor was all red and wrinkled in his little white lace gown. There were about a dozen families—it was a collective baptism, like in the early church. 'Baptism binds us to the church,' said the priest, 'and cleaves us to the body of Christ.' Anne was cradling Victor in her arms—he weighed four kilos. He was very good, he didn't cry at all. 'Are we not then of the same body?' The parents looked at each other and seemed rather dubious. Then the priest poured the baptismal water three times on my son's forehead and anointed him with chrism. 'This perfumed oil, sanctified by the bishop, symbolizes the gift of the Holy Spirit,' said the priest. Then he addressed Victor directly. 'Victor,' he said, 'you are now a Christian and by the power of Holy Unction you have been incorporated into Christ's body. From henceforth you will participate in his holy, apostolic and catholic mission.'

"I was so impressed I joined a 'Living with Faith' group that met every Wednesday. There was a young Korean girl there—she was very pretty, and I wanted to fuck her the first time I saw her. It was a bit delicate because she knew I was married. Anne invited the group to our house one Saturday. The Korean girl sat on the sofa. She was wearing a short dress. I spent the whole afternoon staring at her legs, but nobody noticed.

"Anne took Victor to see her parents for the midterm holidays in February and I stayed in Dijon on my own. I tried again to become a Catholic. I'd lie on my Épéda mattress drinking *pastis* and reading *The Mystery of the Holy Innocents*. It was really beautiful—Péguy is an amazing writer—but in the end it just depressed me. All that stuff about sin and the forgiveness of sin, and God rejoicing more in the return of the sinner than in the thousands of the just . . . I wanted to be a sinner, but I just couldn't do it. I felt like I'd been robbed of my childhood. All I wanted was for some little bitch to put her full lips around my cock and give me a blow-job. I saw a lot of little bitches with pouting lips in the nightclubs, and I went to the Slow Rock and l'Enfer a few times while Anne was away; but they were always going out with someone else, always sucking someone else's cock, and I just couldn't stand it.

"It was around this time that sex sites took off on the Minitel; everyone was talking about it. I used to stay online all night. Victor would be asleep in our room, but he slept through the night, so that wasn't a problem. I was terrified when the first telephone bill arrived. I took it out of the mailbox and opened it on the way to school: fourteen thousand francs. Luckily I still had a savings account at the Caisse d'Épargne from my student days, so I transferred everything into our joint account. Anne didn't notice a thing.

"We only begin to live through other people's eyes. As time went by, I noticed that my colleagues at school looked at me without a trace of bitterness or dislike. I was no longer a threat to them; we were all in the same boat; I was *one of them*. They taught me how the system worked. I got my driver's license and started to get into home-improvement catalogues. When spring came, we spent the afternoons on the lawn at the Guilmards'. They lived in an ugly old house in Fontaine-lès-Dijon, but they had a big garden with a beautiful tree-lined lawn. Guilmard taught math, and we taught the same students, pretty much. He was tall, thin and stooped, with reddish-blonde hair and a drooping mustache—he looked like some German accountant. His wife would help him with the barbecue. There were usually four or five teachers with their partners. In the late afternoons we'd talk about the holidays—we were usually a bit stoned. Guilmard's wife was a nurse and she had the reputation of being a real slut; in fact, when she sat on the grass you could see that she wasn't wearing anything under her dress. They spent their holidays at Cap d'Agde, on the nudist beach. I think they went to a wife-swapping sauna on the Place Bossuet—well, that's what I heard, anyway. I never dared to talk to Anne about it, but I really liked them. They were sort of social democrats, not at all like the aging hippies who used to hang around with Mother in the seventies. Guilmard was a good teacher, and thought nothing of staying behind after class to help a kid who was having problems. He gave to some charity for the handicapped as well, I think."

Abruptly Bruno fell silent. After a minute or two, Michel got up, opened the French doors and went out onto the balcony for a breath of the night air. Most of the people he knew had lived lives very like Bruno's.

Excepting some high-profile businesses like advertising and fashion, it's pretty easy to be accepted physically in professional circles; the dress code is simple and obvious. After a couple of years of working, sexual desire wanes and people turn their attention to gourmet food and wine. Some of Michel's colleagues—many of them much younger—had already started a cellar. Bruno wasn't like that—he hadn't even commented on the wine, Vieux Papes at twelve francs a bottle. Half forgetting that his brother was there, Michel leaned on the railing and looked out at the other buildings. It was dark now and the lights in most of the apartments were out. It was 15 August, a Sunday evening. He came back inside and sat near Bruno, their knees almost touching. Was it possible to think of Bruno as an individual? The decay of his organs was particular to him, and he would suffer his decline and death as an individual. On the other hand, his hedonistic worldview and the forces that shaped his consciousness and desires were common to an entire generation. Just as determining the apparatus for an experiment and choosing one or more observables made it possible to assign a specific behavior to an atomic system—now particle, now wave—so could Bruno be seen as an individual or, from another point of view, as passively caught up in the sweep of history. His motives, values and desires did not distinguish him from his contemporaries in any way.

Generally, the initial reaction of a thwarted animal is to try harder to attain its goal. A starving chicken (*Gallus domesticus*) prevented from reaching its food by a wire fence will make increasingly frantic efforts to get through it. Gradually, however, this behavior is replaced by another which has no obvious purpose. When unable to find food, for example, pigeons (*Columba livia*) will frequently peck the ground even if nothing there is edible. Not only will they peck indiscriminately, but they start to preen their feathers; such inappropriate behavior, frequently observed in situations of frustration or conflict, is known as *displacement activity*. Early in 1986, just after he turned thirty, Bruno began to write.

13

"No metaphysical mutation takes place," Djerzinski would write many years later, "without first being announced. The radical change is preceded by many minor mutations—facilitators whose historic appearance often goes unnoticed at the time. I consider myself to have been one such mutation."

Drifting among the mass of European humanity, Djerzinski was little understood in his lifetime. In the introduction to Djerzinski's posthumously published *Clifden Notes,* Hubczejak writes: "An idea which evolves in a single mind, without the counterbalance of debate, can nonetheless avoid the pitfalls of idiosyncrasy and folly. It is significant, however, that Djerzinski presents his idea in the form of a quasi-Socratic dialogue. It should be added that, until the end, Djerzinski considered himself primarily a scientist. He believed that his principal contribution to human evolution was his work in biophysics, which he had developed within the classical scientific constraints of consistency and refutability. As far as he was concerned, the more philosophical elements of his later works were never more than rash, even crazy conjectures, which he recorded less for their intrinsic claims to truth than out of personal considerations."

. . .

He felt a little tired; the moon glided over the sleeping city. He knew that he only had to say the word and Bruno would get up, put on his jacket and disappear into the elevator. He could easily hail a cab at La Motte-Picquet.

When we think about the present, we veer wildly between the belief in chance and the evidence in favor of determinism. When we think about the past, however, there is no more doubt: it seems obvious that everything happened in the way it was intended. Djerzinski had long since seen through this perceptual illusion, based as it was on an ontology of objects and intrinsic properties and dependent on a strong notion of external reality. It was this realization, rather than any feeling of compassion or respect, which prevented him from uttering the simple, established phrase that would have cut short this broken, tearful creature's confession. This evening, sprawled on the sofa, this animal with whom he shared one half of his genetic code had overstepped the unspoken boundaries of decent human conversation. This evening, Djerzinski had a faint but definite feeling that Bruno's tortuous, pathetic tale was tending toward some conclusion; words would be spoken and—for the first time—these words would have meaning and finality. He stood up and went to the bathroom, where discreetly, without a sound, he vomited. He splashed water on his face and went back to the living room.

"You're not human," Bruno said quietly, looking up at Michel. "I knew it from the start, from the way you behaved with Annabelle. But you're the audience life has given me. At the time, I suppose you weren't surprised when you got my article on John Paul II."

"Every civilization has had to find some way to justify the sacrifices parents make," said Michel sadly. "Under the historical circumstances, you didn't have much choice."

"But I really did admire John Paul II," Bruno protested. "I remember it was in 1986—Canal+ and M6 had just started broadcasting, the *Globe* had just been launched and the Restos du Coeur soup kitchens started up. John Paul II was the only person—the only person—who really understood what was happening in the West. I was stunned when my paper was badly received by my 'Living with Faith' group in Dijon; they criticized the Pope's position on abortion, condoms—all that rubbish. I have to admit I didn't make much of an effort to see their point of view, either. We used to take turns holding the meeting in our houses; everyone would bring something to eat, a salad, a dip, a cake. I used to spend the evenings smiling like a half-wit, nodding my head and knocking back the wine; I wasn't really listening. Anne was really into it, though. She signed up to help with a literacy program. The evenings she was out, I'd put a sedative into Victor's bottle, log on to the Minitel and jerk off, but I never actually met anyone in person.

"In April, for Anne's birthday, I'd bought her a silver lamé bodice and garters. She was a little wary at first, but I persuaded her to try it on. While she was strapping herself into it, I finished the champagne. Then I heard her small trembling voice saying nervously: 'I'm ready . . .' The minute I walked into the bedroom I knew it had been a lousy idea. Her sagging ass was squeezed into the garters and her tits had never really recovered from breast-feeding. She needed liposuction, silicone implants, the works—though she would never have agreed to it. I closed my eyes and slipped a finger into her G-string; I was completely soft. At that moment Victor started howling from the next room—loud, shrill, unendurable screams. She put on a dressing gown and ran into his room. When she got back I just asked her for a blow-job. She wasn't very good at it—you could feel her teeth—but I closed my eyes and imagined it was a Ghanaian girl from my *seconde* class. Thinking about her rough, pink tongue, I managed to come in my wife's mouth. I had no intention of having another child. I wrote the piece about the family the next day—you know, the one that was published."

"I still have a copy of it," said Michel. He got up and took down the magazine from a bookshelf. Bruno thumbed through it, somewhat surprised, and found the page.

There are families still, more or less
(Sparks of faith among atheists,
Sparks of love in the pit of nausea),
And we do not know how
These sparks glow.

Slaves working for incomprehensible organizations,
The only way in which we can live our lives is through sex

(Though only, of course, those for whom sex is still permitted,
Those for whom sex is possible).

Now, marriage and fidelity cut us off from any possibility of existence,
We will not find—in the office or the classroom—that spirit in us which clamors for adventure, for light, for dance;
And so we try to pool our destinies through increasingly difficult loves,
We try to sell a body which is ever more exhausted, mutinous, recalcitrant
And we disappear
In the shadow of sorrow
Into true despair,

We go down the long, solitary road to the place where all is dark,
Without children, without wives,
We enter the lake
In the middle of night
(and the water on our ancient bodies is so cold).

Just after writing this, Bruno had slipped into a kind of alcoholic coma. He was woken some hours later by the screams of his son. Between the ages of two and four, human children acquire a sense of self, which manifests itself in displays of megalomaniacal histrionics. Their aim in this is to control their social environment, making slaves of those around them (specifically, their parents); slaves dedicated to satisfying their every whim. Their egotism knows no bounds—such is the nature of the individual. As Bruno picked himself up from the living room floor, the screaming grew loud and shrill with rage. He crushed two Lexomil, mashed them into a spoonful of jam and headed toward Victor's room. The child had crapped itself. Where the fuck was Anne? These jungle-bunny literacy classes were ending later and later. He took off the soiled diaper and threw it on the floor; the stench was atrocious. The child swallowed the mixture on the spoon easily and his body stiffened as though he'd been struck. Bruno put on his jacket and went to the Madison, an all-night bar on the rue Chaudronnerie. He bought a three-thousand-franc bottle of Dom Pérignon on his credit card and shared it with a pretty blonde. In one of the upstairs rooms, the girl jacked him off slowly, pausing every now and then to heighten his pleasure. Her name was Hélène. She came from Dijon and was studying tourism; she was nineteen. As he slipped inside her, she tightened her vagina and he had three whole minutes of complete contentment. When he left, Bruno kissed her on the lips and insisted on giving her a tip—he only had three hundred francs in cash left.

The following week he decided to show a colleague—a fifty-year-old Marxist who taught literature—what he had written. He was tall and thin; rumor had it he was homosexual. Fajardie was pleasantly surprised. "You're obviously influenced by Claudel—or perhaps Péguy, in his blank verse. But it's very original, and that's something you don't come across much anymore." He was certain as to what should happen next: "*L'Infini*—it's the only serious literary magazine nowadays. Send it to Sollers." A little taken aback, Bruno asked him to repeat the name—he later realized he'd confused it with a brand of mattress—and sent off his work. Three weeks later he telephoned the publisher, Denoël, and was surprised when Philippe Sollers answered and suggested that they meet. Bruno had no classes on Wednesday, so it would be possible to get to Paris and back in a day. On the train, he tried to read Sollers's novel *A Curious Solitude* but quickly gave up, though he did manage to read some of *Women*—mostly the bits about sex. They had arranged to meet in a café on the rue de l'Université. Sollers arrived ten minutes late, brandishing the cigarette holder which would become his trademark. "You're in the suburbs? Pity. You should move to Paris right away. You have talent." He told Bruno that he would publish the piece on John Paul II in the next issue of *L'Infini*. Bruno was stunned; he couldn't have known that Sollers was deep into his "Counter-Reformation" phase and was publishing a variety of impassioned tracts favorable to the Pope. "I really admire Péguy!" said Sollers enthusiastically, "and de Sade, you must read de Sade . . ."

"What about the poem I wrote about families?"

"Excellent, also excellent—you're a real reactionary, that's good. All the great writers were reactionaries: Balzac, Baudelaire, Flaubert, Dostoyevsky. But you have to fuck, too, you know? You have to fuck as much as possible—that's important."

In five minutes Sollers was gone, leaving Bruno in a state of slightly inebriated narcissism. On the way home he calmed down a little. Philippe Sollers was obviously a famous writer, but from reading *Women* it was clear that the only women he managed to screw were cultivated old whores; real chicks preferred rock stars. In which case, what was the point of publishing some shitty poem in some shitty magazine?

"Of course that didn't stop me from buying five copies of *L'Infini* when it was published. Thank God they didn't run the piece on John Paul II in the end, it was terrible . . . Is there any wine left?"

"Just one bottle." Michel went to the kitchen and brought back the final bottle from the six-pack of Vieux Papes; he was beginning to feel really tired. "You're working tomorrow, aren't you?" he asked. Bruno didn't respond. He was staring at a spot on the floor, though there was nothing there, nothing specific, just some lumps of grime. He came to life when he heard the cork pop and held out his glass. He drank slowly, in small sips; his gaze had now fallen on some indistinct point on the radiator. Michel hesitated for a moment and then turned on the television: there was a documentary about rabbits. He turned down the sound. In fact, it might have been a program about hares, he always confused the two. He was surprised when Bruno began to speak again:

"I was trying to remember how long I was in Dijon. Four years? Five? When you work in something like teaching, every year seems the same. The only things that mark out your life are visits to the doctor and watching the kids grow up. Victor was growing up, he was starting to call me Daddy."

Suddenly he started to cry. Curled up on the sofa, he sobbed, snuffling loudly. Michel looked at his watch; it was just after four a.m. On the screen a wildcat had a dead rabbit in its mouth.

Bruno took out a tissue and wiped the corners of his eyes. Tears continued to stream down his face as he thought about his son. Poor little Victor, who drew creatures from the pages of *Strange*, who loved him. He'd given the boy few moments of happiness and fewer still of love—now the boy was fourteen and the time for happiness was over.

"Anne would have liked to have had more children, she actually rather liked the idea of being a mother and a housewife. I was the one who pushed her to apply for a job in Paris so we could move back. She didn't dare say no, of course. At the time everyone believed—or pretended to believe—that a woman's career was essential to her self-esteem, and more than anything, Anne had a need to conform with what other people thought. I knew perfectly well that the real reason we were going back to Paris was to make the divorce easier. In the sticks people still meet and gossip, and I didn't want people talking about our divorce, even if they thought it was a good idea. In the summer of '89 we went away to Club Med—it was our last vacation together. I remember the stupid fucking games before dinner and spending hours checking out girls on the beach. Anne chatted with the other mothers. When she lay on her stomach you could see her cellulite, and when she turned onto her back you could see her stretch marks. This was in Morocco. The Arabs were aggressive and obnoxious and the weather was far too hot. It wasn't really worth getting skin cancer just so I could go back to the room at night and jerk off. Victor really enjoyed himself—he had a great time at the Mini Club . . ." Bruno's voice faltered again.

"I was a bastard; I knew I was being a bastard. Parents usually make sacrifices for their kid—that's how it's supposed to be. I just couldn't cope with the fact that I wasn't young anymore; my son was going to grow up and he would get to be young instead and he might make something of his life, while I had failed in mine. I wanted to be an individual entity again."

"A monad," said Michel softly.

Bruno said nothing. He drained his glass. "The bottle's empty . . ." he remarked absently. He got up, put on his jacket, and Michel walked him to the door. "I do love my son," Bruno said. "If he had an accident, if anything happened to him, I couldn't bear it. I love that kid more than anything, but I've never even been able to accept his existence." Michel nodded. Bruno walked toward the elevator.

Michel went back to his desk and noted on a piece of paper, *Write something about blood;* then lay down to think, but he fell asleep almost immediately. Some days later, when he turned up the piece of paper, he discovered the words "blood is thicker than water" written underneath; for ten minutes he stood there completely mystified.

14

On the morning of the first of September Bruno waited for Christiane at the Gare du Nord. She had taken a bus from Noyon to Amiens and a train from there to Paris. It was a beautiful day. Her train arrived at 11:37. She was wearing a long print dress with lace cuffs and a pattern of scattered flowers. He took her in his arms. Their hearts beat eagerly.

They had lunch in an Indian restaurant, then went back to his apartment and made love. The floor was polished, the curtains had been cleaned and smelled lovely, he'd put flowers in the vases. He managed to hold back for a long time, waiting for her to come; sunlight flickered through the gap in the curtains, glinting on her black hair, where he could see one or two gray hairs. She came, then came again immediately afterward. As she did so, her vagina contracted vigorously and he came inside her. He pressed himself against her and they fell asleep.

When they woke, it was around seven and the sun was sinking between the high-rises. Bruno opened a bottle of white wine. He had never spoken to anyone about the years that followed his return from Dijon; he wanted to now.

"At the beginning of the 1989–1990 academic year, Anne got a job at the Lycée Condorcet. We rented an apartment, a small, dark two-bedroom on the rue Rodier. Victor was going to nursery school by now, so I had my days free. It was about then that I started visiting prostitutes. There were lots of Thai massage parlors in the area—the New Bangkok, the Golden Lotus and the Mai Lin; the girls were polite, always smiling, and everything went well. At about the same time I started seeing an analyst. I don't remember much about the experience—I think the guy had a beard, but I might be confusing him with someone in a film. I talked to him about my adolescence, and a lot about the massage parlors. I felt he had nothing but contempt for me, which made me feel better. In any case, in January I changed shrinks. The new one was good—he had an office near the Strasbourg Saint-Denis metro, so I'd tour the peep shows on the way back. His name was Dr. Azoulay. There were copies of *Paris Match* in his waiting room. Anyway, I thought he was a good doctor. My case didn't really interest him much, but I didn't hold that against him—after all, it was terribly banal. I was just one more frustrated, aging fucker who didn't find his wife attractive anymore. At about the same time, he was called as an expert witness in the trial of a gang of teenage Satanists who had cut up some handicapped kid with a saw and eaten him. You have to admit that was a damn sight more exciting. Anyway, at the end of every session, he'd recommend that I take up a sport—he was obsessed with sports. Though he was getting a little paunch himself. Anyway, the sessions were okay, if a bit depressing; the only thing that seemed to bring him to life was my relationship with my parents. At the beginning of February, I had a really interesting story for him. It was in the waiting room of the Mai Lin; I'd come in and sat down next to some guy whose face seemed familiar—I didn't recognize him, there was just something about him. Anyway, he was sent upstairs and I went up right after him. There were only two massage cabins, separated by a plastic curtain, so he had to be on the other side. When the girl started stroking my belly with her soapy tits, I had a revelation: the guy in the next cabin getting a quick "full body" was my father. He had aged terribly—he looked like a real retiree—but there was no doubt about it, it was him. Just as I realized this, I heard him come with a little noise like a bladder emptying. After I'd shot off myself, I waited a couple of minutes before getting dressed; I didn't fancy running into him on the way out. But the day I told the story to my analyst, I phoned my father when I got home. He seemed surprised to hear from me—but pleased. I was right—he was retired, having sold his shares in the Cannes clinic. He'd lost a lot of money in the last couple of years, but he was still okay financially; there were people a lot worse off. We said we'd meet up someday soon, but we couldn't manage it right away.

"At the beginning of March I got a call from the school superintendent. One of the teachers had taken maternity leave early, so they had a vacancy until the end of the year at the Lycée de Meaux. Well, I thought about it for three hours—after all, I had very bad memories of Meaux—and then figured out that I didn't really give a damn. I suppose that's old age for you. Emotional reactions are dulled; you harbor little resentment and little joy. You spend most of your time worrying about the functioning of your organs, about their precarious equilibrium.

"When I got off the train and walked through the town, I was surprised at how small and ugly it was—there seemed to be nothing of interest in it at all. As a kid, when I got back to Meaux every Sunday night, I felt like I was entering some vast hellish place. Well, I was wrong—it was a pretty small hell, without a single distinguishing feature. The streets and the houses didn't conjure up any memories—even the school had been renovated. I took a tour of the building where the boarders had lived; it had long since been closed and turned into a local history museum. In these rooms, other boys had hit me and humiliated me. They'd spit on me, pissed on me, pushed my head into the toilet and enjoyed it, but I didn't feel anything. Oh, maybe I felt a little sad—but in a very general sort of way. 'God Himself cannot undo that which has been done,' as some Catholic writer said somewhere. When I looked back at what was left of my childhood in Meaux, it didn't look too bad to me.

"I walked around town for several hours, and even went back to the Café de la Plage. I thought about Caroline Yessayan and Patricia Hohweiller, but nothing there particularly reminded me of them. I suppose I'd never really forgotten them. I noticed a lot of young immigrants—blacks, mostly, a lot more than when I was a teenager; that was the only thing that had really changed. Then I went back to the school and introduced myself. The housemaster was delighted to hear I was a former pupil; he said he might go and dig out my file but I changed the subject, so at least I didn't have to go through that. I took three classes:

seconde, première A and *première* S. I realized straightaway that the *première* A would be the worst: there were three boys and about thirty girls. Thirty sixteen-year-old girls—blondes, brunettes, redheads, white girls, Arabs, Asians . . . every one of them lovely and every one of them desirable. And they weren't virgins, either—you could tell. They slept around, swapped boyfriends—enjoying their youth to the full. I used to walk past the condom machine every day and they weren't the slightest bit embarrassed to use it right in front of me.

"The problems started when I decided I might have a chance. A lot of their parents were probably divorced, so I was convinced I could find one who was looking for a father figure. It could work—I was sure of it. But I'd have to be a big, broad-shouldered father figure, so I grew a beard and joined a gym. The beard was a qualified success—it grew in thinly, which made me look like a dirty old man, a little like Salman Rushdie—but the gym was a great idea. Within a couple of months I had well-defined pecs and deltoids. The problem—and it was a new one for me—was my dick. It probably sounds strange now, but in the seventies nobody really cared how big their dick was. When I was a teenager I had every conceivable hang-up about my body except that. I don't know who started it—queers, probably, though you find it a lot in American detective novels, but there's no mention of it in Sartre. Whatever, in the showers at the gym I realized I had a really small dick. I measured it when I got home—it was twelve centimeters, maybe thirteen or fourteen if you measured right to the base. I'd found something new to worry about, something I couldn't do anything about; it was a basic and permanent handicap. It was around then that I started hating blacks. There weren't many of them in the school—most of them went to the technical high school, Lycée Pierre-de-Coubertin, where the eminent Defrance did his philosophical striptease and propounded his pro-youth ass-kissing. I only had one, in my *première* A class, a big, stocky guy who called himself Ben. He always wore a baseball cap and Nikes; I was convinced he had a huge dick. All the girls threw themselves at this big baboon and here I was trying to teach them about Mallarmé—what the fuck was the point? This is the way Western civilization would end, I thought bitterly, people worshiping in front of big dicks, like hamadryas baboons. I got into the habit of coming to class without any underwear on. This black guy was going out with exactly the girl I would have chosen myself: blonde, very pretty, with a childlike face and small firm tits. They would come to class holding hands. I always kept the windows closed while they were working; the girls would get hot and take off their sweaters, their T-shirts sticking to their breasts. Hidden behind my desk, I'd jerk off. I still remember the day I gave them a passage from *Le Côté de Guermantes* to comment on.

> . . . the purity of a bloodline into which for many generations there had flowed only what was greatest in the history of France had rid her manner of everything that the lower orders call "airs" and had endowed her with perfect simplicity . . .

"I looked at Ben: he scratched his head, he scratched his balls, he chewed his gum. What the hell would it mean to him, the big ape? What would it mean to any of them? I was beginning to wonder whether *I* understood what Proust meant, exactly. These dozens of pages about the purity of the bloodline, the nobility of genius compared to the nobility of race, the rarefied atmosphere of great doctors . . . it all seemed bullshit to me. We clearly live in a simpler world. The Duchesse de Guermantes has a lot less dough than Snoop Doggy Dogg; Snoop has less than Bill Gates, but he gets the girls wet. There are two possible criteria, that's it. Of course you could write a Proustian novel about the jet set, about money and fame—a major star brought face to face with a literary legend. It would entrance the literati, but in the end, who cares? Literary fame is a poor substitute for real stardom, media stardom, which is linked to show biz; after all, show biz rakes in more than any other industry in the world. What's a banker or a senator or a CEO next to an actor or a rock star? Financially, sexually, any way you look at it, they're nonentities. The strategies of distinction so subtly described by Proust are completely meaningless nowadays. From the point of view of man as a hierarchical animal, as a builder of hierarchies, the twentieth century had about as much in common with the eighteenth as the GAN insurance tower with the Petit Trianon. Proust was fundamentally European—he and Thomas Mann were the last Europeans—but what he wrote no longer bears any relationship to the world as we know it. The passage about the Duchesse de Guermantes is magnificent, of course, but I found it all rather depressing. I found myself increasingly drawn to Baudelaire. Here were real themes: death, anguish, shame, dissipation, lost childhood and nostalgia—transcendent subjects. It was pretty strange really; it was spring, the weather was beautiful, there were stunning girls everywhere and there I was reading:

Be calm, my pain, and venture to be still.
You clamored for the Night; it falls; is here:
The city shrouds itself in blackest chill,
Brings peace to some, to others fear.

'Neath Pleasure's lash, the grim high executioner,
Mortal souls, that vile and worthless throng,
Reap grim remorse amidst the abject ceremony,
Pain, take my hand; let us now along . . .

"I stopped for a minute. I could tell the poem had moved them; there was total silence. It was my last class of the day, and in half an hour I would be on the train heading home to my wife. Suddenly I heard Ben's voice from the back of the classroom: 'You've got death on the brain, old man . . .' His voice was loud, but he didn't seem to be trying to insult me; in fact, he sounded rather admiring. I don't really know if he was referring to me or to Baudelaire, but as a response to the text it was pretty appropriate. But I had to deal with it somehow. I just said: 'Get out.' He didn't move. I waited thirty seconds, so scared that I was sweating. I knew that if I waited much longer I wouldn't be able to say anything, but I managed to croak 'Get out' again. He stood up, got his things together very slowly and walked toward me. In any conflict, there is a moment of grace when the opposing forces are equally matched. When he got to me, he stopped—he was a good head taller than I was—and for a moment, I thought he was going to deck me, but he didn't, he just walked past me to the door. I had won. It was a small victory, of course; he was in class again the next day. I think he had understood what was going on—maybe he caught me looking at her—but he started feeling his girlfriend up right there in class. He'd push her skirt up, put his hand as high as possible, very high on her thigh, then he'd look right at me and smile, really cool. I wanted the bitch so badly. I spent the weekend writing a racist pamphlet—I had a hard-on all the time I was writing it. Monday, I called *L'Infini*. This time Sollers asked me to come to his office. He was sharp and mischievous, just like he is on television—better, even. 'It's obvious you're a real racist. That's good, it really carries the piece. Well done!' He pointed to one of the pages with a graceful gesture. He had underlined a section: *We envy and admire the Negro because we long to regress, like him, to our animal selves; to be animals with big cocks and small reptilian brains which are no more than appendices to their pricks.* He tapped the page: 'It's strong, spirited, very aristocratic. You've got talent. A gift for words. I'm not keen on the subtitle: "We Become Racist, We Are Not Born That Way." I always think irony is a bit, um . . .' His face darkened, but then he twirled his cigarette holder and smiled again. He was a real clown, but a nice guy. 'It's very original, too, and not too heavy. You're not even anti-Semitic!' He pointed to another passage: *Only Jews are spared the regret of not being Negroes, because they have long since chosen the path of intelligence, shame and guilt. Nothing in Western civilization can equal or even approach what the Jews have made of guilt and shame; this is why Negroes hate the Jews most of all.* He sat back in his chair, seeming really pleased. He folded his arms behind his head; for a second I thought he was going to put his feet up on the desk, but he didn't. He leaned forward again—he just couldn't stay still.

"'So, what are we going to do?'

"'I don't know. You could publish it.'

"'Publish it in *L'Infini*?' He burst out laughing, as though I'd just told a really good joke. 'I don't think you realize what you're suggesting, my good man . . . You might have got away with it in Céline's day. These days, there are some subjects about which you can't just write anything you feel like. Something like this could make life really difficult for me. You think I don't have enough problems? You think that because I'm at Gallimard I can do what I like? People keep an eye on me, you know. They're just waiting for me to make a mistake. No, no—it would be too difficult. Haven't you got anything else?'

"He seemed really surprised that I hadn't brought another piece with me. I was sorry to disappoint him; I really wanted to be his *good man*, I wanted him to take me dancing and buy me whiskey at the Pont-Royal.

Outside, on the sidewalk, I felt a pang of despair. It was late afternoon, the weather was warm, women walked past me along the boulevard Saint-Germain, and I understood that I'd never be a writer, but I also understood that I didn't care. But what was I going to do? I was already spending half my salary on sex; I couldn't believe that Anne hadn't figured out something was wrong by now. I could have joined the National Front—but why bother getting into bed with those stupid assholes? In any case, there aren't any women on the far right, or if there are, they only fuck paratroopers. My article was crazy—I threw it into the first trash can I saw. I had to stick to my 'liberal humanist' position; I knew in my heart it was my only chance of getting laid. I sat on the terrace at the Escurial. My penis was hot, swollen and aching. I had a couple of beers and then walked back to the apartment. As I was crossing the river, I remembered Adjila. She was a pretty little Arab girl in the *seconde*. Good student, serious, a class ahead of her age. She had an intelligent, sensitive face, not at all cynical. She really wanted to make something of herself—you could tell. A lot of girls like that live with thugs and murderers, so all you have to do is show them a little kindness. Again, I started to believe it was possible. For the next two weeks, I talked to her often and called her up to the blackboard. She responded to my glances, she didn't seem to think anything was up. I didn't have much time, it was June already. When she walked back to her desk, I could see her little ass in her tight jeans. I liked her so much I stopped visiting prostitutes. I'd imagine sliding my cock into her long, soft black hair; I even jerked off over her homework once.

"On Wednesday 11 June she turned up in a little black skirt. Class would be over at six. She was sitting in the front row. When she crossed her legs under her desk I thought I'd pass out. She was sitting beside a fat blonde who ran off as soon as the bell rang. I went over and put a hand on her books. She just sat there, and didn't seem to be in any hurry. All the other kids left and the classroom was quiet again. Holding her exercise book in my hand, I could make out a word or two: *Remember . . . hell . . .* I sat next to her and put the book down on the desk, but I couldn't manage to say anything to her. We sat there in silence for more than a minute. I stared into her big black eyes, but I was aware of every little movement of her body, the rise and fall of her breasts. She had turned halfway toward me and then she parted her legs. I don't remember doing what I did next—I think it was half-involuntary—but the next thing I knew I felt her thigh against the palm of my left hand, then it's all a blur. I remembered Caroline Yessayan and froze with shame. I had made the same mistake—twenty years later, I had made the same mistake. Just like Caroline Yessayan twenty years earlier, she did nothing for a second; she blushed a little. Then, very gently, she moved my hand away, but she didn't get up, didn't make any move to leave. Through the bars on the windows I could see a girl in the playground racing off to the station. With my right hand I opened my fly. Her eyes widened and she looked at my penis. Her eyes on me felt like hot vibrations—I nearly came just from her watching me, but I knew that she had to actually do something if this were to be mutual. I moved my right hand toward hers but couldn't go through with it; imploringly, I took my cock in my hand as if to offer it to her. She burst out laughing; I think I laughed, too, as I started to masturbate. I went on laughing and jerking off as she got her things together, as she got up to leave. When she got to the door, she turned around and looked at me one last time; I ejaculated, then everything went black. I heard the door close and her footsteps dying away. I was stunned, as though I'd been struck like a gong. Still, I managed to phone Azoulay from the station. I don't remember the train back to Paris, or the metro; Azoulay saw me at eight. I couldn't stop shaking, and he had to give me an injection to calm me down.

"I spent three days in Saint Anne's and then they transferred me to a Ministry of Education psychiatric clinic at Verrières-le-Buisson. Azoulay was clearly worried. There was a lot of stuff about pedophilia in the papers that year, as if journalists had put the word out to "come down hard on pedophiles." It was starting to become a national obsession, all because they hated old people and loathed old age. The girl was fifteen, I was a teacher, I'd abused a position of authority and, to make matters worse, she was an Arab. His file on me could've got me fired—and probably lynched. After a couple of weeks he began to calm down; the term was almost over, and it was clear that Adjila hadn't said anything. I was back to being a typical case: depressed teacher, a bit suicidal, needs to rebuild his psyche . . . The odd thing is that the Lycée de Meaux wasn't a particularly *tough* school, but he made a big deal of the traumas I'd suffered there as a child, how going back there had brought them back—he did a pretty good job.

"I was in the clinic for about six months; my father came to see me several times, seeming more tired, more considerate. I was so out of it on neuroleptics that I didn't have any sex drive at all, but sometimes one of the nurses would take me in her arms. I'd press myself against her and stay there, not moving, for a minute or two, then I'd lie down again. It seemed to do me so much good that the chief psychiatrist suggested they continue, if they had no problem with it. Though he suspected that Azoulay hadn't told him everything, he had cases a lot more serious than mine—schizophrenics and dangerous psychotics—so he didn't have time to bother with me. As long as I had a doctor treating me, that was enough.

"Of course there was no way I could go back to teaching, but in 1991 the ministry found me a job with the Department of French Curricula. I'd forfeited my teacher's schedule, and school holidays, but I was paid the same salary. I divorced Anne soon afterward. We worked out a pretty standard formula for maintenance and custody; actually, the lawyers don't give you much choice, it's pretty much a boilerplate contract. When we got to the head of the line, the judge read through everything at top speed and the divorce only took about fifteen minutes. We walked out together onto the steps of the Palais de Justice just after noon. It was early in March; I had just turned thirty-five. I knew that the first chapter of my life was over."

Bruno stopped talking. It was completely dark; neither of them had dressed. He looked up at her. Christiane did something surprising: she leaned close, put her arm around his neck and kissed him on both cheeks.

"The next few years, life went on as normal," Bruno continued softly. "I had a hair transplant, which took pretty well—the doctor was a friend of my father's. I kept going to the gym. I tried taking vacations with Nouvelles Frontières, I tried Club Med again and that outdoorsy outfit, UCPA. I had a couple of flings, though not many; women my age aren't really into sex anymore. Of course they pretend they are, and some of them are looking for feelings they once had—passion or desire or something like that—but there was no way I could provide that. I never met a woman like you before. I never even dared to hope that a woman like you could exist."

"We need . . ." she said haltingly, "we need a little generosity. Someone has to start. If I'd been in that Arab girl's place, I don't know how I would have reacted. But I believe there was something genuine about you even then. I think . . . well, I hope I would've consented to give you pleasure." She lay down again, put her head on his thigh and licked the tip of his penis once or twice. "I'd like to get something to eat," she said suddenly. "It's two in the morning, but there must be somewhere in Paris we can go, no?"

"Of course."

"Do you want me to make you come first, or do you want a hand-job in the taxi?"

"No, now."

15

THE MACMILLAN HYPOTHESIS

They took a taxi to Les Halles and ate in an all-night brasserie. Bruno had pickled herring as a first course. Now, he thought, anything is possible. Almost immediately he realized he was wrong, though the possibilities were endless in his imagination: he could imagine himself a sewer rat, a saltcellar or a field of pure energy, but in reality his body was in a slow process of decay; Christiane's body was too. Despite the nights they spent together, each remained trapped in individual consciousness and separate flesh. Pickled herring was clearly not the solution, but then again, had he chosen sea bass with fennel it would've been no different. Christiane was mysteriously, obscurely silent. They shared a *choucroute royale* with traditional Montbéliard sausages. In the pleasantly relaxed state of a man who has just been brought lovingly, sensually to orgasm, Bruno had a fleeting idea. It was a professional preoccupation: what role should Paul Valéry play in the French language instruction of the scientific disciplines? By the time he finished his *choucroute* and ordered some cheese, he was tempted to answer "None."

"I'm useless," he said resignedly. "I couldn't breed pigs, I don't have the faintest idea how to make sausages or forks or mobile phones. I'm surrounded by all this stuff that I eat or use and I couldn't actually make a single thing—couldn't even begin to understand how they're made. If industrial production ceased tomorrow, if all the engineers and the specialist technicians disappeared off the face of the earth, I couldn't do anything to start things over again. In fact, outside the industrialized world, I couldn't even survive; I wouldn't know how to feed or clothe myself, or protect myself from the weather. My technical competence falls far short of Neanderthal man. I'm completely dependent on my society, but I play no useful role in it. The only thing I know how to do is write dubious commentaries on outdated cultural issues. I get paid for it, too, well paid—much more than the average wage. Most of the people I know are exactly the same. In fact, the only useful person I know is my brother."

"What has he done that's so extraordinary?"

Bruno thought for a moment, toying with the cheese on his plate, trying to formulate a suitably impressive response.

"He invented a new cow. That's a simplistic way of putting it, but I do know that his research led to the development of genetically modified cows which produce more milk which is of higher nutritional value. He changed the world. I've never done anything, never invented anything—I've contributed nothing to the world."

"You've done no harm . . ." Christiane's face darkened, and she finished her ice cream quickly. In July 1976 she had spent a fortnight at di Meola's estate in Ventoux, where Bruno had been the previous year with Michel and Annabelle. When she mentioned this, they were both struck by the coincidence, but at once she felt a terrible regret. If they had met there in 1976, when he was twenty and she was sixteen, how different their lives could have been. This, she thought, was the first sign that she was falling in love.

"Well, I suppose it's a coincidence," Christiane said, "but it's not so strange. My idiotic parents were part of the same liberal, vaguely beatnik movement as your mom was in the late fifties. They probably knew each other, though I'd rather not know one way or the other. I have nothing but contempt for them, in fact I hate them. They're evil—everything they've done is evil, and believe me, I know what I'm talking about. I remember the summer of '76 very well. Di Meola died about two weeks after I got there; he had an advanced cancer and didn't seem to be interested in anything much anymore. That didn't stop him from trying something with me—I was quite pretty back then—but he didn't push it, I think by then he was really in pain. For twenty years he'd been playing the wise old sage—using spiritual initiation to try and bed girls. At least he was consistent right up to the end. Two weeks after I got there, he took poison, something mild that took hours to work, and then asked to see everyone on the estate one by one—a private audience, very 'death of Socrates.' In fact, he was going on about Plato and the Upanishads and Lao-tzu—the usual suspects. He talked a lot about Aldous Huxley—he said he knew him—and about the time they'd spent together. I think he embroidered it a little, though I suppose the man was dying. When my turn came I was very moved, but he just asked me to unbutton my blouse. He looked at my breasts and he tried to say something I couldn't make out—he was having trouble speaking by then. Suddenly he sat up in his chair and reached out to touch my breasts. I didn't stop him. He put his face between my breasts for a minute and then fell back in the chair. His hands were shaking. He nodded for me to go. I couldn't see any sign of spiritual initiation or wisdom in his face; the only thing I could see in his eyes was fear.

"He died at nightfall. He'd asked for a funeral pyre to be built up on the hill. We all collected branches and then the ceremony began. His son David lit the fire, a strange glint in his eyes. I didn't know him really, just knew that he played in a rock band. The guys he was with looked dangerous—American bikers with tattoos, dressed in leather. I'd gone there with a girlfriend, and that night we didn't feel particularly secure.

"Some tom-tom players sat in front of the fire and began to play a slow, funereal beat. Everyone started to dance. The fire was really hot and everyone started to take off their clothes. Usually at a cremation there's sandalwood and incense; all we had was branches we'd picked up in the forest and probably some local herbs: thyme, rosemary, savory. After about half an hour it smelled just like a barbecue. It was one of David's friends who pointed that out—a big guy in a leather vest, with long, greasy hair and a couple of front teeth missing. Another guy, who looked a little like a hippie, explained that, in many primitive societies, eating the body of the dead chief was a rite of great spiritual communion. The guy with the teeth nodded and laughed. David went over and said something to them. He had taken all his clothes off. The gleam of the firelight on his body was magnificent; I think he probably lifted weights. I thought that things were likely to degenerate, so I hurried off to go to bed.

"Shortly afterward, a storm broke. I don't know why I got up again, but I went back to the fire. There were still thirty or so of them dancing naked in the rain. Some guy grabbed me roughly by the shoulders, dragged me to the pyre and forced me to look at what was left of the body. You could see the skull, the eye sockets. The flesh hadn't burned completely, and there was some of it on the ground mixed with the dirt like a puddle of mud. I started screaming and the guy let go of me. I ran off. My girlfriend and I left the next day. I never heard anything about the place again."

"You didn't see the article in *Paris Match*?"

"No . . ." Christiane looked surprised. Bruno stopped and ordered two coffees before going on. Over the years he had developed a cynical, hard-bitten, typically masculine view of life. The universe was a battle zone, teeming and bestial, the whole thing enclosed within a hard, fixed landscape—clearly perceptible, but inaccessible: the landscape of the moral law. It was written, however, that love contains and perfects this law. Christiane looked at him tenderly, attentively; her eyes were a little tired.

"It's a really disgusting story," Bruno went on wearily. "Actually, I'm surprised the papers didn't make more of it at the time. Anyway, it was five years ago, satanic abuse was still a novelty in Europe. The trial was in Los Angeles and David di Meola was one of the twelve accused—I recognized the name immediately—and one of the two who had managed to escape. According to the article, he was probably in hiding in Brazil. The charges against him were damning. They'd found hundreds of videos of murder and torture at his house, all neatly labeled and classified. You could see his face in some of them. The video they showed the jury was of the ordeal of an old woman, Mary McNallahan, with her granddaughter, an infant. Di Meola dismembered the baby in front of the grandmother with a pair of clippers, then ripped out one of the old woman's eyes with his fingers and masturbated into the bleeding socket. He had a remote control for the camera in his other hand and used it to zoom right in on her face. She was crouched on the floor, manacled to the wall in what looked like a garage. At the end of the film she was lying in her own excrement. The video was three quarters of an hour long, but the police were the only ones to see it all—the jury asked for it to be turned off after ten minutes.

"The article in *Paris Match* was basically just the translation of an interview that the district attorney, David Macmillan, had given in *Newsweek*. According to him, it was not just a group of young men on trial but society as a whole; he believed that the case was symptomatic of America's social and moral decay since the late 1950s. On more than one occasion the judge had instructed him to stick to the facts of the case; he thought the parallels Macmillan was drawing with the Manson family were spurious, especially as di Meola was the only one for whom they could establish a vague connection to the beatnik or hippie scene.

"The following year Macmillan published a book called *From Lust to Murder: A Generation*, translated into French as *Génération meurtre*. The book shocked me; I was expecting the usual right-wing fundamentalist rant about the return of the Antichrist and how there should be prayer in school. In fact, it was a precise, well-documented book which examined a number of cases. Macmillan was particularly interested in David di Meola and had done a lot of research to put together a full biography.

"Just after the death of his father in September 1976, David had sold the seventy-five-acre estate and bought a lot of property in old buildings in Paris. He lived in a big studio on the rue Visconti, and he had the rest renovated to be rented out. He divided up the old apartments; the *chambres de bonne* were knocked together and kitchenettes and showers added. When the work was done, he had about twenty studio apartments, which would themselves guarantee him a comfortable income. He hadn't given up on the idea of being a rock star and thought that maybe in Paris he might get the break he'd been looking for. But he was already twenty-six. He took two years off his age before touring the record studios; all he had to do was tell them he was twenty-four—no one ever checked. Brian Jones had the same idea long before. Once, at a party in Cannes—according to Macmillan's witnesses—David had run into Mick Jagger and recoiled as though he'd come face to face with a cobra. Jagger was *the* biggest rock star in the world: rich, adored, cynical—he was everything David longed to be. To be so seductive, he had to personify evil, to be its perfect embodiment—and what the masses adored above everything was the image of evil unpunished. Only once had Jagger's power been threatened, a clash of egos within the group—with Brian Jones. But the problem had been resolved in Brian Jones's swimming pool. Though it wasn't the official version, David *knew* Jagger had pushed Brian into the pool; he could see it happening. It was this original murder which made him leader of the greatest rock band in the world. David was convinced that man's greatest achievements were based on murder, and by the end of 1976 he was ready to push as many people as he had to into as many swimming pools as he could find in order to succeed. In the years that followed he only managed to appear as a session bassist on a couple of records—none of which was at all successful. On the other hand, women continued to find him attractive. Sexually, he became more demanding. He got used to sleeping with two women at a time—preferably a blonde and a brunette. Most of them agreed because he was exceptionally handsome, with a strong, virile, almost animal beauty. He was proud of his long, thick phallus and his big, hairy balls. He became less and less interested in penetration, but he still got off on watching a girl get on her knees to suck his cock.

"Early in 1981 he met a California guy visiting Paris and looking for bands to put together a heavy-metal tribute album to Charles Manson. He decided to go for it. He sold the studio apartments—which had quadrupled in price—and moved to Los Angeles. He was thirty-one now; officially he was twenty-nine, but even that was too old. Before meeting the American producers, he decided to lose another three years. Physically, he could easily pass for twenty-six.

"Production was delayed, and from his prison cell Manson demanded huge sums for the rights. David took up jogging and began to hang out with Satanist groups. California had always had more than its fair share of Satanists, from the very first ones—the First Church of Satan was founded by Anton La Vey in Los Angeles in 1966, and the Process Church of the Final Judgment was founded in Haight-Ashbury in San Francisco in 1967. These sects still existed, and David sought them out. Most of them just indulged in ritualistic orgies with the occasional animal sacrifice thrown in, but through them he was able to get in touch with more secretive and extreme groups. Notably, he got in touch with John di Giorno, a surgeon who organized 'abortion parties.' After the procedure, the fetus was ground up and kneaded into bread dough to be shared among the communicants. David quickly realized that the most advanced Satanists didn't believe in Satan at all. Like him, they were pure materialists who quickly abandoned all the ritualistic kitsch of pentagrams, candles and long black robes, trappings which were mostly there to help initiates overcome their moral inhibitions. In 1983 he took part in his first ritual murder—a Puerto Rican baby. While he castrated the baby using a serrated knife, John di Giorno ripped out and ate the eyeballs.

"By now David had more or less given up on the rock star dream, though he still felt a twinge whenever he saw Mick Jagger on MTV. The *Tribute to Charles Manson* had gone belly-up, and though he pretended to be twenty-eight, he was actually five years older and beginning to feel too old. In his fantasies of domination and power, he began to identify with Napoleon. He admired this man who had rained fire and blood upon Europe and killed hundreds of thousands of people without even a fig leaf of ideology, faith or political conviction. Unlike Hitler, unlike Stalin, the only thing Napoleon believed in was himself. He had succeeded in establishing a radical separation between himself and the rest of the world, and considered others mere tools in the service of his imperious will. Thinking about his distant Genoese origins, David imagined that he was related to the dictator who, walking through a battlefield at dawn and surveying the thousands of mutilated and eviscerated corpses, said nonchalantly: 'Bah! One night in Paris will replace these men.'

"As the months went by, David and some of the others plunged deeper into cruelty and horror. Sometimes they wore masks and filmed these scenes of carnage—one of them was a producer for a video company and could get the tapes duplicated. A good snuff movie was worth a lot—about twenty thousand dollars a copy. One night, at an orgy held by a lawyer friend, he saw one of his films being shown in a bedroom. It had been filmed about a month before, and in this one he'd cut off a man's penis with a chain saw. He was very aroused and dragged a young girl of about twelve—a friend of the lawyer's daughter—and forced her to her knees in front of him. The girl struggled a bit, but in the end she started to suck him off. On the screen, he watched himself slide the chain saw gently along the thighs of a forty-year-old man. The guy was tied up, his arms spread-eagled, screaming in terror. David ejaculated into the girl's mouth just as the blade cut through the man's penis. He grabbed the girl by the hair and jerked her head around brutally, forcing her to watch the long close-up of the stump as it pissed blood."

"That was the end of the evidence against David. The police got hold of a master copy of one of the torture videos, but David had probably been warned in advance; in any case, he managed to get away in time. At this point, David Macmillan puts forward his theory. What he had proved in his book was that these self-professed Satanists didn't believe in God or Satan or any supernatural power. Blasphemy was simply something they used to spice up their rituals, and most of them quickly lost the taste for it. In fact, like their master the Marquis de Sade, they were pure materialists—libertines forever in search of new and more violent sensations. According to Macmillan, the progressive destruction of moral values in the sixties, seventies, eighties and nineties was a logical, inevitable process. Having exhausted the possibilities of sexual pleasure, it was reasonable that individuals, liberated from the constraints of ordinary morality, should turn their attentions to the wider pleasures of cruelty. Two hundred years earlier, de Sade had done precisely the same thing. In a sense, the serial killers of the 1990s were the spiritual children of the hippies of the sixties, and their common ancestors would be the Viennese Actionists of the fifties. In the guise of performance art, Actionists like Nitsch, Muehl and Schwarzkögler had conducted animal sacrifices in public. They would rip out and tear apart an animal's organs and viscera in front of an audience of cretins, plunge their arms into the flesh and blood—drawing out the innocent animal's suffering to the limit—while someone photographed or filmed the carnage so it could be exhibited in an art gallery. This Dionysian pleasure in the release of bestiality and evil, begun by the Viennese Actionists, can be traced through every succeeding decade. According to Macmillan, this shift in Western civilization since 1945 was simply a return to the brutal cult of power, a rejection of the secular rules slowly built up in the name of right and morality. Actionists, beatniks, hippies and serial killers were all pure libertarians who affirmed the rights of the individual against social norms and against what they believed to be the hypocrisy of morality, sentiment, justice and pity. From this point of view, Charles Manson was not some monstrous aberration in the hippie movement, but its logical conclusion; and what David di Meola had done was nothing more than to extend and to put into practice the principles of individual freedom advocated by his father. Macmillan was a member of the Republican party, and some of his diatribes against individual liberty caused much gnashing of teeth within the party, but his book had a tremendous impact. With his royalties, he went into politics full-time and, the following year, was elected to Congress."

Bruno fell silent. He had long since finished his coffee; it was four a.m. and there wasn't a single Viennese Actionist in the house. In fact, Otto Muehl was currently languishing in an Austrian prison for raping a child. He was in his sixties now, and hopefully would die soon, thereby eliminating one source of evil from the world. There was no reason to get so worked up. Everything was calm now; a single waiter moved between the tables. They were the only customers left, but the brasserie was open twenty-four hours a day—it said so above the door and again on the menu—in what was practically a contractual obligation. "They better not try to hassle us, the bastards," Bruno remarked distractedly. In contemporary society, a human life inevitably goes through one or two crises of self-doubt. It's hardly surprising, therefore, to find at least one establishment in any major European city which is open all night. He ordered a raspberry *bavarois* and two glasses of kirsch. Christiane had listened closely to his story; her silence was pained. It was time to return to simple pleasures.

16

TOWARD AN AESTHETIC OF GOODWILL

With the dawn, young girls go picking roses. A whisper of wisdom breathes over the valleys and the capitals, stirring the intellect of the most ardent poets, strewing safekeeping to cradles, crowns to youth and to old men an intimation of immortality.

—LAUTRÉAMONT,
Poésies II

Most of the people Bruno had encountered in his life had been motivated solely by the pursuit of pleasure—if one includes in the definition those narcissistic pleasures so central to the esteem or admiration of others. And thus different strategies are adopted, and these are called human lives.

To this rule, however, he had to make an exception for his half brother; it seemed impossible to associate the notion of pleasure with him; but what, if anything, did motivate Michel? A uniform rectilinear motion will continue indefinitely in the absence of friction or any other external force. Orderly, rational, sociologically situated at the median of the higher social stratum, Michel's life did not so far seem to have encountered any friction. It was possible that there were dark and terrible power struggles among molecular biologists, but Bruno doubted it.

. . .

"You have a very pessimistic view of the world . . ." said Christiane, ending the oppressive silence between them. "Nietzschean," corrected Bruno. "Pretty second-rate Nietzsche at that," he felt he should add. "I'll read you a poem." He took a notebook out of his pocket and recited the following verse:

It's always the same old shit of course,
The eternal return, et cetera,
And here I am eating raspberry mousse
In a café called Zarathustra.

"I know what we should do," she said after a long silence. "We should go and have an orgy on the nudist beach at the Cap d'Agde. You get a lot of Dutch nurses and German businessmen there, all very proper, very middle-class—the Northern European or Benelux types. Why don't we go fuck around with some Luxembourgeois policemen."

"I haven't got any vacation left."

"Neither have I, school starts again on Tuesday, but I *need* a holiday. I'm tired of teaching, the kids are all little fuckers. You need a holiday too, and you need to get off with a lot of different women. It's possible—I know you don't believe me, but it is. I've got a friend who's a doctor; he can give us sick leave."

They arrived at the station at Agde on Monday morning and took a taxi to the nudist colony. Christiane hadn't had time to go back to Noyon and had very little luggage with her. "I have to send my son some cash," she said. "He can't stand me, but I still have to support him for another couple of years. I just hope he doesn't turn violent. He hangs out with a lot of shady people—neo-Nazis and Muslims . . . You know, if he had an accident on his motorbike and was killed, I'd be sad, but I think I'd probably feel relieved."

It was September, so they found a rental easily. The nudist colony at Cap d'Agde was divided into five separate condominiums built in the late seventies and early eighties with a capacity of ten thousand beds—the largest in the world. Their apartment was twenty-two square meters:

a living room with a sofa bed, a kitchenette, two bunk beds, a bathroom, separate toilet and a balcony. It had a maximum occupancy of four people—usually a family with two children. Bruno and Christiane felt at home immediately. The balcony was west-facing, with a view over the harbor, so they could drink their aperitifs while watching the sun set.

Though it boasted three shopping centers, a mini-golf course and bicycle rental, the primary attractions for vacationers at the colony were sex and sunbathing. It was an archetype of a particular sociological concept, which was all the more surprising in that it was the result not of some preestablished plan but the convergence of individual desires.

That, at least, was how Bruno portrayed it in his article "The Dunes of Marseillan Beach: Toward an Aesthetic of Goodwill," a distillation of his two-week vacation. The article was narrowly rejected by *Esprit*.

"What first strikes the visitor to Cap d'Agde," he wrote, "is the juxtaposition of the consumer outlets typical of any European seaside resort with shops openly selling erotica and sex. It is surprising to see a bakery or a supermarket next to a shop selling transparent miniskirts, latex underwear and dresses cut away to reveal breasts and buttocks. It is equally surprising to see women and couples, some with their children, moving casually from shop to shop, aisle to aisle. At the resort, the newsstands offer the usual array of papers and magazines alongside a particularly extensive assortment of porn and wife-swapping magazines as well as sex toys without raising so much as an eyebrow.

"Vacation clubs usually run the gamut from 'family' concerns (Mini Clubs, Kids' Clubs—bottle warmers and changing tables) to more trendy alternatives (boogie boarding, nightclubs for ravers, 'not recommended for under 12s'). The nudist colony at Cap d'Agde—with its high proportion of families and the focus on sexual activity divorced from traditional pickup rituals—escaped this standard dichotomy. What is most surprising is how different it is from traditional nudist colonies, which tend to stress the 'healthy' aspects of naturism, avoiding any direct allusion to sexuality. They are big on macrobiotic food and smoking is practically forbidden. Their outlook is very environmentalist: vacationers study yoga, painting on silk and oriental exercise and are satisfied with rough-and-ready accommodation in a wilderness environment. The apartments on the Cap d'Agde, on the other hand, correspond to the standards of comfort prevalent at other resorts. The only allusion to nature is the manicured lawns and lavish flower beds. The food is standard fare, pizzerias jostling with seafood restaurants, French fry stands and ice cream parlors. Even nudity, dare one say it, wears a coat of a different color. In traditional colonies, nudity is obligatory whenever the weather permits; this is strictly monitored, and any behavior deemed to be voyeuristic is severely reprimanded. At Cap d'Agde, however, there is no dress code, and from the supermarkets to the bars, attire ranges from traditional dress to full nudity by way of overtly fetishistic outfits (fishnet miniskirts, lingerie, thigh-high boots). Voyeurism is tacitly condoned: it is commonplace to see men on the beach stop to admire the female genitalia on show; women make even this contemplation more intimate by shaving to make it easier to see the vulva and sometimes the clitoris. Even if one does not partake in the activities of the center, all this makes for a singular atmosphere, as far removed from the erotic, narcissistic ambience of an Italian disco as from the sleazy ambience of the red-light districts of major cities. What we have here is a traditional, rather genial seaside resort with the single distinction that sexual pleasure is recognized as an important commodity. It is tempting to suggest that this is a sexual 'social democracy,' especially as foreign visitors to the resort are principally German, Dutch and Scandinavian."

On the second day, Bruno and Christiane met a couple on the beach. Rudi and Hannelore gave them an insight into the sociology of the resort. Rudi was an engineer in a satellite tracking station responsible for the geostationary position of satellite Astra; Hannelore worked in a big bookshop in Hamburg. They had been coming to the Cap d' Agde for ten years or so. They had two small children but had decided to leave them with Hannelore's parents and treat themselves to a nice vacation this year. The four of them had dinner together that evening in a seafood restaurant famous for its bouillabaisse. Afterward they went back to the German couple's apartment. Bruno and Rudi took turns penetrating Hannelore while she licked Christiane's vagina, before getting the women to swap positions. Then Hannelore fellated Bruno. She had a beautiful body, buxom but firm and visibly toned through regular exercise. She sucked very sensitively; turned on by the whole situation, Bruno came a little too quickly. Rudi, more experienced, managed to delay his orgasm for twenty minutes while Christiane and Hannelore sucked him off together, their tongues sliding over each other around the glans of his penis. Hannelore offered them a glass of kirsch to round out the evening.

The Germans spent little time in the nightclubs at the colony. The Cleopatra and the Absolute could not compete with the Extasia, which was outside the nudist area, on the Marseillan resort, spectacularly equipped with a "black room," peep shows, heated swimming pool, Jacuzzi and, recently, the most magnificent mirror room in Languedoc-Roussillon. Far from resting on the laurels it had earned in the early seventies, and helped by the enchanting surroundings, the Extasia had managed to preserve its reputation as a nightclub legend. Nonetheless, Hannelore and Rudi suggested they meet up the following evening in the Cleopatra. Though smaller, it was situated in the heart of the complex and had a warm, convivial atmosphere ideally suited to the novice couple. It was the perfect place to have a no-frills after-dinner drink with friends and for women to try out their daring new clothing in a supportive environment.

Rudi passed the bottle of kirsch around once more. None of them had dressed. Bruno was excited to discover that he was hard again, less than an hour after coming in Hannelore's mouth; he mentioned this, his voice naively enthusiastic. Touched, Christiane began to masturbate him under the tender gaze of their new friends. As he neared climax, Hannelore knelt between his thighs and started fellating him gently as Christiane continued to stroke him. Somewhat absently, Rudi murmured, "*Gut . . . gut . . .*" They left, a little drunk but in good spirits. Bruno said that together they reminded him of the Famous Five. He told Christiane she was exactly as he had always imagined George; all they needed now was Timmy the dog.

The following afternoon they went to the beach together. The weather was beautiful and, for September, very hot. Bruno thought how pleasant it was, the four of them walking naked along the shoreline. It was nice to know there would be no problems, that all the sexual issues had been resolved; it was good to know that each of them would do their best to bring pleasure to the others.

. . .

The nudist beach at Cap d'Agde is about three kilometers long, on a gentle slope that makes for very safe swimming even for young children. Most of its length is reserved for family bathing and beach activities (windsurfing, badminton, kite-flying). It is tacitly accepted that couples looking for adventure meet on the eastern part of the beach, just past the refreshment stand. The dunes are shored up at the sides by a fence, creating a slight hill. From the top of the hill, to one side you see the beach sloping gently to the sea; to the other, which is more hilly, the dunes enclose flat expanses of sand dotted with clumps of holly oak. They settled themselves on the beach side, just below the rise. About two hundred couples were there, concentrated in the limited space. Some single men had sat down among the couples; others paced up and down the line of dunes, looking from side to side.

"During our two-week vacation, we went to the beach every afternoon," Bruno's article continued. "Of course death, or the thought that one might die, could make one judgmental about such human pleasures. I intend to show that if we ignore such an extremist notion, the dunes of Marseillan beach are a defining example of the humanist proposition: striving to maximize individual pleasure without causing unbearable moral suffering to anyone. Sexual pleasure—the most intense feeling of which human beings are capable—is principally dependent on the sense of touch, in particular, on the deliberate stimulation of specific areas of the epidermis rich in Krause's corpuscles. These activate neurons capable of triggering an abundant flow of endorphins in the hypothalamus. This simple neocortical system has evolved over generations of cultural change and a richer construct has been superimposed, one based on *fantasies* and (particularly in women) on *love*. My hypothesis is that the dunes of Marseillan beach, far from wildly exacerbating fantasies, even out the sexual odds, and serve as the geographic medium for a return to a norm in which sex is based on the notion of *goodwill*. To be specific, in this space between the dunes and the shoreline, any couple can take the initiative and begin public fondling; often the woman begins to stroke or lick her partner's sexual organs and the man returns the favor. Neighboring couples watch with interest, move closer to better observe their caresses and slowly begin to follow their example. From the original couple, a wave of affection and sexual excitement will quickly ripple across the beach. Sexual passion begins to grow, and couples come together to indulge in group sex—though it must be stressed that each waits for acknowledgment or explicit consent. If a woman wishes to decline an unwanted caress, she indicates this with a simple shake of the head, and the man makes a formal—almost comic—apology.

"The extreme decorum among the men is even more striking farther inland, above the dunes. This area is dedicated to fans of the *gang bang*, usually involving multiple male partners. Here, too, the germ is a couple who begin an intimate caress—commonly fellatio. Rapidly, the couple find themselves surrounded by ten or twenty single men. Sitting, standing or crouched on their haunches, they masturbate as they watch. Often things go no further; the couple return to their embrace and the crowd slowly disperses. Sometimes the woman will gesture to indicate that she would like to masturbate, fellate or be penetrated by other men. In this case, the men take turns—in no apparent hurry. When she wishes to stop, another simple gesture is sufficient. No words are exchanged; one can hear the wind whistling through the dunes, bowing the great tufts of coarse grass. Now and then the wind dies away and the silence is almost total, broken only by cries of pleasure.

"It is not my intention to depict the naturist resort at Cap d'Agde as some sort of idyllic phalanstery out of Fourier. In Cap d'Agde, as anywhere, beautiful, firm young women and seductive, virile men will find themselves inundated by flattering propositions. In Cap d'Agde, as anywhere, the obese, the old and the ugly are condemned to solitary masturbation—the sole difference being that whereas masturbation is generally prohibited in public, here it is looked upon with kindly compassion. What is most surprising is that so many diverse sexual practices—many far more arousing than one might witness in a pornographic film—can take place with such exemplary courtesy and not so much as an undertone of violence. In my opinion, this 'sexual social democracy' is an uncommon example of the qualities of discipline and respect for the social contract which allowed Germany to conduct two appallingly murderous wars a generation apart before building a powerful international economy from the ruins of their country. Indeed, it would be interesting to see what countries which traditionally honor the values of discipline and respect (Japan and Korea, for example) might make of the application of such principles in the Cap d'Agde. This respectful and legalistic attitude, which pleasurably rewards those who fulfill the contract, is a powerful incentive, in that it can, even without a written code, easily be enforced on the multifarious minorities at the resort (National Front yahoos, Arab delinquents, Italians from Rimini)."

At the end of his first week, Bruno stopped writing. What remained to be said was more tender, fragile and uncertain. After spending the afternoon at the beach, they were in the habit of going back to their apartment for an aperitif at about seven o'clock. He usually had a Campari, Christiane a vodka martini. He watched the sunlight play on the stucco—white inside, pinkish outside—and enjoyed seeing Christiane wander naked through the apartment, fetching ice or olives. What he felt was strange, very strange: his breathing was easier, and sometimes he found he could spend minutes at a time without thinking, without being so afraid. One afternoon, about a week after they arrived, he said to Christiane, "I think I'm happy." She stopped dead, her hand on the ice bucket tensing visibly, and breathed out slowly.

"I want to live with you," he went on. "I think we've both had enough, that we've both been too miserable for too long. Later we'll have to deal with sickness and infirmity and death, but I think we could be happy together right to the end. I'd like to try, anyway. I think I love you."

Christiane started to cry. Later, over seafood at the Neptune, they tried to work out the practical side. She could come and stay on weekends, that would be easy, but it would be difficult for her to get a transfer to Paris. Allowing for alimony, Bruno's salary was not enough for them to live on. In any case, there was Christiane's son to think of; they would have to wait. All the same, it was feasible. For the first time in many years, something seemed feasible.

The following morning Bruno wrote a short, emotional letter to Michel. He declared himself happy, and regretted that they had never truly understood each other. He hoped that Michel, too, might find a measure of happiness. He signed the letter: *Your brother, Bruno.*

17

When Michel received the letter he was in despair over a theoretical crisis. According to Margenau's theory, human consciousness could be compared to a field of probabilities in a Fock space, defined as a direct sum of Hilbert spaces. Such a space could be created by elementary electrical activity at a microscopic, synaptic level. Normal behavior could therefore be seen as the elastic warping of the field and free will as a rupture within it; but in what topology? There was nothing in the natural topography of Hilbert spaces that might give rise to free will. Michel was not entirely convinced that the problem could even be posed except in the most metaphorical sense. Of one thing he was certain: that a new conceptual framework was needed. Every night, before switching off his PC, he sent a request over the Internet for the daily experimental results. The following morning, he would digest them. As he did so, he remarked that around the world, research centers were groping their way along in a senseless empiricism. Nothing in their results brought them closer to a conclusion, nor did they provide support for any particular hypothesis. Individual consciousness seemed to emerge among animals for no apparent reason, and clearly predated the capacity for language. Darwinians, with their unconscious teleology, as usual put forward hypotheses about the possible selective advantages of the emergence of consciousness, but, as usual, these didn't explain anything; they were just-so stories, no more. Then again, the anthropogenic model was hardly more convincing: life had thrown up something which could contemplate it, a mind capable of understanding it, but so what? That in itself did not make understanding human consciousness any easier. Self-consciousness, which is absent in nematodes, was clearly observable in inferior lizards like *Lacerta agilis,* implying the presence of both a central nervous system and something more. What that something was remained completely mysterious. Consciousness did not seem to depend on any single factor, whether anatomical, biochemical or cellular. It was all rather dsicouraging.

What would Heisenberg have done? What would Niels Bohr have done? Step back from the problem, take time to think, take a walk in the country, listen to music. The new was never simply a reworking of the old; information was added like handfuls of sand, predefined in their nature by the conceptual framework of the experiments. Now, more than ever, a new paradigm was essential.

The short, hot days went by sadly. On the night of 15 September Michel had an unusually happy dream. He was with a little girl as she gamboled through the forest, surrounded by flowers and butterflies. (An image, he realized later, that had floated to the surface from a thirty-year-old memory of the credits of *Prince Sapphire,* a television series he used to watch at his grandmother's every Sunday afternoon, and which so accurately found an echo in his own heart.) A moment later, he was walking alone across an immense, undulating meadow through tall grasses. He could not see the horizon; the grassy hills seemed to stretch out to infinity under the brilliant gray sky. He walked on, however, purposeful and unhurried; he knew that some way beneath his feet ran an underground river, and that his feet instinctively would follow its path. All around him the breeze ruffled the long grass.

Upon waking he felt joyful and alive, something he hadn't felt in the two months since he left work. He went out and walked under the linden trees down the avenue Émile-Zola. He was alone, but not lonely. He stopped at the corner of the rue des Entrepreneurs. It was about nine o'clock. Zolacolor was opening up; Asian girls sat behind the cash registers. Between the Beaugrenelle towers, the sky seemed strangely luminous; there seemed no solution. Perhaps he should have talked to his neighbor across the street, the girl who worked at *Vingt Ans*. Working for a lifestyle magazine, informed about cultural trends, she would surely know how to fit in. She would know about psychology, too. There was probably much that she could teach him. He walked back quickly, almost breaking into a run, and bounded up the stairs to the door of his neighbor's apartment. He rang the doorbell three times. No one answered. Flustered, he retreated to his own building; as he waited for the elevator, he questioned himself. Was he depressed, and did such a question have any meaning? For years he had seen posters appear in the area, asking people to be vigilant and warning them about the National Front. The fact that he had no opinion on such a subject one way or the other was already a worrying sign. *Depressive lucidity*, usually described as a radical withdrawal from ordinary human concerns, generally manifests itself by a profound indifference to things which are genuinely of minor interest. Thus it is possible to imagine a depressed lover, while the idea of a depressed patriot seems frankly inconceivable.

Back in his kitchen, he realized that belief in the free and rational determination of human actions—which was the natural foundation of democracy—and, in particular, the belief in the free and rational determination of individual political choices, probably resulted from a confusion between the concepts of freedom and unpredictability. The turbulence of a river flowing around the supporting pillars of a bridge is structurally unpredictable, but no one would think to describe it as being *free*. He poured himself a glass of white wine, opened the curtains and lay down to think. The equations of chaos theory made no reference to the physical space in which their effects took place; their ubiquity meant that they applied as effectively to hydrodynamics as to meteorology, group sociology or the genetics of a population. As a tool for devising morphological models they were excellent, but their predictive capacities were nonexistent. On the other hand, the equations of quantum mechanics made it possible to predict the behavior of microphysical systems with exceptional, even perfect precision if one was prepared to give up any hope of a return to a materialist ontology. Certainly it was premature to establish a mathematical link between the two; it might even prove impossible. But Michel was convinced that the formation of attractors in the evolving network of neurons and synapses held the key to understanding human actions and opinions.

Looking for a list of recent publications on the subject, he noticed he hadn't opened his mail for more than a week. Naturally, most of it was junk mail. With the launch of the *Costa Romantica,* a company called TMR hoped to completely redefine the luxury-cruise concept; the ship was described as an "authentic floating paradise." The first moments of his cruise—"the decision is yours!"—might be described thus: "You step into the great hall. Sunlight streams through the great glass cupola. You take one of the panoramic elevators to the upper deck. Here, from the immense atrium situated on the prow, you can stare out to sea as though you were watching it *on a gigantic screen*." He put the brochure to one side, thinking to study it in detail later. "Walk along the deck, contemplate the ocean through a transparent bulkhead, sail for weeks under a changeless sky . . ." Why not? While they sailed, Western Europe might well be atomized under a hail of bombs. They would disembark, tanned and sleek, onto a new continent.

In the meantime he had to live, and that was something he could do intelligently, responsibly, joyously. The most recent issue of *Dernières Nouvelles de Monoprix* stressed more than ever the image of a socially responsible company. Once again the editor took issue with the notion that gastronomy and watching your weight were incompatible. Their scrupulous choice of recommended dishes, their range of produce, their store-label products—everything, in fact, that Monoprix had stood for since the beginning—was based on exactly the opposite conviction. "It is possible to have gourmet food, a balanced diet and to have it now," the editor boldly affirmed. After this first contentious, even combative article, the rest of the magazine was filled with "handy hints," educational games and "useful information." Michel was therefore able to calculate his average daily caloric intake. In the past weeks he hadn't once swept or ironed, gone swimming, played tennis or made love; the only three activities he could actually tick off were sitting, lying down and sleeping. All told, he needed only 1,750 calories a day. From Bruno's letter, it was clear that he'd been doing rather more swimming and lovemaking. He recalculated, using these new parameters, and discovered he would require 2,700 calories a day.

There was a second letter, this one from the town council at Crécy-en-Brie. In the light of development plans for a new parking lot, it was necessary to move the local cemetery; a number of graves, among them his grandmother's, would have to be moved. According to regulations, a family member had to be present for the relocation of the remains. He could arrange a meeting with the funeral directors between the hours of ten-thirty and noon.

18

REUNIONS

The railcar to Crécy-la-Chapelle had been replaced by a commuter train. The village itself had changed considerably. He stopped for a moment in the square outside the station and looked around in surprise. There was a Casino superstore on the outskirts of Crécy on avenue Général-Leclerc. In every direction he could see new houses and office buildings.

It had all happened around the time EuroDisney opened, explained a clerk at the town hall, and the extension of the commuter railway as far as Marne-la-Vallée. Many Parisians chose to move here; land prices had more than tripled, and the last of the farmers sold off their fields. Now there was a complex comprising a gym, community center and two swimming pools. Delinquency posed some problems, but no more than anywhere else.

As he passed the old houses and the canals on his way to the cemetery, he felt the sadness and confusion of anyone returning to his childhood home. Crossing the covered way, he found himself opposite the windmill. The seat where he and Annabelle liked to sit after school was still there. In the dark waters, huge fish swam against the current. Sunshine briefly broke through the clouds.

. . .

The man was waiting for Michel at the cemetery gates. "Are you the . . ."

"Yes." What did they call gravediggers nowadays? He was carrying a spade and a black plastic bag. Michel walked close behind him. "You don't have to look . . ." he muttered as they approached the open grave.

Death is difficult to understand; only reluctantly does a person resign himself to face a precise image of it. Michel had seen the body of his grandmother twenty years before and had kissed her for the last time. Nevertheless, he was at first surprised by what he saw in the excavation. His grandmother had been buried in a coffin, but among the freshly dug earth there remained only fragments of broken wood, a rotting board and indistinct white fragments. When he realized what he was looking at he quickly turned his head and forced himself to look the other way, but it was too late. He had seen the skull caked with earth, clumps of white hair falling over empty sockets. He had seen her vertebrae scattered in the clay. He understood.

The man continued to fill the plastic bag, glancing over at Michel, devastated, beside him. "Always the same," he muttered. "Can't help themselves, they have to look. Coffin's not going to last twenty years, is it?" he said almost angrily. Michel walked a few paces behind as the gravedigger poured the contents of the bag into their new resting place. Once he finished his work, the man stood up, came over and asked, "You all right?" Michel nodded. "We'll move the headstone tomorrow. Sign here for me."

That was that. After twenty years, that was that. Bones and earth mingled together and the mass of white hair, so much of it, so alive. He could see his grandmother embroidering in front of the television, walking toward the kitchen. That was that. As he passed the Bar des Sports, he realized he was trembling. He went in and ordered a *pastis*. When he sat down he noticed the interior was completely different from the way he remembered it. There was a pool table and video games; a television tuned to MTV was blaring out music; the cover of *Newlook* pinned to the bulletin board featured the Fantasies of Zara Whites and the great white shark in Australia. He gradually slipped into a gentle doze.

. . .

It was Annabelle who recognized him first. She'd just bought cigarettes and was heading for the door when she saw him slumped on the bench. She hesitated for a second or two before coming up to him. He looked up. "This is a surprise," she said softly; then she sat across from him on the leatherette seat. She had hardly changed. Her face was still incredibly smooth and pure, her hair dazzlingly blonde. It seemed impossible that she could be forty; at most she looked twenty-seven or twenty-eight.

She was in Crécy for reasons similar to his own. "My father died a week ago," she said. "Cancer of the bowel. It was long and difficult—and excruciatingly painful. I stayed for a bit to help Mom out. The rest of the time I live in Paris, like you."

Michel looked down. There was a moment's silence. At the next table, two young guys were talking about karate.

"I ran into Bruno about three years ago, at an airport. He told me you were a scientist—and important, well known in your field. He told me you'd never married. My life is less brilliant—I'm a librarian in a local library. I never married either. I've often thought about you. I hated you when you didn't answer my letters. That was twenty-three years ago, but I still think about it sometimes."

She walked him to the station. It was almost six and getting dark. They stopped on the bridge over the Grand Morin. There were plants in the water, chestnut trees, willows; the water was still and green. Corot loved this scene and had painted it many times. An old man in his garden looked like a scarecrow. "We're at the same point now," said Annabelle, "the same distance from death."

She stood on the step of the train and kissed him on both cheeks just before it pulled out. "I'll see you again," he said. She answered: "Yes."

She invited him to dinner the following Saturday. She was living in a studio apartment on the rue Legendre. It was very small, but the place seemed warm and inviting—the walls and the ceiling were paneled in dark wood like the cabin of a boat. "I've been living here for eight years," she said. "I moved in when I passed my library exams. Before that I worked in the coproduction unit at TF1. I'd had enough—I didn't like working in television. I lost two thirds of my salary when I changed jobs, but I like it much better. I work in the children's section in the public library in the seventeenth arrondissement."

She had made a lamb curry with dal. Michel said little as they ate. He asked Annabelle about her family. Her elder brother had taken over the family business. He was married with three children—a boy and two girls. Unfortunately, the business was in trouble; competition in precision optics was fierce, and on more than one occasion he had almost filed for bankruptcy. He drowned his sorrows drinking *pastis* and voting for Le Pen. Her younger brother had gone into the marketing department at L'Oréal and had recently been made marketing director for North America; they didn't see much of him. He was divorced, childless. Two completely different fates, but both somehow equally archetypal.

"I haven't really had a happy life," said Annabelle. "I think I was too obsessed with love. I fell for guys too easily; once they got what they wanted, they dumped me and I got hurt. It took me years to come to terms with the cliché that men don't make love because they're in love, but because they're turned on. Everyone around me knew that and lived like that—I grew up in a liberated environment—but I never enjoyed the game for its own sake. In the end, even the sex started to disgust me; I couldn't stand their triumphant little smiles when I took off my dress, or their idiot leers when they came and especially their boorishness once it was all over and done with. They were spineless, pathetic and pretentious. In the end, it was too painful to know they thought of me as just another piece of meat. I was a prime cut, I suppose, because I was physically perfect, and they were proud to take me out and show me off in a restaurant. Only once did I think I was involved in a serious relationship; I even moved in with him. He was an actor, and there was something very imposing about him physically, but he never really made it—in fact I paid most of the bills. We lived together for two years and then I got pregnant. He asked me to have an abortion. I did. But as I was coming back from the hospital I knew it was over. I moved out that night and checked into a hotel for a while. I was thirty. It was my second abortion and I couldn't take much more. This was in 1988 and everyone was starting to worry about AIDS. For me it was a salvation. I'd slept with dozens of men and there wasn't one of them worth remembering. People think that when you're young you go out and have fun, and only later do you start to think about death. But every man I ever met was terrified of getting old. They worried all the time about how old they were. They get obsessed about it when they're quite young—I've seen twenty-five-year-olds worried about getting old—and it just gets worse. I decided to give up, to stop playing the game. I live a quiet, joyless life. In the evening I read, I make herbal tea and hot drinks. I go to see my parents every weekend and spend a lot of time looking after my nephew and my nieces. Sometimes I get scared at night; I have trouble sleeping; it's true I need a man around. I take tranquilizers and sleeping pills, but they're never really enough. I just want life to go by as quickly as possible."

Michel said nothing; he wasn't surprised. For many women, adolescence is exciting—they're really interested in boys and sex. But gradually they lose interest; they're not so keen to open their legs or to get on their knees and wiggle their ass. They're looking for a tender relationship they never will find, for a passion they're no longer capable of feeling. Thus they begin the difficult years.

Folded out, the sofa bed took up most of the room. "I've never actually used it before," Annabelle said. They lay down side by side and held each other.

"I haven't been on the pill for a long time, and I haven't got any condoms. Do you have any?"

"No." He smiled at the very idea.

"Would you like me to take you in my mouth?"

He thought for a moment and at last said "Yes." It was pleasant, though not intensely so; in fact, it never had been. Sexual pleasure that's so intense for some is faint, almost insignificant for others (a result of culture, neural connections or what?). There was a poignancy in the act, which symbolized their reunion, their interrupted destiny. But afterward, it was wonderful to take Annabelle in his arms when she turned away to sleep. Her body was soft and pliant, warm and perfectly smooth; she had a slim waist, big hips and small, firm breasts. He slipped a leg between hers and placed his hands on her stomach and breasts; in this warmth, this softness, he was at the dawn of the world. He fell asleep almost immediately.

At first he saw a man, a form in space, only his face was visible. The expression in his eyes as they flashed in the darkness was difficult to decipher. There was a mirror facing him. When he first looked into it, the man felt as though he were falling into an abyss. But then he sat down and studied his reflection as though it were a thing apart, a mental image unrelated to him, transferable to others. After a minute, he began to feel more or less indifferent, though if he turned away, even for a few seconds, he had to begin again. Once more, he had to force himself, painfully—as one begins to focus on a nearby object—to shatter the feeling of identification with his reflection. The self is an intermittent neurosis, and this man was far from cured.

Then he saw a smooth, white wall and, as though from within, letters began to form upon it. Little by little they rose, creating a moving bas-relief in time to a nauseating throb. At first it resolved into the word PEACE, then into WAR, then PEACE reappeared. Then, suddenly, the phenomenon ceased and the surface of the wall was as smooth as before. The atmosphere seemed to liquefy, pulsing in waves; the sun was an immense yellow. He could see to a distant point, the root of time itself. This root sent out tendrils across the universe, knotty at the center, their tips cold and sticky. They wound around, encircled and encapsulated portions of space.

He saw the brain of the dead man as a part of space, containing space.

Last, he saw the mental aggregate of space and its opposite. He saw the mental conflict through which space was structured, and saw it disappear. He saw space as a thin line separating two spheres. In the first sphere there was being and separation, and in the second was nonbeing and the destruction of the individual. Calmly, without a moment's hesitation, he turned and walked toward the second sphere.

He extricated himself from their embrace and sat up. Annabelle's breathing was deep and regular. She had a cube-shaped Sony alarm clock which read 3:37. Could he get back to sleep? He had to get back to sleep. He had some Xanax with him.

In the morning, she made him coffee while she had tea and toast. The weather was beautiful, though it was already a little cold. She looked at his naked body; his still skinny frame seemed strangely adolescent. They were both forty, which was difficult to believe. Nonetheless, she could no longer have children without running the risk that they would be genetically malformed; his virility had already largely ebbed. From the point of view of the good of the species, they were a couple of aging human beings of middling genetic value. She had lived a bit: taken cocaine, participated in orgies, stayed in luxury hotels. Her beauty had put her at the epicenter of the movement of moral liberation which was such a major part of her youth. As a result, she had suffered greatly—in the end, she would almost give her life for it. His indifference had left him on the periphery both of that movement, and of life, and of everything, so he barely had been touched by it. He had been content to be faithful to his local Monoprix and to coordinate research in molecular biology.

Their different existences had left few visible marks on their separate bodies, but life itself had long since begun its work of destruction, slowly overburdening the capacity of cells and their organelles to replicate. Intelligent mammals capable of loving one another, they looked at each other on this autumn morning. "I know we've left it a bit late," she said, "but I'd still like to try. I still have my train pass from 1974–75, the last year we were at school together. Every time I look at it, I feel like crying. I can't understand how things can have gotten so fucked up. I just can't accept it."

19

In the midst of the suicide of the West, it was clear they had no chance. They continued to see each other, however, once or twice a week. Annabelle visited her gynecologist and went back on the pill. Michel proved able to penetrate her, but what he liked most was simply sleeping next to her, feeling her living flesh. One night he dreamed of a carnival in Rouen, on the right bank of the Seine. There was a Ferris wheel, almost empty, turning slowly against a livid sky, dominating a landscape of decrepit freighters and metallic structures eaten away by rust. He walked past the sideshows, the colors alternately dim and garish; a glacial wind whipped rain against his face. As he came to the exit, he was attacked by a number of razor-wielding youths in leather. They laid into him for some minutes and then let him go on. His eyes were bleeding; he knew that he would be blind, and his right hand was almost severed. In spite of the blood and pain, still he knew that Annabelle would stand by him, shielding him forever with her love.

For All Saints' Day weekend they went to Soulac and stayed in a summer house belonging to Annabelle's brother. The morning after they arrived, they walked down to the beach together. He was tired and sat on a bench while Annabelle walked on. In the distance the sea roared and heaved, a gray and silver flux. As they broke against the sandbanks on the horizon, the waves threw spray against the sun in a dazzling, beautiful haze. Annabelle's silhouette, barely visible in her pale jacket, walked along the water's edge. Circling around the plastic furniture of the Café de la Plage, an old Alsatian was also hard to make out, half erased by a mist of air, water and sunlight.

For dinner she grilled a sea bass; the society in which they lived accorded them a surplus above and beyond their basic nutrional needs, so they could live a little, but in fact they no longer really wanted to. He felt compassion for her, for the boundless reserve of love simmering inside her, which the world had wasted; it was perhaps the only human emotion which could still touch him. As to the rest, a glacial reticence had taken over his body. He simply could no longer love.

Back in Paris they had happy moments together, like stills from a perfume ad (dashing hand in hand down the steps of Montmartre; or suddenly revealed in motionless embrace on the Pont des Arts by the lights of a *bateau-mouche* as it turned). There were the Sunday afternoon half-arguments, too, the moments of silence when bodies curl up beneath the sheets on the long shores of silence and apathy where life founders. Annabelle's studio was so dark they had to turn on the lights at four in the afternoon. They sometimes were sad, but mostly they were serious. Both of them knew that this would be their last human relationship, and this feeling lacerated every moment they spent together. They had a great respect and a profound sympathy for each other, and there were days when, caught up in some sudden magic, they knew moments of fresh air and glorious, bracing sunshine. For the most part, however, they could feel a gray shadow moving over them, on the earth that supported them, and in everything they could glimpse the end.

20

Bruno and Christiane had also returned to Paris, as it was inconceivable not to. On the day they went back to work, he stopped and thought about the unknown doctor who had given them this singular gift, two weeks of unmerited sick leave; then he set off again toward his office on the rue de Grenelle. As he got to his floor, he realized he looked tanned and healthy—which was ridiculous—but he didn't really care. His colleagues, the thought-provoking seminars, the social development of the adolescent, multiculturalism . . . none of it had the slightest importance for him anymore. Christiane sucked his cock and looked after him when he was ill; Christiane was important. At that moment, he knew he would never see his son again.

Christiane's son, Patrice, had left her apartment a complete mess: pizza ground into the carpet, empty Coke cans, cigarette butts strewn about, and there were scorchmarks on the floor. She hesitated for a moment, thought about checking into a hotel, but then decided to clean up, to make the place her own again. Noyon was a dirty, dull and dangerous town: she got into the habit of going to Paris every weekend. Most Saturdays, they would go to a club for couples—the 2+2, Chris et Manu, the Chandelles. Their first night at Chris et Manu left a vivid impression on Bruno. Along the dance floor, a number of rooms were bathed in a strange purple glow; beds were set up side by side. All around them couples were fucking, stroking and licking each other. Most of the women were naked, though some wore a blouse or a T-shirt, or had simply hiked up their skirts. In the largest room there were about twenty couples. No one spoke, there was only the steady hum of the air-conditioning and the panting of women as they approached orgasm. He sat on one of the beds next to a tall dark-haired woman with heavy breasts who was being tongued by a man of about fifty who was still wearing a shirt and tie. Christiane opened his trousers and began to jerk him off, glancing around her as she did so. A man came up to them and slipped his hand under her skirt. She unhooked it and let it slip to the floor; she was wearing nothing underneath. The man knelt and began to stroke her as she continued to masturbate Bruno. Beside him on the bed, the dark-haired woman started to moan louder, and he cupped her breasts. He was hard as a rock. Christiane leaned over and began to tease the ridge of his penis and the frenum with the tip of her tongue. Another couple came over and sat beside them; the woman, a redhead of about twenty, was wearing a black fake-leather miniskirt. She watched as Christiane licked his cock; Christiane smiled at her and pulled up her T-shirt to show off her breasts. The other woman hiked up her skirt, revealing her cunt; her lush pubic hair, too, was red. Christiane took her hand and guided it to Bruno's penis. The woman began to jerk him off while Christiane continued to lick the glans. In a matter of seconds he shuddered with a spasm of pleasure and came all over her face. He sat up quickly and took her in his arms. "I'm sorry," he said, "really sorry." She kissed him, pulling him close to her, and he could smell the sperm on her cheeks. "It doesn't matter," she said gently, "it really doesn't." A little later she said, "Do you want to go?" He nodded sadly, his excitement completely dissipated. They dressed quickly and left immediately.

In the weeks that followed he learned to control himself a little better. It was the beginning of a good time for them, a happy time. His life had meaning now, though it was limited to the weekends he spent with Christiane. In the health section of FNAC he found a book by an American sexologist on how to postpone ejaculation using a series of gradual exercises. Essentially they helped develop the pubococcygeal muscle, a small arc-shaped muscle at the base of the testicles. By violently contracting the muscle and inhaling deeply just before orgasm, it was possible to avoid ejaculating. Bruno began the exercises; it was a goal, something worth working toward. Every time they went out he was astonished to see men, sometimes much older than he, penetrate several women one after another, to see them masturbated or sucked for hours on end without ever losing their erections. He was also embarrassed to discover that most had pricks much bigger than his. Christiane told him time and again it didn't matter, that it made no difference to her. He believed her—he could see that she was in love with him—but couldn't help feeling that many of the women they met in clubs were somewhat disappointed when they saw his cock. No one ever commented; their courtesy was exemplary, and the atmosphere always friendly and polite, but their looks couldn't lie and slowly he realized that from a sexual viewpoint, too, he just didn't make the grade. Yet there were moments of dazzling, unbelievable pleasure in which he would almost swoon or cry out with complete gratification, but these had less to do with his potency than with his genital sensitivity. On the other hand, Christiane told him he was very tactile, and it was true; he knew it was rare for him not to bring a woman to orgasm.

In mid-December, he noticed Christiane was losing weight and that there were red marks on her face. She was still having problems with her back, she told him, and had increased her medication; the weight loss and the red spots were just side effects of the drugs. She quickly changed the subject, and he thought she seemed embarrassed. He felt uneasy about the whole thing. She certainly was capable of lying to protect him: she was too gentle, too good-natured. On Saturday nights she usually cooked, and they had a nice meal together before going out. She wore skirts slit up the side and small see-through tops or garter belts and sometimes a body suit open at the crotch. Her pussy was soft, exciting and instantly wet. They were wonderful nights of the sort he scarcely had dreamed of before. Sometimes, when she let herself be fucked by several people, Christiane's heartbeat became irregular. Her heart would begin to beat a little too fast, and she would suddenly start to sweat. At such times Bruno was afraid. They would stop, then; she would press herself against him, kiss him and stroke his neck and his hair.

21

Of course, even here there was no escape. The men and women who frequented clubs for couples quickly abandoned their search for pleasure (which required time, finesse and sensitivity) in favor of prodigal sexual abandon—rather insincere in its nature and, in fact, lifted directly from the gang-bang scenes in the fashionable porn movies shown on Canal+. In homage to Marx's "tendency for the general rate of profit to decline," the cryptic law at the heart of his system, it would be tempting to propose a corresponding "tendency for the general rate of pleasure to decline" for the libertine system in which Bruno and Christiane found themselves, but that would be simplistic and inaccurate. As secondary cultural and anthropological phenomena, pleasure and desire explain almost nothing about sexuality itself; far from being determining factors, they are in fact themselves sociologically determined. In the context of a monogamous system based on romance and love, they can be attained only through the intermediary of the loved one. In the liberal system which Bruno and Christiane had joined, the sexual model proposed by the dominant culture (advertising, magazines, social and public health organizations) was governed by the principle of *adventure*: in such a system, pleasure and desire occur as a result of a process of *seduction*, which emphasizes novelty, passion and individual creativity (all qualities also required of employees in their professional capacities). The diminishing importance of intellectual and moral criteria of seduction in favor of purely physical criteria led regulars of such clubs, little by little, to a slightly different system, which can be considered the fantasy of the dominant culture: the *Sadean* system. In this fantasy world, cocks are invariably enormous and rock hard, breasts enhanced, cunts wet and shaven. Female regulars, often readers of *Connexion* and *Hot Video*, go out with the sole aim of being impaled on as many pricks as possible. For them, the logical next step would be S&M clubs. Orgasm is a matter of custom, as Pascal would undoubtedly have said if he had been interested in such things.

With his five-inch cock and his inability to maintain an erection between orgasms (he had never really been able to sustain one for any length of time, except perhaps as a teenager, and the time between ejaculations had grown considerably since then: he wasn't getting any younger), Bruno wasn't really in his element in such places. He was happy, however, to have more cunts and mouths open to him than he had ever dreamed possible; he felt indebted to Christiane for that. The gentlest moments were those when she caressed another woman; they were invariably delighted by the deftness of her tongue and the agility of her fingers in finding and stimulating their clitorises; their stimulation of him, however, was usually disappointing. Gaping from multiple penetrations and brutal fingering (often using several fingers, or indeed the whole hand), their cunts had all the sensitivity of blocks of lard. Imitating the frenetic rhythm of porn actresses, they brutally jerked his cock in a ridiculous piston motion, as though it were a piece of dead meat (the ubiquity of techno in the clubs, rather than more sensual rhythms, probably contributed to the excessively mechanical nature of their technique). He came quickly, with no real pleasure, and after that the evening was over as far as he was concerned. They usually stayed for another half hour or hour; Christiane would let herself be fucked by several men while trying—usually in vain—to get him hard again. When they woke, they would make love again and images of the previous night would flood back, softened by his half-sleep; these were moments of extraordinary tenderness.

The ideal scenario would have been to invite a number of chosen couples to spend the evening at their apartment and chat pleasantly while fondling one another. Bruno felt sure that this was the way forward; he knew, too, that he should go back to the exercises recommended by the American sexologist. His relationship with Christiane, which had brought him more joy than anything in his life, was deep and serious. That, at least, is what he told himself sometimes, as he watched her dress or putter around in the kitchen. But more often, during the week, when she was away from him, he had a premonition that it was a bad farce, one last sordid joke life was playing on him. Unhappiness isn't at its most acute point until a realistic chance of happiness, sufficiently close, has been envisioned.

The accident happened one night in February at Chris et Manu. Bruno was lying on a mattress in the main room, his head raised on several cushions, holding Christiane's hand as she gave him a blow-job. She was kneeling over him, legs apart, offering herself to any man who might pass. They slipped on condoms and took her from behind. Five men had already fucked her without Christiane even glancing back at them; eyes half-closed, dreamlike, she let her tongue play on Bruno's penis, exploring every centimeter of its length. Suddenly she gave a single short cry. The man behind her, a well-built guy with curly hair, continued conscientiously to pump her hard and fast, his eyes glazed and distant. "Stop! Stop!" said Bruno; he thought he'd screamed, but his voice didn't seem to carry, and only a feeble croak had escaped his lips. He got up and brutally pushed the guy away. The man stood, stunned, his cock rigid, his arms hanging loose. Christiane had fallen onto her side, her face contorted in a rictus of pain. "Can you move?" he asked her. She shook her head. He ran to the bar and asked to use the telephone. The ambulance arrived ten minutes later. Everyone in the club had dressed, and in complete silence they watched the paramedics lift Christiane onto a stretcher. Bruno rode with her in the ambulance to the Hôtel-Dieu nearby. For hours he waited in the linoleum-tiled corridor until the duty nurse came to speak to him: she was asleep now; she was out of danger.

On Sunday they took a bone marrow sample. Bruno came back at six. It was dark already, and a chill, fine rain was falling over the Seine. Christiane was sitting up in bed, her back supported on a pile of pillows. She smiled when she saw him. The diagnosis was simple: the necrosis in the vertebrae of her coccyx was so advanced that nothing could be done. She had known for several months that it could happen at any moment; her medication had slowed its progress, but could not stop it. It would get no worse, and there were no complications to fear, but she would be permanently paralyzed from the waist down.

When she was discharged ten days later, Bruno was with her. Things were different now; life in general is a series of long stretches of dazed monotony, and for the most part remarkably miserable. Then, suddenly, things take a decisive turn. Christiane would never have to work again; she was entitled to a disability pension, even to free home care. She wheeled herself toward him, still a little awkward—you had to get the hang of it, and her forearms were not yet strong enough. He kissed her on both cheeks, then on the lips. "Now you can come to Paris and move in with me," he said. She looked up at him but he could not hold her gaze. "Are you sure?" she asked softly. "Are you sure that's what you want?" He didn't answer, or at least he hesitated. There was silence for thirty seconds, then she added: "You don't have to. You've still got your life ahead of you, you don't have to spend it looking after a cripple."

Contemporary consciousness is no longer equipped to deal with our mortality. Never in any other time, or any other civilization, have people thought so much or so contantly about aging. Each individual has a simple view of the future: a time will come when the sum of pleasures that life has left to offer is outweighed by the sum of pain (one can actually feel the meter ticking, and it ticks always in the same direction). This weighing up of pleasure and pain, which everyone is forced to make sooner or later, leads logically, at a certain age, to suicide. On this subject, it's amusing to note that two highly respected *fin-de-siècle* intellectuals, Gilles Deleuze and Guy Debord, both committed suicide for no reason other than that they could not bear the idea of their own physical decline. Their suicides provoked neither surprise nor comment; generally, the suicide of elderly people—by far the most commonplace—seems to us perfectly rational. It is perhaps also useful to cite public reaction to the prospect of a terrorist attack as symptomatic: the overwhelming majority of people would prefer to be killed outright rather than tortured, maimed or even disfigured. In part, this is because they are somewhat tired of life; but the principal reason is that nothing—not even death—seems worse than the prospect of living in a broken body.

He turned off at La-Chapelle-en-Serval. The easiest thing would be to plow the car into a tree as he drove through the forest of Compiègne. He had hesitated a couple of seconds too long; poor Christiane. Then he had hesitated a couple of days too long before calling her; he knew she was alone in her low-income apartment with her son, he could picture her there in her wheelchair, not far from the phone. There was nothing forcing him to look after a cripple, that's what she'd said, and he knew that she hadn't died hating him. Her broken wheelchair had been found at the bottom of the stairs near the mailbox. Her face was swollen and her neck broken. Bruno's name was on a form in the box marked "in the event of an accident, please contact . . ." She had died on the way to the hospital.

The funeral complex was just outside Noyon, on the road to Chauny; you turn off just after Baboeuf. In a white prefab shed, two employees in overalls were waiting for him. It was stuffy and overheated with radiators everywhere, like a classroom in a technical school. The bay windows opened onto a series of low-rise modern buildings in a semiresidential zone. The coffin, still open, lay on a trestle table. Bruno approached it, saw Christiane's corpse and felt himself fall backward; his head hit the ground hard. The men helped him up carefully. "Cry! Go on, let it all out!" the older man urged him. He shook his head; he knew he couldn't bring himself to. Christiane's body would never again breathe or move or speak, her body would never again love. Nothing now was possible for Christiane, and it was all his fault. This time all the cards had been dealt, all the hands played, the last one face-up on the table, and he had lost. He had no more been capable of love than his parents before him. He floated in a strange state of sensory detachment, as though he were floating several centimeters off the ground. He watched as they placed the lid on the coffin and closed it tight with an electric screwdriver. He followed them to the "wall of silence," a gray concrete wall three meters high with funerary trays set into it, about half of which were empty. The older man checked his instruction sheet and went to compartment 632; behind him, his colleague rolled the coffin on a hand truck. It was cold and damp, beginning to rain. Compartment 632 was halfway up the wall about a meter and half off the ground. In a quick, efficient motion that lasted only seconds, the workers lifted the coffin and slid it into the hole. Using a pneumatic gun they sealed the compartment with quick-drying cement, then the elder of the two asked Bruno to sign the register. If he wanted, the man said as he left, he could stay and collect his thoughts.

Bruno drove back along the expressway, arriving at the *périphérique* at about eleven. He had taken the day off; it hadn't occurred to him that the ceremony would be so brief. He took the Porte de Châtillon exit and found a place to park on the rue Albert-Sorel just opposite his ex-wife's apartment. He did not have to wait long. Ten minutes later, his son turned the corner of the avenue Ernest-Reyer, his satchel on his back. He seemed worried, and was talking to himself as he walked. What could he be thinking about? Anne had told him that Victor was a solitary boy; he would come home at lunchtime and heat up something she'd left out for him rather than eat with his classmates at school. Had he missed Bruno? Probably, though he had never said anything. Children suffer the world that adults create for them and try their best to adapt to it; in time, usually, they will replicate it. Victor reached the door, keyed in the security code; he was only a couple of meters from the car, but he hadn't noticed his father. Bruno sat up in his seat and put his hand on the handle. The door to the building closed behind the boy; Bruno remained motionless for a few seconds, then sat back heavily in his seat. What could he possibly say to his son, what message did he have to give? Nothing. There was nothing. He knew his life was over, but he didn't understand the ending. Everything was dark, indistinct and painful.

He started the car and took the expressway south. Just past the exit for Antony, he turned off toward Vauhallan. The psychiatric clinic run by the Ministry of Education was just outside Verrières-le-Buisson, near the forest of Verrières; he remembered the park well. He parked on rue Victor-Considérant, walked the short distance to the gates. He recognized the duty nurse. He said: "I've come back."

22

SAORGE — TERMINUS

Advertising is so focused on attracting the youth market that it has often blundered into campaigns in which age is treated with condescension, caricature and ridicule. To compensate for the inability of such a society to listen, it is necessary to ensure that every member of every sales force become an "ambassador" to the elderly.

—CORINNE MÉGY,
Le Vrai Visage des seniors

Perhaps it was always going to end like this; perhaps there was no other solution. Perhaps it was necessary to unravel everything that had become tangled, complete everything that had been started. And so Djerzinski had to come to this place: Saorge, latitude 44° north, longitude 7°30' east, at an altitude of just over 500 meters. At Nice he checked into the Windsor, a midrange hotel with a foul ambience, one of whose rooms had been decorated by the mediocre artist Philippe Perrin. The following morning he took the famously picturesque Nice–Tende train. The train wound its way through Nice's northern suburbs of housing projects full of Arabs, billboards for Minitel sex sites and a sixty percent National Front majority. After Peillon-Saint-Thècle station the train entered a tunnel, and when it emerged into the brilliant sunshine

Djerzinski could see the fantastical silhouette of the town of Peillon perched high in the hills. This was what was called the *niçois* back country; people came from as far as Chicago and Denver to contemplate the beauty of the hinterland of Nice. Then the train rushed through the gorges of the Roya, and Djerzinski disembarked at Fanton-Saorge. He had no luggage; it was the end of May. He walked for half an hour or so. About halfway, he had to go through a tunnel; there was no traffic whatsoever.

According to the *Guide du Routard* he'd bought at Orly airport, the village of Saorge, dominating the whole valley from a vertiginous slope, its tall houses built into the terraced hillside, had "something Tibetan about it"; you could put it that way. In any case, it was here that his mother—Janine, rechristened Jane—had chosen to die, after spending five years in Goa on the west coast of the Indian subcontinent.

"Well, she chose to come here," Bruno corrected him, "but I'm sure she didn't choose to die. Apparently the old whore converted to Islam, to Sufi mysticism or some such bullshit. She moved into an abandoned house outside the village with a crowd of hippies. You'd think hippies had disappeared by now, given how little you hear about them in the magazines and papers, but actually there's more of them than ever; what with high unemployment, their numbers have increased considerably; you could even say the place is swarming with them. I did my own little survey . . ." he lowered his voice—"and the thing is, now they call themselves 'neo-rurals,' but actually they don't do a goddamn thing. They just collect their unemployment and some idiotic subsidy supposed to promote hill farming." He nodded his head with a knowing air, drained his glass and ordered another. He had arranged to meet Michel at Chez Gilou, the only café in the village. With its dirty postcards, framed pictures of trout and a poster for "Saorge Boules" (with its steering committee of no less than fourteen members), it evoked an olde-world hunting/fishing/nature/historic atmosphere completely at odds with the neo-Woodstock scene Bruno vilified. Out of his pocket he carefully took a pamphlet entitled *Solidarity with the Brigasque Sheep!* "I wrote it last night," he said conspiratorially. "I was talking to some of the breeders yesterday. They're struggling to make ends meet. They're really angry—

their sheep have been decimated. It's all because of the eco-movement and the National Park at Mercantour. They've reintroduced wolves into the wild, hordes of wolves, and they eat the lambs!" His voice became strangulated and suddenly broke into sobs. In his letter to Michel, Bruno had mentioned that he had moved back to the psychiatric clinic at Verrières-le-Buisson "probably for good." Obviously they had let him out for the occasion.

"So our mother is dying," Michel interrupted, anxious to get to the point.

"Absolutely! It's the same at Cap d'Agde—apparently they've closed the dunes to the public. The decision was taken by the Society for the Protection of the Coast, which is completely run by the eco-warriors. People weren't doing any harm, they were just having a nice orgy, but apparently they were disturbing the terns. Terns are a type of sparrow. Well, fuck the terns!" Bruno shouted. "They're trying to stop us fucking, and now they want to stop us eating sheep's cheese, the fucking Nazis. The Socialists are in on it too. They hate sheep because sheep are conservative, whereas everyone knows wolves are left-wing—which is kind of strange, because wolves look like German shepherds and they're clearly on the extreme right. Who're you gonna trust?" He shook his head solemnly. "What hotel are you staying at in Nice?" he asked suddenly.

"The Windsor."

"The Windsor? Why?" Bruno was agitated again. "When did you start staying in high-class hotels? Who do you think you are? Personally"—he stressed each sentence, with increasing energy—"I always stay at a Mercure hotel! Did you at least bother to check it out? Did you know that the Hôtel Mercure at Baie des Anges has attractive seasonal rates? Off-peak, the room costs only three hundred and thirty francs—the price of a two-star hotel—with all the comfort of three-star service, a view over the Promenade des Anglais and twenty-four-hour room service!"

Bruno was practically screaming now. Despite his customer's somewhat eccentric behavior, the manager of Chez Gilou (was his name Gilou? It was likely) was listening carefully. Men are always interested in finance and value for money, it's one of their characteristic traits.

. . .

"Oh, here's Twat!" said Bruno sharply, his tone completely changed as he nodded to a young man who had just come into the café. About twenty-two, dressed in fatigues and a Greenpeace T-shirt, he had a dark complexion and wore his black hair in dreadlocks. In short, he was doing the Rasta thing. "Hi, Twat," Bruno said cheerfully. "This is my brother. On your way to see the old bitch?" The boy nodded without saying anything; for some reason or other he had decided not to let Bruno get to him.

The road led out of the village and gently sloped up the mountainside toward Italy. Over the first hill they found themselves in a large valley flanked by forest; the border could not have been more than ten kilometers away. To the east it was possible to make out snow-capped peaks. The deserted landscape seemed serene and abundant. "The doctor came around," explained the Rasta-Hippie. "She can't be moved. Anyway, there's nothing more they can do for her. It's nature's way," he said gravely.

"Did you hear that?" yelled Bruno. "Did you hear that clown? Going on about *nature*—that's all they talk about. Now that she's sick, they can't wait for her to snuff it, like she's an animal in its hole. That's my mother you're talking about, Twat!" he said haughtily. "Look at his get-up!" he went on. "The rest of them are the same—worse, probably. They're total jerk-offs."

"It's pretty around here . . ." Michel said absently.

The house was large and squat beside a spring, built of rough-hewn stone with a slate roof. Before going in Michel took out his Canon Prima Mini (retractable zoom lens, 38–105 mm, 1,290 FF at FNAC). He turned around completely and focused on a long shot before pressing the button, then he joined the others.

Apart from Rasta-Hippie and Bruno, the only people in the front room were an indeterminate, probably Dutch creature with blondish hair, knitting a poncho by the fireplace, and an old hippie with long gray hair, a gray beard and an intelligent goatlike face. "She's in here . . ." said Rasta-Hippie, pulling back a piece of fabric nailed to the wall and ushering them into the next room.

Certainly Michel was curious to see the dark-haired figure huddled at the end of its bed, watching as they came in. After all, this was only the second time he'd ever seen his mother, and everything led him to believe that it would be the last. The first thing that struck him was her extreme thinness, which made her cheekbones prominent and her arms look twisted. Her skin was dark, earth-colored, and she was breathing with difficulty; clearly not long for this world; but over her nose, which seemed hooked, her huge, pale eyes shone in the dim light. Cautiously, he walked toward the stretched-out form. "Don't worry," said Bruno. "She can't talk anymore." She might not have been able to talk, but she was certainly still alert. Did she recognize him? Probably not. Maybe she was confusing him with his father, it was possible; Michel knew he looked a lot like his father had at his age. There are people who have a profound effect on one's life, who leave their mark for better or worse; for Janine, now Jane, there was life *before* Michel's father and life *after*. Before she met him, she was just a degenerate little rich girl; afterward she was to become something else, something much more disastrous. In fact, "meet" was the wrong word; they hadn't met, as such, simply had run into each other, procreated and gone their separate ways. She had never succeeded in understanding the enigma that was Marc Djerzinski; she had never even come close. Did she think of him now, in the final hours of her calamitous life? It wasn't impossible.

Bruno collapsed heavily into a chair beside her bed. "You're just an old whore," he said in a pedantic tone. "You deserve to croak." Michel sat opposite him at the head of the bed and lit a cigarette. "Do you want to be cremated?" Bruno went on jovially. "Well, when the time comes, I'll make sure they incinerate you. I'll put what's left of you in a little pot and every morning when I get up, I'll piss on your ashes." He nodded contentedly; Jane let out a throaty howl. Just then Rasta-Hippie reappeared. "Would you like something to drink?" he offered coldly. "Of course, my good man!" Bruno shouted. "What kind of question is that? Go open a bottle, Twat!" The young man went out and came back with a bottle of whiskey and two glasses. Bruno poured himself a large glass and knocked it back quickly. "You'll have to forgive him, he's upset," said Michel in a barely audible voice. "That's right," said his half brother, "you just leave us to our misery, Twat." He emptied the glass, clicked his tongue and poured himself another. "They better keep out of my way, the fuckers . . ." he said. "She's left everything to them and they fucking know that the children are absolutely entitled to their inheritance. If we wanted to contest the will, we'd win hands down." Michel said nothing, not wanting to discuss the subject. There was a marked silence. In the next room, no one said a word either; they could hear the weak but raucous breathing of the dying.

"She just wanted to stay young, that's all . . ." said Michel, his voice tired and forgiving. "She wanted to be with young people—though certainly not her kids, who just reminded her that she was part of an older generation. It's not so difficult to understand. I want to go now. Do you think she'll die soon?"

Bruno shrugged his shoulders. Michel got up and went into the other room; Gray-Hippie was on his own now, peeling organic carrots. He tried to talk to him, to find out what the doctor had actually said, but the old fool could come up with only vague details that were completely off the subject. "She was a radiant woman," he said emphatically, carrot in hand. "We think she's ready for death, having reached a sufficiently advanced level of spiritual awareness." What the fuck did that mean? There was no point in getting into it. It was obvious the old guy wasn't actually saying anything, just making noises with his mouth. Michel impatiently turned on his heel and went back to Bruno. "Fucking hippies . . ." he said as he sat down again. "They're still convinced that religion is some sort of individual experience based on meditation, spiritual exploration and all that. They don't understand that, on the contrary, it's a purely social activity about rites and rituals, ceremonies and rules. According to Auguste Comte, the sole purpose of religion is to bring humanity to a state of perfect unity."

"Auguste Comte yourself!" interrupted Bruno angrily. "As soon as people stop believing in life after death, religion is impossible. If society is impossible without religion, which is what you're saying, then society isn't possible either. You're just like those sociologists who go on about how the youth culture is just some passing fad from the fifties that had its finest hour in the eighties, and so on. Actually, man has always been terrified by death—he's never been able to face the idea of his own disappearance, or even physical decline, without horror. Of all worldly goods, youth is clearly the most precious, and today we don't believe in anything but worldly goods. 'If Christ did not rise from the dead,' says Saint Paul bluntly, 'then our faith is vain.' Christ didn't rise from the dead, he lost his fight with death. I even wrote a utopian script on the theme of the New Jerusalem. The film takes place on an island entirely populated by naked women and small dogs. Men have been wiped out by some biological disaster, along with nearly every species of animal. Time has stood still, the weather is constant and mild, trees bear fruit all year long. The women are eternally young and nubile, and the little dogs forever lively and happy. The women swim and stroke each other while the little dogs frolic and play around them. The dogs come in all shapes and sizes: poodles, fox terriers, Shih-Tzus, King Charles spaniels, Yorkshire terriers, Westies, beagles. The only big dog is a clever, gentle Labrador who acts as a counselor to the others. The only sign that men have ever existed is a video of speeches by Édouard Balladur, which has a soothing effect on the dogs and some of the women. There's also a video of *The Animal Kingdom*, presented by Claude Darget; no one ever watches it, but it is there as a testimony to the barbarism of previous eras."

"So they let you . . . write," Michel said quietly. He was not surprised. Most psychiatrists were particularly interested in their patients' scribblings. Not that they ascribe particular therapeutic value to them, but it's something to do and anything is better than slashing your wrists with a razor.

"There is drama on this little island," Bruno went on, his voice filled with emotion. "For example, one day one of the little dogs swims too far out to sea. Luckily his mistress notices that he's in difficulty, jumps in a boat and quickly rows out, just in time to save him. The poor dog has swallowed too much water and passed out; it looks like he's dead, but his mistress revives him by performing CPR and everything ends well. The little dog is happy again." Suddenly he was silent. He seemed serene now, almost rapt.

Michel looked at his watch and glanced around. His mother was quiet. It was almost noon; everything seemed too calm. He got up and went back into the other room. Gray-Hippie had disappeared, leaving his carrots on the table. Michel poured himself a beer and walked over to the window. He could see for kilometers across pine-covered hills. Between the snow-capped peaks it was just possible to see the shimmering blue of a lake. The air was warm and full of fragrance; it was a beautiful spring morning.

It was difficult to tell how long he'd been standing there. His mind had left his body and was floating peacefully among the peaks when he was brought back to reality by what he at first thought was a yell. It took him several seconds to focus on what he was hearing; then he walked quickly into the other room. Still seated at the end of the bed, Bruno was singing at the top of his voice:

They've all come
the boy and his brother
the screams have brought them running
To see their dying mother . . .

Inconsequential; inconsequential, shallow and ridiculous: such is man. Bruno stood up and belted out the next verse:

They've all come
The wop and the bum
Bringing gifts
To their dear old mum

The silence which followed this vocal performance was broken only by the buzzing of a fly as it crossed the room, before it landed on Jane's face. *Diptera* can be recognized by its single pair of membranous wings attached at the second thoracic ring, a pair of balancing antennae (to stabilize flight) on the third thoracic ring and a proboscis which pierces or sucks. When the fly began to move across Jane's eye, Michel knew something was wrong. He leaned over Jane without touching her. "I think she's dead," he said after a brief examination.

The doctor had no trouble confirming this diagnosis. He was accompanied by a county clerk, and that was when the problems started. Where was the body to be transferred? A family mausoleum, perhaps?

Michel didn't have the faintest idea, and felt confused and exhausted. If they had known how to form warm, affectionate relationships in his family, they wouldn't be in this position—making themselves ridiculous in front of some functionary who remained icily polite. Bruno was clearly uninterested in the proceedings; he sat off to one side playing Tetris on his GameBoy. "Well . . ." said the clerk, "we could offer you a plot at Saorge cemetery. It would be a little far for you to come if you don't live in the area, but from the point of view of transport it's obviously the most practical solution. The burial could take place as early as this afternoon, we're not too busy at the moment. I don't suppose there'll be any problems with the death certificate . . ." "No problem at all," the doctor said a bit too enthusiastically. "I've brought the paperwork." With a bright smile, he brandished a sheaf of forms. "Fuck," Bruno said to himself, "I'm dead," as the GameBoy played a cheerful little tune. "Are you satisfied with the idea of burial, Mr. Clément?" said the clerk, his voice sounding a little strained. "Absolutely not!" Bruno jumped up. "My mother wanted to be cremated, it was very important to her!" The clerk frowned. The cemetery at Saorge was not equipped to deal with cremation; it required specialized equipment, and there simply wasn't enough demand to justify it. Cremation would make things very difficult indeed. "It was my mother's dying wish," Bruno said importantly. There was silence. The county clerk thought quickly. "There is, of course, a crematorium in Nice," he said timidly. "We could arrange transport there and back if you'd still like to have her buried here. Of course, you would be responsible for the expense . . ." No one spoke. "I'll give them a call," he went on. "I'll have to find out when they might have an opening." He checked his address book, took out a mobile phone and had begun to dial when Bruno interrupted him again. "Oh, don't worry about it . . ." He made a large gesture. "Let's just bury her here. Who gives a shit about her last wishes? You're paying for it!" he said authoritatively, turning to Michel. Michel said nothing, but took out his checkbook and inquired as to the price of a plot on a thirty-year lease. "A very good choice," said the clerk. "With a thirty-year lease, you've got time to wait and see."

. . .

The cemetery was about a hundred meters above the village. Two men in overalls carried the coffin. They'd gone for the basic white-pine model stocked at the local undertaker's; the funeral business seemed to be remarkably well organized in Saorge. It was late in the afternoon, but the sun was still warm. Bruno and Michel walked side by side two paces behind the men; Gray-Hippie walked beside them, having insisted on going with Jane to her final resting place. The path was stony and arid; all this had to make some kind of sense. A bird of prey—probably a buzzard—glided slowly, low in the sky. "The place is probably full of snakes . . ." Bruno muttered. He picked up a sharp white stone. Then, just as they turned into the cemetery, as if to confirm his statement, an adder appeared between two bushes along the cemetery wall; Bruno aimed and threw the stone with all his strength. It shattered against the wall, just missing the reptile's head.

"Snakes have their place in nature too," said Gray-Hippie sharply.

"Nature? I wouldn't piss on it if it was on fire." Bruno again was beside himself with anger. "I'd shit on its face. Fucking nature . . . nature my ass!" he muttered angrily to himself for several minutes. However, he behaved himself as the coffin was lowered, content to make clucking sounds and nod his head, as though the event had evoked thoughts which were as yet too vague to be put into words. After the ceremony, Michel tipped the two men generously—he assumed it was customary. He had fifteen minutes to catch his train, and Bruno decided to go at the same time.

They parted on the platform at Nice. Though they didn't know it yet, they would never see each other again.

"How are things at the clinic?" Michel asked.

"Yeah, not bad, nice and cushy. They've got me on lithium." Bruno smiled mischievously. "I'm not going to go back to the clinic just yet. I've got another night left. I'm going to go to a whorehouse, there are loads of them in Nice." He frowned and his face darkened. "Since they put me on lithium I can't get it up at all, but that doesn't matter, I'd still like to go."

Michel nodded distractedly and climbed aboard; he had reserved a sleeping car.

PART THREE
Emotional Infinity

1

When he got back to Paris he found a letter from Desplechin. According to Article 66 of the National Scientific Research Center code, Michel had to apply to be reinstated, or ask that his leave be prolonged, no later than sixty days before the end of the original term of leave. The letter was polite and witty, with Desplechin's caustic comments about bureaucracy; Michel realized the deadline had passed three weeks earlier. He put the letter on his desk, feeling deeply uncertain. For a year he'd been completely free to determine the direction of his research, and what had he come up with? Nothing, absolutely nothing. He turned on his computer and felt queasy when he discovered he had received another eighty e-mails, though he'd been away only for two days. One of them was from the Institute of Molecular Biology at Palaiseau. The colleague who had taken his position had initiated a research program on mitochondrial DNA; unlike cellular DNA, it seemed to have no mechanisms for repairing code damaged by radical attacks—hardly a surprise. The most interesting message was from the University of Ohio: as a study of *Saccharomyces* demonstrated, the varieties that reproduced sexually evolved more slowly than those that reproduced by cloning; random mutation, in this case, seemed to be more efficient than natural selection. This engaging experimental model completely contradicted the standard hypothesis that sexual reproduction was the driving force behind evolution; but actually, it was only of anecdotal interest. As soon as the genome had been completely decoded (which would be in a matter of months), humanity would be in a position to control its own evolution, and when that happened sexuality would be seen for what it really was: a useless, dangerous and regressive function. But even if one could detect the incidence of mutations and even calculate their possible deleterious effects, nothing yet shed any light on what they determined; therefore nothing provided a definitive meaning or practical application for them. Obviously this should be the focus of research.

Cleared of all the books and files which had cluttered the shelves, Desplechin's office seemed vast. "Yep"—he smiled discreetly—"I'm retiring at the end of the month." Djerzinski stood openmouthed. It is possible to know someone for years, decades even, learning little by little how to avoid personal questions and anything of real importance, but the hope remains that someday, in different circumstances, one could talk about such things, ask such questions. Though it may be indefinitely postponed, the idea of a more personal, human relationship never fades, quite simply because human relationships do not fit easily into narrow, fixed compartments. Human beings therefore think of relationships as potentially "deep and meaningful"—an idea that can persist for years, until a single brutal act (usually something like death) makes it plain that it's too late, that the "deep, meaningful" relationship they had cherished will never exist, any more than any of the others had. In his fifteen years of professional experience, Desplechin was the one person with whom Michel would've liked to have a relationship beyond the utilitarian, infinitely irritating chance juxtapositions of office life. Well, now it was too late. Devastated, he glanced at the boxes of books piled on the floor of the office. "I think it might be better if we went for a drink somewhere," Desplechin suggested, aptly summing up the mood of the moment.

They walked past the Musée d'Orsay and settled themselves at a table on a nineteenth-century terrace. At the next table, half a dozen Italian tourists were babbling excitedly like innocent birds; Djerzinski ordered a beer and Desplechin a dry whiskey.

"What are you going to do, then?"

"I don't know." Desplechin looked as if he genuinely did not know. "Travel . . . probably a bit of sexual tourism." When he smiled, his face still had great charm; disillusioned, certainly—there could be no doubt he was a broken man—but charming nonetheless. "I'm joking. Truth is, I'm just not interested in sex anymore. Knowledge, on the other hand . . . There's still a desire for knowledge. It's a curious thing, the thirst for knowledge . . . very few people have it, you know, even among scientists. Most of them are happy to make a career for themselves and move into management, but it's incredibly important to the history of humanity. It's easy to imagine a fable in which a small group of men—a couple hundred, at most, in the whole world—work intensively on something very difficult, very abstract, completely incomprehensible to the uninitiated. These men remain completely unknown to the rest of the world; they have no apparent power, no money, no honors; nobody can understand the pleasure they get from their work. In fact, they are the most powerful men in the world, for one simple reason: they hold the keys to rational certainty. Everything they declare to be true will be accepted, sooner or later, by the whole population. There is no power in the world—economic, political, religious or social—that can compete with rational certainty. Western society is interested beyond all measure in philosophy and politics, and the most vicious, ridiculous conflicts have been about philosophy and politics; it has also had a passionate love affair with literature and the arts, but nothing in its history has been as important as the need for rational certainty. The West has sacrificed everything to this need: religion, happiness, hope—and, finally, its own life. You have to remember that when passing judgment on Western civilization." He fell silent, deep in thought. He let his gaze wander around the tables for a moment, then settle on his glass.

"I remember a boy I knew in the *première* when I was sixteen. He was very confused, very tortured. His family were rich, extremely traditional; and actually he completely accepted their values. One day when we were talking he said to me, 'The value of any religion depends on the quality of the moral system founded upon it.' I stood there, speechless with surprise and admiration. I didn't know if he'd come to this conclusion by himself, or whether he'd read it in a book somewhere; all I know is that it impressed me deeply. I've been thinking about it for forty years, and now I think he was wrong. It seems impossible to me to think of religion from a purely moral standpoint; Kant was right, though, when he said that the Savior of mankind should himself be judged by the same universal ethics as the rest of us. But I've come to believe that religions are basically an attempt to explain the world; and no attempt to explain the world can survive if it clashes with our need for rational certainty. Mathematical proofs and experimental methods are the highest expressions of human consciousness. I realize that the facts seem to contradict me. I know that Islam—by far the most stupid, false and obfuscating of all religions—currently seems to be gaining ground, but it's a transitory and superficial phenomenon: in the long term, Islam is even more doomed than Christianity."

Djerzinski looked up, having listened closely; he would never have imagined that Desplechin was interested in such things. Desplechin hesitated, then went on:

"I lost touch with Philippe after the baccalauréat, but a couple of years later I found out that he'd committed suicide. Anyway, I don't think the two things are connected: being homosexual, strictly Catholic and a monarchist can't exactly have been easy."

At that moment, Djerzinski realized he'd never really thought seriously about religion. This despite knowing that materialism, having destroyed the religious faiths of previous centuries, had itself been destroyed by recent advances in physics. It was curious that neither he nor any of the physicists he'd ever met had the slightest spiritual doubts.

"Personally," said Michel, the idea coming to him only as he spoke, "I think I needed to stick to the basic, pragmatic positivism that most researchers have. Facts exist and are linked together by laws; the notion of cause simply isn't scientific. The world is equal to the sum of the information we have about it."

"I'm no longer a researcher," Desplechin said with disarming simplicity. "Maybe that's why I'm starting to think about metaphysical questions rather late in the day. But you're right, of course. We have to go on investigating, experimenting, finding new laws—nothing else is important. Remember Pascal: 'We must say summarily: This is made by figure and motion, for it is true. But to say what these are, and to compose the machine, is ridiculous. For it is useless, uncertain, and painful.' Once again, he's right and Descartes is wrong. So tell me . . . have you decided what you're going to do? I'm sorry about"—he made an apologetic gesture—"all this trouble with deadlines."

"Yes. I need to get a position at the Galway Center for Genetic Research in Ireland. I need to quickly set up simple experiments, in very specific conditions of temperature and pressure, with a good range of radioactive markers. What I need more than anything is a lot of processing power, but if I remember correctly they have two Crays running in tandem."

"Are you thinking of taking your research in a new direction?" Desplechin's voice betrayed his excitement. Realizing this, he smiled his small, discreet smile again, almost in self-mockery. "The thirst for knowledge . . ." he said quietly.

"I think that it's a mistake to work only from natural DNA. DNA is a complex molecule that evolved more or less by chance; there are redundancies, long sequences of junk DNA, a little bit of everything. If you really want to test the general conditions for mutation, you have to start with simpler self-replicating molecules with a maximum of a hundred bonds."

Desplechin nodded, his eyes shining; he was no longer trying to hide his excitement. The Italian tourists had left, and they were the only people left in the café.

"It will be a long haul," Michel went on. "There's nothing in principle to distinguish configurations prone to mutation, but there have to be some conditions for structural stability at a subatomic level. If we can work out a stable configuration with even a couple hundred atoms, it's just a matter of the power of the processor. But I'm getting a bit ahead of myself."

"Maybe not . . ." Desplechin's voice had the slow, dreamy quality of a man who has just glimpsed phantasmagorical new ideas from a great distance.

"My work would have to be completely independent of the center's bureaucracy. Some of this is no more than pure speculation: too long and too complicated to explain."

"Of course. I'll write to Walcott, the director there. He's a good man, he'll leave you in peace. You've already done some work with them, haven't you? Something about cows?"

"Something small, yes."

"Don't worry. I'm retiring anyway"—this time there was a trace of bitterness in his smile—"but I still have some influence. From an administrative point of view, you'll have a completely independent position which can be extended year by year for as long as you like. Regardless of who gets my job, I'll make sure there's no way the decision can be reversed."

They parted just past the Pont Royal. Desplechin extended his hand. He had never had a son; his sexual preference precluded it, and he'd always found the idea of a marriage of convenience ridiculous. For the several seconds they shook hands, he thought that this kind of relationship was infinitely more satisfying; then, realizing he was very tired, he turned and started back along the quai past the bookstalls. For a minute or two, Djerzinski watched as the man walked away in the fading light.

2

He had dinner at Annabelle's the following evening and explained clearly and precisely why he had to move to Ireland. His research had been mapped out, everything was coming together. The important thing was not to become fixated on DNA, but to look at the living being as its own self-replicating system.

At first Annabelle didn't say anything, though she couldn't keep the corners of her mouth from turning down. Then she poured him another glass of wine; she'd cooked fish that evening, and more than ever her little studio seemed like a ship's cabin.

"You weren't planning to take me with you . . ." Her words resounded in the silence; the silence continued. "It didn't even occur to you," she said, her voice a mixture of surprise and childish petulance; then she burst into tears. He didn't move, and if he'd made a gesture at that moment she would certainly have pushed him away; you have to let people cry, it's the only way. "It's strange," she said through her sobs. "We got along well when we were twelve . . ."

She looked up at him. Her face was pure and extraordinarily beautiful. She was talking without thinking: "I want to have your child. I need someone to be close to me. You don't have to help raise him or look after him, you don't even have to acknowledge him. I'm not asking you to love him, or even to love me; I just want you to give me a baby. I know

I'm forty, but so what? I'm prepared to take the risk. This is my last chance. Sometimes I regret having the abortions, even though the first guy who got me pregnant was a shit and the second was an irresponsible fool. When I was seventeen, I never imagined that life would be so constrained, that there would be so few opportunities."

Michel lit a cigarette to give himself time to think. "It's a strange idea . . ." he said between his teeth. "It's a curious idea to reproduce when you don't even like life."

Annabelle stood up and began to take off her clothes. "Let's make love anyway," she said. "It must be more than a month since we made love. I stopped taking the pill a couple of weeks ago; I'll be fertile about now." She put her hands on her stomach and moved them up to her breasts, parted her thighs slightly. She was beautiful, desirable, loving: why then did he feel nothing? It was inexplicable. He lit another cigarette, then suddenly realized that thinking about it would get him nowhere. You make a baby, or you don't; it's not a decision one can make rationally. He stubbed the cigarette out in the ashtray and murmured: "All right."

Annabelle helped him off with his clothes and masturbated him until he could penetrate her. He felt nothing except the softness and the warmth of her vagina. He quickly stopped moving, fascinated by the geometry of copulation, entranced by the suppleness and richness of her juices. Annabelle pressed her mouth to his and wrapped her arms around him. He closed his eyes and, feeling the presence of his penis more acutely, started to move inside her once again. Just before he ejaculated he had a vision—crystal clear—of fusing gametes, followed immediately by the first cell divisions. It felt like a headlong rush, a little suicide. A wave of sensation flowed back along his penis and his sperm pumped out of him; Annabelle felt it too, and exhaled slowly. They lay there, motionless.

"You were supposed to come in for a smear about a month ago," the gynecologist said in a weary voice. "Instead of which you stop taking the pill without consulting me and then go get yourself pregnant. You're not a girl anymore, after all!" The office seemed cold and humid; when she left Annabelle was surprised by the June sunshine.

She telephoned the following morning. The smear had shown "pretty serious" anomalies; they would have to do a biopsy and a D&C. "As for getting pregnant, now would not be a good time. Let's take one thing at a time, okay?" He didn't sound worried, just a little annoyed.

Annabelle had her third abortion—the fetus was only two weeks old, so a little suction was enough. The technology had advanced since her last termination and, to her surprise, it was all over in less than ten minutes. The results arrived three days later. "Well . . ." The doctor seemed terribly old, sad and wise. "I'm afraid there's no doubt about it. I'm afraid you have stage one uterine cancer." He resettled his glasses on his nose and looked at the papers again; the impression of general competence was greatly enhanced. He was not surprised: cancer of the uterus often attacks women in the years before menopause, and not having had children simply increased the risk. There was no question as to the treatment. "We have to do a hysterectomy and a bilateral salpingo-oophorectomy. They're standard surgical procedures nowadays, and complications are almost unheard of." He glanced at Annabelle; that she hadn't reacted was irritating. She simply sat there openmouthed; she probably would have a breakdown. It was standard procedure for practitioners to refer patients to a therapist for counseling—he'd prepared a list of addresses. Above all, it was important to emphasize the main point: that the end of fertility did not mean that one's sex life was over; on the contrary, many patients found their desire increased.

"You mean they're going to remove my uterus . . ." she said incredulously.

"The uterus, the ovaries and the fallopian tubes; it's best to avoid any risk of the cancer spreading. I'll prescribe hormone replacement therapy for you—in fact it's commonplace to prescribe it even for menopause nowadays."

She went back to her family's house in Crécy-en-Brie. The operation was scheduled for 17 July. Michel and her mother went with her to the hospital in Meaux. She wasn't scared. The operation lasted a little more than two hours. When Annabelle woke up the following morning, through her window she could see blue sky and the wind in the trees. She barely felt anything. She wanted to see the scar on her abdomen, but didn't dare ask the nurse. It was strange to think she was still the same woman, except that her reproductive organs had been removed. The word "ablation" hung in her mind for a moment before giving way to a more visceral image. They've gutted me, she thought, gutted me like a chicken.

She left the hospital a week later. Michel had written to Walcott to tell him that his departure had been postponed; after some vacillation, he agreed to stay at her parents' house in her brother's old room. Annabelle noticed that he and her mother had become closer while she had been in the hospital. Her older brother also dropped by more often, now that Michel was there. In fact they had nothing much to say to each other; Michel knew nothing about small businesses, and Jean-Pierre was completely ignorant as to the issues raised by research in molecular biology. Nevertheless, over a nightly aperitif they'd managed to establish a semi-illusory male bond. She needed to rest and to avoid lifting heavy objects, but at least she could now wash herself and eat normally. In the afternoons she would sit in the garden; Michel and her mother would pick strawberries or plums. It was strange, as if she were on vacation or a child again. She felt the sun caress her face and arms. More often than not she did nothing, though sometimes she did a little embroidery or made stuffed toys for her nephew and nieces. A psychiatrist in Meaux had given her a prescription for sleeping pills and some strong tranquilizers. For whatever reason, she slept a lot and her dreams were happy and peaceful; the mind is a very powerful thing, as long as it remains in its sphere. Michel lay beside her in bed, his hand on her waist, feeling her abdomen rise and fall regularly. The psychiatrist came to see her frequently, and muttered, worried, talked about "dissociation." She had become very gentle, and her behavior a little strange; sometimes she would laugh for no reason, other times her eyes would suddenly fill with tears. Then she would take another Percodan.

After the third week she was allowed out, and would take short walks along the river or in the surrounding woods. It was August, and the weather was exceptionally beautiful: day after day, each one identically radiant, without so much as the murmur of a storm or anything that might signal an ending. Michel held her hand; often they would sit together on the bench beside the Grand Morin. The grass on the river-bank was scorched, almost white; in the shadow of the beech trees, the river wound on forever in dark green ripples. The world outside had its own rules, and those rules were not human.

3

On 25 August, a routine examination revealed metastases in the abdomen; under normal circumstances, she could expect it to spread. Radiation therapy was a possibility—in fact, it was the only possibility—but it was important to realize that it was an arduous treatment and the chances of success were only fifty percent.

The meal was a silent affair. "You'll get better, darling," said Annabelle's mother, her voice trembling a little. Annabelle put her arm around her mother's neck and pressed her forehead to hers; they sat like that for almost a minute. After her mother had gone to bed, she stayed in the living room, leafing through some books. Michel watched her every move from the armchair. "We could get a second opinion," he said after a long silence. "Yes, we could," she said lightly.

She could not make love—the scar was too fresh, too painful, but she held him in her arms for a long time. In the silence, she could hear him grinding his teeth. Once, as she stroked his face, she found it wet with tears. She stroked his penis gently; it was exciting and calming all at once. He took two Halcion and at last fell asleep.

At about three a.m. she got up, put on a dressing gown and went down to the kitchen. She rummaged in the dresser and found the bowl, inscribed with her name, that her godmother had given her for her tenth birthday. She emptied the contents of a tube of Rohypnol into the bowl, then added a little sugar and water. She didn't feel anything, unless perhaps a very general, almost metaphysical sadness. That was life, she thought; her body had taken a turn which was unfair and unexpected, and now could no longer be a source of joy or pleasure. On the contrary, it would gradually but quite quickly become another source of pain and embarrassment to her and others. And so she would have to destroy her body. A big wooden clock loudly counted off the seconds; her mother had been given it by *her* mother, and she'd had it since before she got married. It was the oldest piece of furniture in the house. Annabelle added some more sugar to the bowl. She was far from accepting; life seemed to her like a bad joke, an unacceptable joke, but acceptable or not, that was what it was. In a few short weeks her illness had brought her to the feeling so common in the elderly: she did not want to be a burden to others. Toward the end of her adolescence, her life had speeded up, then there had been a long dull period. Now, at the end, everything was speeding up again.

Just before daybreak, as he turned over in bed, Michel noticed that Annabelle was gone. He dressed and went downstairs: her motionless body was lying on the sofa in the living room. Nearby, on the table, she had left a note. The first line read: "I prefer to die surrounded by those I love."

The head of emergency services at the hospital in Meaux was a man of about thirty, with dark curly hair and an honest face; he immediately made a good impression on them. There was little chance that she would regain consciousness, he explained, but they could stay with her if they wished, he had no problem with that. Coma was a strange condition, and one which was poorly understood. It was probable that Annabelle was unaware of their presence. There was, however, some weak electrical activity in the brain, which had to correspond to some mental process, but as to what that process might be, nature was defiantly enigmatic. The medical prognosis was far from certain; there were cases where a patient remained in a coma for weeks, even months, before suddenly regaining consciousness; more often, unfortunately, coma slipped just as suddenly toward death. She was only forty, and at least they knew that her heart was strong; that was the only thing they could say for sure.

Day was breaking over the town. Sitting beside Michel, Annabelle's brother shook his head and muttered. "It's not possible . . . It's not possible," he repeated endlessly, as though the words themselves had some power. But it was, obviously. Anything was possible. A nurse walked past pushing a trolley full of rattling bottles of serum.

Later, the sun ripped through the clouds and the sky turned blue. It would be a beautiful day, as beautiful as the previous ones. Annabelle's mother stood up with difficulty. "We should get some rest," she said, struggling to control her voice. Her son rose too, his arms hanging limply by his sides, and followed her like a robot. Michel shook his head to indicate that he wasn't coming. He didn't feel in the least tired. In the moments that followed, he was strangely aware of the visible world. He was sitting on a plastic chair in a sunlit corridor. This wing of the hospital was very quiet. From time to time, a faraway door opened and a nurse came out and hurried toward another corridor. The noise of the town some floors below was greatly muted. In a state of complete mental detachment, he went over the events, the circumstances and the stages of the destruction of their lives. Seen in the frozen light of a restrictive past, everything seemed clear, conclusive and indisputable. Now it seemed unthinkable that a girl of seventeen should be so naïve; it was particularly unbelievable that a girl of seventeen should set so much store by love. If the surveys in magazines were to be believed, things had changed a great deal in the twenty-five years since Annabelle was a teenager. Young girls today were more sensible, more sophisticated. Nowadays they worried more about their exam results and did their best to ensure they would have a decent career. For them, going out with boys was simply a game, a distraction motivated as much by narcissism as by sexual pleasure. They later would try to make a good marriage, basing their decision on a range of social and professional criteria, as well as on shared interests and tastes. Of course, in doing this they cut themselves off from any possibility of happiness—a condition indissociable from the outdated, intensely close bonds so incompatible with the exercise of reason—but this was their attempt to escape the moral and emotional suffering which had so tortured their forebears. This hope was, unfortunately, rapidly disappointed; the passing of love's torments simply left the field clear for boredom, emptiness and an anguished wait for old age and death. The second part of Annabelle's life therefore had been much more dismal and sad than the first, of which, in the end, she had no memory at all.

Toward noon, Michel pushed open the door to her room. Her breathing was very shallow, the sheet covering her chest almost still—though, according to the doctor, it was sufficient for oxygenation. If her respiratory rate dropped further, they intended to put her on a respirator. For the time being, a drip was hooked up to her arm just above the elbow and an electrode fixed to her temple, that was all. A ray of sunlight crossed the immaculate sheet and lit a lock of her magnificent blonde hair. A little paler than usual, her face, eyes closed, seemed completely at peace. All fear seemed to have disappeared; to Michel, she had never looked so happy. It is true that he'd always had a tendency to confuse happiness with coma; nonetheless she seemed to him completely happy. He stroked her hair, kissed her forehead and her warm lips. It was too late, of course, but it was nice. He stayed in the room with her until nightfall. Back in the corridor, he opened a book of Buddhist meditations compiled by Dr. Evans-Wentz (the book had been in his pocket for some weeks; a small book with a dark red cover).

May all creatures in the east,
May all creatures in the west,
May all creatures in the north,
May all creatures in the south,
Be happy, and remain happy;
And may they live in friendship.

It wasn't entirely their fault, he thought: they had lived in a painful world, a world of struggle and rivalry, vanity and violence; they had not lived in a peaceful world. On the other hand, they had done nothing to change it, had contributed nothing that might make it a better place. He should have given Annabelle a child, he thought, and then he remembered that he had, or tried to, that at least he had accepted the idea; and this thought filled him with joy. Now he began to understand the peace and gentleness he had felt in these last weeks. He could do nothing more now, as one could not battle against the empire of sickness and death; but at least for some weeks she must have felt loved.

If a man practices the thoughts of love
And does not abandon himself to wantonness;
If he severs the bonds of passion
And turns his gaze toward Faith,

Because he was able to practice love,
He will be born again in the sky a Brahma
And soon will merit deliverance
And forever inherit Nirvana.

If he does not kill nor think of harm,
Nor seek glory in the humiliation of others,
If he practices universal love
At his death will he have no thoughts of hatred.

In the evening, Annabelle's mother came by to see if there was any change. No, there were no developments; deep coma could be a very stable condition, the nurse reminded her patiently, and it might be weeks before a prognosis could be made. She went in to see her daughter and after a minute came out sobbing. "I don't understand . . ." she said, shaking her head. "I don't understand how life can be like this. She was a lovely girl, you know, always very affectionate, she never gave me any trouble. She never complained, but I knew she wasn't happy. She deserved better from life."

She left shortly afterward, visibly shattered. Strangely, Michel was neither hungry nor tired. He paced up and down the corridor, then went down to the lobby. The West Indian at the information desk was doing a crossword; he nodded to him, then got a hot chocolate from the vending machine and walked to the windows. The moon hung between the buildings; a few cars drove along the avenue de Châlons. He knew enough about medicine to understand that Annabelle was but a whisper away from death. Her mother was right to refuse to understand; man is not made to grasp death, neither his own nor that of others. He walked up to the security guard and asked for a piece of paper; a little surprised, the man handed him a sheaf of hospital stationery. (Later, the letterhead helped Hubczejak identify this text among all the other papers at the Clifden house.) Some people cling fiercely to life; they leave it, as Rousseau said, with bad grace. Michel already knew that such would not be the case with Annabelle.

She was a child intended for happiness
And gave to everyone her heart's treasure
She could have given her life for others,
Among the newborn of her bed.

By the cry of children,
By the blood of the race
Her ever-present dream
Will leave a trace
Written in time,
Written in space

Written on flesh
Forever sanctified
In the mountains, in the air
In the river waters clear,
And in the changed sky.

Now you are here
On your deathbed
Still in your coma
You love here still.

Our bodies will become cold, my Annabelle,
Simply present in the grass,
Such will be the death
Of every individual.

We will have loved little
In our human forms
Perhaps the sun, the rain on our graves,
The wind and frost
Will end all our pain.

4

Annabelle died two days later, and from the family's point of view it was probably for the best. When death occurs people tend to say shit like that, but it's true that her mother and brother would have found it difficult to cope with prolonged uncertainty.

In the steel and white concrete building, the same place where his grandmother had died, Djerzinski became conscious for the second time of the power of emptiness. He crossed the room to where Annabelle lay. The body was the same one he had known, yet its warmth was slowly ebbing away. Now her skin was almost cold.

Some people live to be seventy, sometimes eighty years old believing there is always something new just around the corner, as they say; in the end they practically have to be killed or at least reduced to a state of serious incapacity to get them to see reason. This was not how it was for Michel Djerzinski. He had lived alone all his adult life, in a vacuum. He had contributed to the sum of human knowledge—that was his vocation, the way he'd found to express his talents—but love was something he had never known. And Annabelle, despite her beauty, had not known love either; and now she was dead. Her body lay useless, like pure weight in the light. They sealed the coffin.

. . .

In her final note she had asked to be cremated. Before the ceremony, they had coffee at the Relais H in the hospital waiting room; at the next table a Gypsy on a drip talked about cars with two friends who'd come to visit him. The lighting was poor—just a couple of bulbs in the ceiling, set into an ugly plaster relief that looked like huge corks.

They walked out into the sunshine. The crematorium was not far from the hospital building, in the same complex. The incinerator itself was a large white concrete cube set in the middle of an equally white courtyard; the reflected light was blinding. Currents of warm air wove around them like a multitude of small snakes.

The coffin was placed on a moving platform leading to the furnace. They had thirty seconds of silent thought, then one of the staff started the motor. The cogs that moved the platform grated a little; the door closed. It was possible to watch the blaze through a Pyrex porthole. At the moment the flames leapt from the huge burners, Michel turned his head away. For about twenty seconds, a red smudge persisted in his field of vision and then was gone. One of the staff collected the ashes in a small rectangular box of white pine and gave it to Annabelle's elder brother.

They drove slowly back to Crécy. The sun shone through the leaves of the chestnut trees along the allée de l'Hôtel de Ville. He and Annabelle had walked along that same road after school twenty-five years before. A dozen people were gathered in the garden of her mother's house. Her younger brother had come from the States for the occasion; he was thin, nervous, visibly stressed and dressed a little too elegantly.

Annabelle had asked that her ashes be scattered in the garden of her parents' house; that, too, was done. The sun was beginning to sink. Like powder—a whitish powder—she settled as gently as a veil on the ground between the rosebushes. At that moment they heard the bells at the train crossing ringing in the distance. Michel remembered the afternoons when he was nearly fifteen and Annabelle used to come to the station to meet him and take him in her arms. He looked at the earth, the sun, the roses; the suppleness of the grass. It was incomprehensible. Everyone was silent. Annabelle's mother had poured wine for a toast. She offered him a glass and looked into his eyes. "You can stay for a couple of days if you like, Michel," she said in a low voice. No, he would go; he would go back to work. He didn't know how to do anything else. The sky was streaked with sunlight; he realized that he was crying.

5

As the airplane dipped toward the clouds that seemed to stretch out endlessly beneath the sky, he had the feeling that his whole life had been leading up to this moment. For several seconds more, there was only the enormous blue vault and a vast expanse in which matte and brilliant white alternated, and then the plane dropped into a middle zone, gray and fluid, where his senses were confused. Below, in the world of men, there were fields and trees and animals; everything was green, damp and infinitely detailed.

Walcott was waiting for him at Shannon airport. He was a stocky man with rapid gestures, his pronounced baldness surrounded by a crown of reddish blonde hair. He drove the Toyota Starlet quickly past misty hills and meadows. The center was situated just north of Galway on land adjoining the village of Rosscahill. Walcott took him on a tour of the facilities and introduced him to the technicians who would work with him on programming the calculations of the molecular configurations for his experiments. The equipment was all ultramodern, the rooms immaculately clean—all of it financed with money from the EU. In a refrigeration room, Djerzinski took a look at the two huge Crays, built like towers, whose control panels glowed in the darkness.

Their millions of parallel processors were simply waiting to integrate Lagrangian models, wave functions, spectral analyses, Hermite operators; this was the universe he would now inhabit. He folded his arms across his chest and squeezed them against his body but could not dispel the feeling of sadness, of inner cold. Walcott offered him a coffee from the vending machine. Through the windows it was possible to make out the lush slopes plunging toward the dark waters of Lough Corrib.

On the road down to Rosscahill they passed a long sloping field with a herd of fine-looking dun cows, somewhat smaller than average. "Recognize them?" asked Walcott with a smile. "Yep . . . those are the descendants of the first cattle you worked on, ten years ago now. The center was very small at the time and none too well equipped; we were really grateful for your help. The cattle are strong, they've had no trouble breeding and they give excellent milk. Do you want a look?" He parked in a lane. Djerzinski stood at the stone wall that enclosed the field. The cows were grazing calmly, rubbing their heads against each other's flanks; two or three of them were lying down. It was he who had created the genetic code which governed their cell reproduction, or, at least, he had improved on it. To them he should be like God, but they seemed completely indifferent to his presence. A bank of fog rolled slowly down the mountain, gradually shrouding them as it went. He walked back to the car.

At the steering wheel, Walcott was smoking a Craven A; the windshield was blurred with rain. In his soft, discreet voice (its discretion in no way seemed indifferent), he asked: "I believe you had a death in the family?" So Michel told him about Annabelle, and about her death. Walcott listened, nodding from time to time or letting out a soft sigh. When Michel finished, he was silent for a while; then lit and stubbed out another cigarette and said: "I'm not Irish myself. I was born in Cambridge. I'm still very English, they tell me. People often say that the English are very cold fish, very reserved, that they have a way of looking at things—even tragedy—with a sense of irony. There's some truth in it; it's pretty stupid of them, though. Humor won't save you; it doesn't really do anything at all. You can look at life ironically for years, maybe decades; there are people who seem to go through most of their lives seeing the funny side, but in the end, life always breaks your heart. Doesn't matter how brave you are, or how reserved, or how much you've developed a sense of humor, you still end up with your heart broken. That's when you stop laughing. In the end there's just the cold, the silence and the loneliness. In the end there's only death."

He turned on the windshield wipers and restarted the engine. "Most of them around here are Catholics," he said. "Well, that's all changing now. Ireland is coming into the modern world. Quite a few hi-tech companies have set up here to take advantage of the tax breaks and the low social-security payments. Round here, there's Roche and Lilly. And Microsoft, of course; every kid in the country dreams of working for Microsoft. People don't go to mass as much as they used to, there's more sexual freedom than there was a couple of years ago, there are more nightclubs, more antidepressants. The classic story . . ."

They drove along the lake again. The sun emerged from behind the bank of mist, scattering iridescent glints on the water. "All the same," Walcott went on, "Catholicism is still a powerful force here. Most of the technicians at the center are Catholic. It doesn't make my working relationship with them any easier. They're nice enough, very polite, but they think of me as someone apart, someone you can't really talk to."

The sun emerged from the fog, forming a perfect white disk; the whole lake was bathed in light. On the horizon, the Twelve Bens Mountains formed a palette of grays like images from a dream. The men said nothing. As they came into Galway, Walcott spoke again: "I'm an atheist, always have been, but I can understand why they're Catholic here. There's something very special about this country. Everything seems constantly trembling: the grass in the fields or the water on the lake, everything signals its presence. The light is soft, shifting, like a mutable substance. You'll see. The sky itself is alive."

6

He rented an apartment on Sky Road near Clifden, in an old coast guard house which had been converted into tourist apartments. The rooms were decorated with wheels and storm lamps, anything they thought might please the tourists; this didn't bother him. In this apartment, as in his whole life now, he knew he would always feel as though he were staying in a hotel.

He had no intention of returning to France, but in the first weeks he had to go to Paris a number of times to arrange the sale of his apartment and the transfer of his bank accounts. He would take the 11:50 a.m. from Shannon. The plane flew over the sea, the sun blistering white on the water, the waves snaking and twisting like worms far below. Beneath this writhing mass, he knew, mollusks were breeding, and fish with sharp, fine teeth fed on the mollusks only to be devoured by bigger fish. Often, he slept; he had nightmares. When he woke, the plane was flying over the countryside. Half-awake, he would stare in astonishment at the uniform color of the fields. The fields were brown, sometimes green, but the tones always muted. The suburbs of Paris were gray. The plane fell slowly, gently nosing its way down, irresistibly drawn to this life, to the beating of millions of lives.

. . .

By mid-October the Clifden peninsula was completely covered by a thick blanket of fog rolling in from the Atlantic. The last of the tourists had gone. Though it was not cold, everything was bathed in a deep, soft gray. Djerzinski did not go out much. He had imported three DVDs, representing more than forty gigabytes of data. From time to time he would turn on his computer and study a molecular configuration, then he would lie down on his huge bed, his cigarettes always within reach. He had not gone back to the center yet. Outside the window, the mass of fog shifted slowly.

Around 20 November the sky cleared and the weather became colder and drier. He began taking long walks along the coast road. He would pass Gortrumnagh and Knockavally, usually continuing on to Claddaghduff and sometimes as far as Aughrus Point. This was the westernmost point of Europe, the very edge of the Western world. Before him stretched the Atlantic, four thousand kilometers of ocean between him and America.

According to Hubczejak, these two or three months of solitary reflection—during which Djerzinski did no apparent work, set up no experiments and programmed no calculations—should be considered as a key period during which the principal elements of his later work fell into place. The last months of 1999 were, in any case, a strange period for Western civilization as a whole, marked as they were by a sense of waiting, a sort of dull preoccupation.

The thirty-first of December 1999 fell on a Friday. In the clinic at Verrières-le-Buisson, where Bruno would spend the rest of his life, there was a small party for the patients and the staff. They drank champagne and ate paprika-flavored chips. Later that evening Bruno danced with one of the nurses. He wasn't unhappy; the medication was working, and all desire was dead in him. He enjoyed the afternoon snack, and watching game shows on television with the others before the evening meal. He expected nothing, now, of the progression of days, and the last night of the second millennium was a pleasant one for him.

In cemeteries all across the world, the recently deceased continued to rot in their graves, slowly becoming skeletons.

Michel spent the evening at home. He was too isolated to hear the noise of the party in the village. Many warm, peaceful images of Annabelle flitted across his memory; and images, too, of his grandmother.

He remembered that when he was thirteen or fourteen he used to buy flashlights, and small mechanical objects he liked to take apart and put together again endlessly. And he remembered the airplane, with an actual motor, his grandmother had given him, which he had never succeeded in flying. It was a beautiful plane, painted in camouflage; in the end, it stayed in its box. Percolating through the slow drift of his consciousness, certain things seemed to characterize his life. There were people and thoughts. Thoughts occupy no space; people occupy a portion of space, and can be seen. Their images form on the lens, pass through the choroid and strike the retina. Alone in the empty house, Michel watched his modest parade of memories. Throughout the evening, a single conviction slowly filled his mind: soon he would be able to get back to work.

All across the surface of the globe, a weary, exhausted humanity, filled with self-doubt and uncertain of its history, prepared itself as best it could to enter a new millennium.

7

Some say:
"The civilization we have built is still fragile,
We are only just emerging from the darkness.
We carry with us still the terrible image of centuries of misery;
Would it not be better to leave such things buried?"

The narrator stands, gathers himself and recalls
Patiently but firmly he rises and recalls
That a metaphysical revolution has taken place.

Just as the Christians could visualize ancient civilizations, could form a complete image of these civilizations unassailed by questions or by doubt,
Because they had crossed a line,
A threshold,
They had stepped over the fracture;

Just as the men of the age of materialism could take part, unknowing, unseeing, in the ceremonial rituals of Christianity,
Just as they could read and reread the literature of their former

Christian age, without ever abandoning their quasi-anthropological perspective,
Unable to comprehend the arguments which had inflamed their ancestors about the vacillations between grace and sin;

So, we now can listen to this story of a materialist era
As an ancient human story.
It is a sad story, but we will not be saddened by it
Because we are no longer like these men.
Born of their flesh and their desires, we have cast aside their categories and their affiliations,
We do not feel their joys, neither do we feel their sufferings,
We have set aside
Indifferently
And without the least effort
Their universe of death.

These centuries of pain which are our heritage,
We can now bring out of the half-light.
Something has happened, like a second chance,
And we have the right to live our lives.

Between 1905 and 1915, working almost entirely alone and with limited mathematical knowledge, Albert Einstein succeeded in elaborating a general theory of gravity, space and time, from a first intuition which was the specific theory of relativity. In doing so, he had a decisive influence on the future evolution of astrophysics. This risky, solitary labor—accomplished, according to Hilbert, "for the glory of the human spirit"—had no obvious practical application and remained inaccessible to the scientists of his time. It can be compared to Georg Cantor's work to establish a typology of the infinite, which created set theory, or the work of Gottlob Frege, which redefined the basis of logic. According to Hubczejak in his introduction to *Clifden Notes,* it can also be compared to the solitary intellectual work of Djerzinski at Clifden between 2000 and 2009—especially as, like Einstein, Djerzinski did not have the mathematical resources necessary to test his idea rigorously.

His first work, *The Topology of Meiosis*, published in 2002, had a considerable impact. It established, for the first time, on the basis of irrefutable thermodynamic arguments, that the chromosomal separation at the moment of meiosis which creates haploid gametes is in itself a source of structural instability. In other words, all species dependent on sexual reproduction are by definition mortal.

Three Conjectures on Topology in Hilbert Spaces, published in 2004, was a shock. Some interpreted it as a reaction against a continuous dynamic, as an attempt—with strangely Platonic resonances—to redefine an algebra of forms. While they accepted the significance of his conjectures, many serious mathematicians gleefully pointed out the absence of rigor in Djerzinski's propositions and the somewhat anachronistic character of his approach. In fact, as Hubczejak confirms, Djerzinski didn't have access to recent mathematical publications at the time, and it would seem that he wasn't very interested in them. There is little information on his work between 2004 and 2007. He was a regular visitor to the Galway center, but his relationships with the staff were purely utilitarian. He had developed a working knowledge of Cray assembly code and could therefore dispense with the services of programmers. Only Walcott seems to have maintained a more personal rapport with him. He, too, lived near Clifden and would often come to spend the afternoon with Djerzinski. According to him, Djerzinski talked often about Auguste Comte, in particular the letters to Clotilde de Vaux and *Subjective Synthesis*, the philosopher's last, unfinished work. Even from the standpoint of the scientific method, Comte could be considered the true founder of positivism. No metaphysical or ontological system of the time appealed to him. It is probable, as Djerzinski points out, that if Comte had been in the intellectual circle of Niels Bohr between 1924 and 1927, he would have maintained his position of intransigent positivism and allied himself to the Copenhagen interpretation. In any case, the philosopher's insistence on the reality of social structures as opposed to the fiction of individual existence, his continued interest in historical processes and currents of public opinion, and his deep sentimentality lead one to think he might have been at home with a more recent ontological overhaul, the replacement of an ontology of objects with an ontology of states, established by the work of Zurek, Zeh and Hardcastle. Only the latter ontology was capable of restoring the practical possibility of human relationships. In an ontology of states the particles are indiscernible, and only a limited number are observable. The only entities which can be identified and named are wave functions and, through them, state vectors—from which arose the analogous possibility of giving new meaning to fraternity, sympathy and love.

They walked along the Ballyconnelly road; the ocean glittered at their feet. Far off on the horizon, the sun sank over the Atlantic. More and more often, Walcott got the impression that Djerzinski's thinking was straying into uncertain, even mystical territory. He himself remained steadfast to a radical instrumentalism in the pragmatic Anglo-Saxon tradition, and influenced by the Vienna school. He was slightly suspicious of Comte's work, which he considered romantic. Contrary to the materialism it sought to replace, positivism could, he insisted, provide the foundation for a new humanism; in fact, this would be a first, since materialism was antithetical to humanism and would eventually destroy it. Nonetheless, materialism had had a historic importance: to break down the first barrier, which was God. Man, having done this, found himself plunged into doubt and distress. But now a second barrier had been broken down—this time in Copenhagen. Man no longer needed God, nor even the idea of an underlying reality. "There are human perceptions," said Walcott, "human testimonies, human experiences; reason links them, and emotion brings them alive. All of this happens without any metaphysical intervention, without any ontology at all. We don't need concepts of God or nature or reality anymore. In experiments, it is possible to get a group of observers to agree on the basis of reasonable intersubjectivity; these experiments are linked by theories which should, as far as possible, be succinct and must, by definition, be refutable. There is a perceived world, a felt world, a human world."

Djerzinski knew this position was unassailable: was the need to find meaning simply a childish defect of the human mind? On a trip to

Dublin at the end of 2005, he first saw the Book of Kells. Hubczejak is convinced that this encounter with this illuminated manuscript of great formal complexity, which was probably the work of seventh-century Irish monks, was a decisive moment in the evolution of Djerzinski's ideas. According to Hubczejak, his long study of the book likely allowed him—in a series of intuitions which in retrospect seem miraculous—to overcome the complexities of calculating energy stability in biological macromolecules. Without necessarily subscribing to Hubczejak's statement, it is certainly true that the Book of Kells has, through the ages, elicited from its admirers a response akin to ecstasy. In 1185, Giraldus Cambrensis made the following description of the book:

> The book is a concordance of the four Gospels according to the text of Saint Jerome, with almost as many drawings as there are pages, each decorated in wondrous colors. Here one can contemplate the visage of divine majesty miraculously rendered; there, the mystical representations of the Evangelists, some having six wings, some four, some two. Here we see the eagle, there the bull, here the face of a man, there that of a lion, and innumerable other drawings. In looking at them casually, it might appear that they are no more than idle scribblings rather than formal compositions. One might not see the subtleties, whereas all is subtlety. But if one takes pains to study the book attentively, to penetrate the innermost secrets of the art, one will find embellishments of such intricacy, such delicacy and density, such a wealth of knots and interlacing links in such fresh and lustrous hues, that one will unequivocally pronounce it the work not of man but of angels.

Hubczejak might be right when he affirms that any new philosophy, even one which claims to be axiomatic and founded on pure logic, is in fact bound to a new visual conception of the universe. In giving mankind the gift of physical immortality, Djerzinski has clearly modified our perception of time; but his greatest contribution, according to Hubczejak, is to have laid the foundations for a new philosophy of space. Just as the world of Tibetan Buddhism is inseparable from the prolonged contemplation of the infinite circular forms of mandalas, just as one can get an accurate idea of Democritus's thought by watching sunlight burst upon white stones on a Greek island on an August afternoon, so one comes closer to the thinking of Djerzinski by studying the infinite architecture of cross and spiral, which are the basic ornamental forms used in the Book of Kells, or by rereading *Meditations on Interweaving,* inspired by it and published separately from *Clifden Notes.*

"Natural forms," wrote Djerzinski, "are human forms. Triangles, interweavings, branchings, appear in our minds. We recognize them and admire them; we live among them. We grow among our creations—human creations, which we can communicate to men—and among them we die. In the midst of space, human space, we make our measurements, and with these measurements we create space, the space between our instruments.

"Uneducated man," Djerzinski went on, "is terrified of the idea of space; he imagines it to be vast, dark and yawning. He imagines beings in the elementary form of spheres, isolated in space, curled up in space, crushed by the eternal presence of three dimensions. Terrified of the idea of space, human beings curl up; they feel cold, they feel afraid. At best, they move in space and greet one another sadly. And yet this space is within them, it is nothing but their mental creation.

"In this space of which they are so afraid, human beings learn how to live and to die; in their mental space, separation, distance and suffering are born. There is little to add to this: the lover hears his beloved's voice over mountains and oceans; over mountains and oceans a mother hears the cry of her child. Love binds, and it binds forever. Good binds, while evil unravels. Separation is another word for evil; it is also another word for deceit. All that exists is a magnificent interweaving, vast and reciprocal."

Hubczejak rightly notes that Djerzinski's great leap lay not in his rejection of the idea of personal freedom (a concept which had already been much devalued in his time, and which everyone agreed, at least tacitly, could not form the basis for any kind of human progress), but in the fact that he was able, through somewhat risky interpretations of the postulates of quantum mechanics, to restore the conditions which make love possible. It is important here to evoke once more the image of

Annabelle: though Djerzinski had not known love himself, through Annabelle he had succeeded in forming an image of it. He was capable of realizing that love, in some way, through some still unknown process, was possible. This was probably his guiding thought in the last months of his theoretical work, about which we know so little.

According to the testimony of those few people who visited Djerzinski in Ireland during those final weeks, he appeared to have made his peace. His anxious, changing expression seemed to have been stilled. He often took long, dreamy, aimless walks along Sky Road with only the sky itself as witness. The road snaked west across the hills, some gentle, others steep. The ocean glittered, refracting a shifting light onto the last rocky islands. On the horizon, the mass of cloud seemed luminous and confused, its presence strangely physical. He walked effortlessly for a long time, his face bathed by the delicate mist. His work, he knew, was done. In the room he had converted into a study, its window overlooking Errislannan Point, he had put his notes in order. There were hundreds of pages on an extraordinary diversity of subjects. The results of his actual scientific work were contained in eighty typed pages. He had not thought it necessary to include his calculations.

On 27 March 2009, in the late afternoon, he went to the central post office in Galway. He sent a copy of his work to the Académie des Sciences in Paris, and another to the British magazine *Nature*. No one can be certain of what happened next. The fact that his car was found near Aughrus Point led many to think of suicide—and indeed neither Walcott nor his colleagues at the center seemed surprised by this. "There was something about him," said Walcott, "something monstrously sad. I think he was probably the saddest man I have ever met, and even the word 'sadness' seems inadequate; there was something broken in him, something completely devastated. I always got the impression that life was a burden to him, that he no longer knew how to make contact with any living thing. I think he held out for exactly as long as was necessary to finish his work, and I don't think any of us will ever know the effort he had to make in order to do so."

Djerzinski's disappearance remains a mystery. When a body could not be found, rumors sprang up that he had gone to live in Asia, probably in Tibet, to compare his work with Buddhist teachings. This hypothesis is now discredited. In part because there is no trace of his leaving Ireland, and in part because the drawings on the last pages of his notebook, which some had interpreted as mandalas, were later found to be combinations of Celtic symbols much like those in the Book of Kells.

We now believe that Michel Djerzinski died in Ireland, where he had chosen to live out his last years. We also believe that, having completed his work, and with no human ties to bind him, he chose to die. Many witnesses attest to his fascination with this distant edge of the Western world, constantly bathed in a soft shifting light, where he liked to walk, where, as he wrote in one of his last notes, "the sky, the sea and the light converge." We now believe that Michel Djerzinski went into the sea.

Epilogue

Though we know much about the lives, physical appearances and personalities of the characters in this book, it must nonetheless be considered a fiction—a plausible re-creation based on partial recollections, rather than a definite, attestable truth. Though *Clifden Notes*—a complex blend of memories, personal impressions and theoretical reflections jotted down by Djerzinski while he was working on his theory between 2000 and 2009—tells us much about the events in his life, and the choices, conflicts and dramas which were to shape his distinctive view of existence, there are many areas in his biography and his personality which remain obscure. What follows, however, belongs to History, and the events which followed the publication of Djerzinski's work have been pored over, commented on and analyzed so often that a brief résumé seems sufficient.

In 2009, the magazine *Nature* published a separate section entitled "Toward Perfect Reproduction," eighty pages synthesizing Djerzinski's last works. This was to send shock waves throughout the scientific community. Around the world, dozens of molecular biologists tried to duplicate his experiments and verify the details of his calculations. After several months, the first results came in and then, week after week, more and more experiments confirmed his original hypotheses with exact precision. At the end of 2009 there could no longer be any doubt:

Djerzinski's conclusions were valid and could be considered to have been proven. The practical consequences were dizzying: any genetic code, however complex, could be noted in a standard, structurally stable form, isolated from disturbances or mutations. This meant that every cell contained within it the possibility of being infinitely copied. Every animal species, however highly evolved, could be transformed into a similar species reproduced by cloning, and immortal.

Hubczejak was twenty-seven when he, like hundreds of researchers all over the world, discovered Djerzinski's work. He was completing his doctorate in biochemistry at Cambridge and was nervous, distracted, always on the move; for a number of years he had been roaming Europe, where he studied at the universities of Prague, Göttingen, Montpellier and Vienna—searching, as he put it, "for a new paradigm, yet also for something more: not just a way of seeing the world but a way of situating myself within it." He was certainly the first and, for many years, the only defender of the most radical of Djerzinski's proposals: that mankind must disappear and give way to a new species which was asexual and immortal, a species which had outgrown individuality, separation and evolution. It is superfluous to note the hostility with which such a project was greeted by the defenders of revealed religion; Judaism, Christianity and Islam were for once agreed, and heaped derision and opprobrium on work which "gravely undermines human dignity in its unique relationship with the Creator." Only Buddhists demurred, noting that all of the Buddha's teachings were founded on the awareness of the three impediments of old age, sickness and death, and that the Enlightened One, if he had meditated on it, would not necessarily have rejected a technical solution. Nonetheless, Hubczejak could count on little support from organized religion. It is perhaps more surprising to note that traditional humanists also rejected the idea out of hand. Though it may be difficult for us to understand this now, it is important to remember how central the notions of "personal freedom," "human dignity" and "progress" were to people in the age of materialism (defined as the centuries between the decline of medieval Christianity and the publication of Djerzinski's work). The confused and arbitrary nature of these ideas meant, of course, that they had little practical or social function—which might explain why human history from the fifteenth to the twentieth century was characterized by progressive decline and disintegration. Nonetheless, the educated or semieducated classes, having more or less succeeded in inculcating these ideas, clung desperately to them. It is hardly surprising that Frédéric Hubczejak had such difficulty in making himself heard in those early years.

The story of the period in which Hubczejak finally managed to have his project, initially greeted with unanimous disgust and condemnation, accepted by a growing proportion of global opinion to the degree that it was eventually granted funding by UNESCO, reveals an extraordinarily brilliant and pugnacious individual, a pragmatic and agile mind, the archetype of an intellectual propagandist. Certainly he was not of the stuff of great researchers, but he was capable of turning to his advantage the enormous respect the scientific community had for Djerzinski and his work. Though he was neither an original nor a profound thinker, in annotating and prefacing *Meditations on Interweaving* and *Clifden Notes*, he presented Djerzinski's thought with precision and incisiveness, making them accessible to a wider public. Hubczejak's first article, "Michel Djerzinski and the Copenhagen Interpretation," is, despite its title, a long meditation on a quotation from Parmenides: "That which is there to be spoken and thought of must be." In his next paper, "A Treatise on Concrete Limitations," and the more soberly titled "On Reality," he attempts a curious synthesis of the logical positivism of the Vienna circle and the religious positivism of Comte, and he is not averse to flights of lyricism, as evinced by the oft-quoted passage "There is no *endless silence of infinite space*, for in reality there is no space, no silence and no void. The world we know, the world we create, the human world, is as round, smooth, simple and warm as a woman's breast." Whatever his failings, he understood how to communicate to a growing public the idea that humanity in its current state could and should control the evolution of the world's species—and in particular its own evolution. In his struggle, he had the support of a number of neo-Kantians who, making use of the sudden unpopularity of Nietzschean ideas, had taken control of the wellsprings of power among the intelligentsia, the universities and the press.

The general consensus is that Hubczejak's real genius lay in his precisely calculated ability to marshal the confused, bastardized, late-twentieth-century ideology known as "New Age thinking" to his advantage. He was the first of his generation to see beyond the ridiculous, contradictory and outmoded superstitions it adopted to the fact that New Age thought appealed to a very real suffering symptomatic of psychological, ontological and social breakdown. Beyond the repellent mix of fundamentalist eco-babble, attraction to tradition and the "sacred" which they inherited from their spiritual forebears, the Esalen commune and the hippie movement, New Agers had a genuine desire to break with the twentieth century, its immorality, its individualism and its libertarian and antisocial aspects. It testified to the anguished awareness that a society cannot function without the unifying axis of some kind of religion; it was, in effect, a call for a new paradigm.

Hubczejak was keenly aware that some compromise is essential. And when he founded the Movement for Human Potential in late 2011, he did not hesitate to openly recycle some New Age themes, ranging from what he referred to as "the formation of the cortex of Gaia" to his celebrated comparison "ten billion people on the face of the planet, ten billion neurons in the human brain," from his appeal for a world government based on a "new alliance" to the almost commercial THE FUTURE IS FEMININE. This was done with an agility which generally drew admiration from commentators. He was careful to avoid any drift toward the nonrational and the sectarian and, on the contrary, secured strong support from the scientific community.

A certain cynicism in the study of human history tends to identify "artfulness" as a key component in success, although in the absence of strongly held convictions it is by itself incapable of producing any significant change. All those who had the opportunity to meet Hubczejak, or to debate him, are agreed that his persuasiveness, magnetism and extraordinary charisma were all rooted in a profound simplicity and an authentic personal conviction. He said exactly what he believed, regardless of the circumstances—and to his critics, tangled up in the limitations of outdated ideologies, such simplicity was devastating. One of the principal objections to his project concerned the suppression of sexual difference, which is so central to human identity. To this Hubczejak responded that his intention was not to re-create the human species down to the smallest detail, but to create a new, rational species, and that the end of sexuality as a means of reproduction in no way heralded the end of sexual pleasure—quite the contrary. The coding sequences responsible for the formation of Krause's corpuscles in the embryo had recently been identified. At the time, such corpuscles were sparsely spread on the surface of the glans penis and the clitoris. There was nothing, however, to prevent these from being multiplied in the future to cover the entirety of the epidermis, offering new and undreamed-of erotic possibilities.

Probably the most profound criticisms focused on the fact that every member of the species created by making use of Djerzinski's work would carry the same genetic code, meaning that one of the fundamental elements of human individuality would disappear. To this Hubczejak responded that this unique genetic code—of which, by some tragic perversity, we were so ridiculously proud—was precisely the source of so much human unhappiness. To the notion that human personality was in danger of disappearing, he proposed the concrete example of identical human twins who, through their individual experiences and despite their shared genetic code, developed different personalities while maintaining a mysterious fraternity—which, as Hubczejak pointed out, was exactly the element necessary if humanity were to be reconciled.

There can be no doubt that Hubczejak was sincere when he presented himself as a logical successor to Djerzinski, like an executor whose sole purpose was to put into practice the ideas of his master. Evidence for this might be found in his staunch loyalty to the bizarre idea proposed on page 342 of *Clifden Notes:* the number of individuals in the new species must always be a prime number; it is therefore necessary to create one person, then two, then three, then five . . . in short, to scrupulously follow the sequence of prime numbers. The purpose of having a population divisible only by itself and one was meant to draw symbolic attention to the dangers which subgroups constitute in any society; but it would appear that Hubczejak accepted this at face value without having the slightest idea what it might mean. More generally, his relentlessly positivist reading of Djerzinski led him constantly to underestimate the extent of metaphysical change which would necessarily accompany such a profound biological mutation—a mutation which had, in truth, no precedent in the history of humanity.

This gross ignorance of the philosophical subtleties of the project, and even his inability to recognize philosophical subtleties in general, in no way hampered or even delayed its implementation. This reveals the extent to which, in all Western societies and particularly in the most advanced segments represented by the New Age movement, there had been an acceptance of the idea that a fundamental shift was indispensable if society was to survive—a shift which would credibly restore a sense of community, of permanence and of the sacred. It is also a measure of how little the public understood or cared about questions of philosophy. The global ridicule in which the works of Foucault, Lacan, Derrida and Deleuze had suddenly foundered, after decades of inane reverence, far from leaving the field clear for new ideas, simply heaped contempt on all those intellectuals active in the "human sciences." The rise to dominance of scientists in all fields of thought became inevitable. Even the occasional, sporadic and contradictory interest which New Age devotees pretended to take in this or that belief or "ancient spiritual tradition" was nothing more than further evidence of a poignant, almost schizophrenic despair. Like others in society, and perhaps more so, they truly believed only in science; science was to them the arbiter of unique, irrefutable truth. Like others in society, they believed in their hearts that the solution to every problem—whether psychological, sociological or more broadly human—could only be a technical solution. Thus it was without any great risk of contradiction that Hubczejak launched his 2013 campaign—the first to unleash public opinion on a planetary level—with the slogan THE MUTATION WILL NOT BE MENTAL, BUT GENETIC.

The first fund of credit was voted through by UNESCO in 2021, and a group of scientists immediately set to work under Hubczejak's direction. In practice, from a scientific standpoint, he had very little to do with the project, but he was to prove himself stunningly effective in the domain of public relations. The extraordinary speed with which the results came in was a surprise; only later did it become apparent that many of the scientists, already members or sympathizers of the Movement for Human Potential, rather than waiting for the green light from UNESCO, had been working on the project for some time in laboratories in Australia, Brazil, Canada and Japan.

The creation of the first being, the first member of the new intelligent species made by man "in his own image," took place on 27 March

2029, twenty years to the day after Michel Djerzinski's disappearance. In homage to Djerzinski, and though no French nationals were on the team, this synthesis took place at the Institute of Molecular Biology in Palaiseau. The worldwide broadcast of the event reached a huge audience—dwarfing that, almost sixty years earlier in July 1969, of man's first steps on the moon. Hubczejak prefaced the broadcast with a short speech in which, with typical directness, he declared that humanity should be honored to be "the first species in the universe to develop the conditions for its own replacement."

Today, some fifty years later, reality has largely confirmed the prophetic tone of Hubczejak's speech—more so than perhaps even he envisaged. There remain some humans of the old species, particularly in areas long dominated by religious doctrine. Their reproductive levels fall year by year, however, and at present their extinction seems inevitable. Contrary to the doomsayers, this extinction is taking place peaceably, despite occasional acts of violence, which also continue to decline. It has been surprising to note the meekness, resignation, perhaps even secret relief with which humans have consented to their own passing.

Having broken the filial chain that linked us to humanity, we live on. Men consider us to be happy; it is certainly true that we have succeeded in overcoming the forces of egotism, cruelty and anger which they could not. We live very different lives. Science and art are still a part of our society; but without the stimulus of personal vanity, the pursuit of Truth and Beauty has taken on a less urgent aspect. To humans of the old species, our world seems a paradise. We have even been known to refer to ourselves—with a certain humor—by the name they so long dreamed of: gods.

History exists; it is elemental, it dominates, its rule is inexorable. Yet outside the strict confines of history, the ultimate ambition of this book is to salute the brave and unfortunate species which created us. This vile, unhappy race, barely different from the apes, which nevertheless carried within it such noble aspirations. Tortured, contradictory, individualistic, quarrelsome and infinitely selfish, it was sometimes capable of extraordinary explosions of violence, but never quite abandoned its belief in love. This species which, for the first time in history, was able to envision the possibility of its succession and, some years later, proved capable of bringing it about. As the last members of this race are extinguished, we think it just to render this last tribute to humanity, an homage which itself will one day disappear, buried beneath the sands of time. It is necessary that this tribute be made, if only once. This book is dedicated to mankind.